S0-AQD-431

Half-Truths, Total Lies

LIN WEICH

enjoy

Lin Weich

Copyright © 2012 by Lin Weich
First Edition – April 2012

ISBN
978-1-77097-387-9 (Hardcover)
978-1-77097-388-6 (Paperback)
978-1-77097-389-3 (eBook)

All rights reserved.

No part of this publication may be reproduced in any form, or by any means, electronic or mechanical, including photocopying, recording, or any information browsing, storage, or retrieval system, without permission in writing from the publisher.

Published by:

FriesenPress

Suite 300 – 852 Fort Street
Victoria, BC, Canada V8W 1H8

www.friesenpress.com

Distributed to the trade by The Ingram Book Company

Moving On

I Am All I Have Ever Been

and more—

Resurfacing from the bottom
of a lake gone dry.
The weight of passing days and obligations,
that rounded me full well,
have shifted
with time and initiative.
Sun warms my skin now
as in former days;
wind fluffs my hair
as it ever did. At night,
I no longer gaze at stars.
In that split and changing world
of then and now,
I was compelled
to follow a one-track existence
in a world of many roads,
as if I were impersonating the past
that only the children knew
who their mother was.
He never did call me
by my name
but only by the one he
gave to me.
And as he became more like himself,
in time,
that I no longer could carry him,
and he no longer could hold on to me,
so did I emerge once more,
a seedling seeking light.

I am all I have ever been—
and more.

Patterns

A small box of patterns
is all that remains
of drawers once full of sewing projects.
The old order of things,
days planning, measuring,
studying techniques and methods,
fitting, and stitching dreams
into children's clothes
and my own,
had run itself out with the times—
and children growing up.

The art, as Wolfgang called it,
of creating fashion and decor,
sought to expand.
As work became routine,
it sent the mind to wander,
while I sat at the machine.
As time changes fashion,
so growth changes people.
Distracted by wondering,
I soon stitched
wrong pieces together, resulting
in ripped seams that needed
reworking.

We saw the world change
with the fashions, but not ourselves,
we only noticed the fit was no longer
there—the fit
in the changing order of things.
He said of business, change was good.
We both took college courses,

helped blaze a trail for the children
of the new age. In time,
clothes were outgrown,
became too tight,
the house too large,
life empty.

>Quickly, I discarded patterns
>held dearly for so long,
>quickly, before I changed my mind
>before I returned to a style
>that confined.

After years of deferring,
I thought my turn would come.
Rather than second-guessing designers,
or retaining out-of-style comfort,
I sought patterns of new fit and style
to drape this way and that
woven of the new threads of the age
into the fabric of newly shaped
months and years,
the design of a new life.
But it never came.

Little by little, I had changed over
from needle to pen—
for the sensation's the same—
yet the pen travels further,
beyond possibility into new space.

>Now purpose lies in finding
>pieces of old and new fabric
>to join together into new designs
>to punctuate and fit
>the changing wardrobe of time
>for a future of new promise.

Along Lake Geneva

Some people built their homes
after they became successful
in business
Maytag and Marshall Fields
movie star
German immigrant
They built mansions so big
a person could lose
herself in them
From the boat's distance
we are free
to inhabit and relish
for a time
someone else's dream
of our popcorn cloud

Into a silent valley
we built a house
keeping up with—
built it large
but not inviting
like someone else's dream,
not far from where we began
The woods took the light
out of the vision
split the name
and held the tears
that brought us back
past the beginning

St. Croix

From the wooden dock
at the end of a concrete road
evening sun spreads
its apricot carpet
imagination's bridge
across the river

Hidden beneath river's depth
lie changing colors
Current sweeps away
everyday intrusions
Carpet welcomes Sunday traveler
to ascend the cloud-framed sphere
almost within reach

The river shoots
blinding arrow lights
illuminating more
of what lies inside and out
I carry the light
all the way home.

The Poet

Evelyn Klein's poetry, set primarily against a backdrop of Wisconsin and Minnesota landscapes, explores the ebb and flow of family life, its pleasures and transformations, with the practiced eye of a veteran observer. They offer us a look into a mind that, through a lengthy process of reflection, has succeeded in illuminating the subtle interplay of professional, spiritual, and personal life, fearlessly exploring its dark corners while also celebrating its moments of discovery and communion.

A prize-winning poet, Klein's work has appeared in many anthologies, journals, newspapers, and other publications. She edited and published the multicultural anthology, *Stage Two: Poetic Lives,* (also illustrated by Wolfgang Klein). She is currently at work on a book on linguistics entitled *Essentials of Language and Writing* and another book of poems, *Neighborhood Stories*. Her prize-winning poem, "A Place Called Home" was recently chosen by the Family Housing Fund for inclusion in an exhibit circulating the Twin Cities.

Klein went to high school in Milwaukee, Wisconsin, and earned her bachelor of science in Secondary Education at the University of Wisconsin–Milwaukee, and her masters degree in the Teaching of English at the University of Wisconsin–River Falls. She taught language arts and German in the public schools of western Wisconsin and Minnesota for many years. She also taught at the Germanic American Institute. She has led a poetry group at the Loft in Minneapolis for seven years and currently teaches there.

The Artist

Wolfgang Klein enjoyed a long and distinguished career as a visual artist. He studied with Ernst Ludwig Kirchner in Davos, Switzerland, at the age of thirteen, and later at the Academy of Fine and Applied Arts in Frankfurt, Germany, working with such well known expressionists as Max Pechstein, Käthe Kollwitz, and Max Beckman. He had his first one-man showing at Frankfurt at the age of nineteen, and later had exhibits in Paris, Vienna, Darmstadt, and other cities. In time, woodcuts became his favorite medium of expression.

Klein first taught art at the Academy of Fine and Applied Arts in Berlin. After emigrating to Milwaukee with his wife and four children, he worked as a commercial artist and subsequently taught art at Marquette University, where he wrote his book, *Basics in the Visual Arts,* and at Alverno College and the Milwaukee YWCA.

In the United States his work has been exhibited in Chicago, Milwaukee, Minneapolis, St. Paul, Atlanta, Santa Barbara, and other cities. Many of his landmark woodcuts have found a permanent home at the Milwaukee County Historical Society. His largest woodcut, the four-by-six-foot Bicentennial picture, currently hangs in the Commerce Building in Washington, D. C.

Klein was artist-in-residence in Milwaukee, Wisconsin, his last place of residence, where he lived with his wife, Henrietta, for over forty years. Wolfgang and Henrietta both died in 1999.

Acknowledgements

Thank you to my twin sister, Tishy, who for many years has taught in some of the more interesting and isolated schools in British Columbia.

Although the book is entirely fictional, many of the stories gleaned from both your experiences and mine were seeds for this twisted tale.

Thanks to my husband Brian, my friends and family for their continued support and encouragement.

Chapter One

Lost in thought, he kicked at a discarded coat in front of the entrance to Riverside Elementary. A low guttural moan disturbed the early morning stillness. Malcolm jolted into awareness.

As he bent down gingerly reaching into the tattered garment, a sickening odour of bloody meat wafted from the clothing. His hand touched a warm, wet, slimy mess. Reeling as his senses were dealt another blow, he uncovered the inert body.

Hardly recognizable, Susan lay semiconscious, bleeding from massive facial trauma. Her eyes, mere slits, framed the pulpy mass that was once a perky, upturned nose. Blood eked its way down her chin, then soaked her matted hair. Once again, the low animal sound escaped from her lips.

***

Concealed behind the large dumpster at the edge of the playground, he watched, grinning with satisfaction. His plan was working.

He saw Malcolm reach into his packsack and root around for his cell phone. The teachers coming up the walkway hurried when they heard Malcolm calling for their help, their chatter extinguished by the desperate tone in his voice.

Cautiously exiting from his hiding place, he flicked his fingers over his jacket to remove any dirt and leaves that might have clung to the brushed wool. Nonchalantly, Robert began walking along the dirt road that led to the school entrance. As he neared the school, he raised his head and broke into a run. Dashing up the front path, he joined the group as they stood around the beaten woman.

"What gives? What's the matter? Oh my God, it's Susan!" he exclaimed.

"I've called 911, but it'll be a hell of a long time before the ambulance gets here. Town is over an hour away, so they're sending the first responders from Melville Creek. Help me check her over," ordered Malcolm. "Support her neck. I've got to find out where all this blood is coming from."

Ben pushed through the anxious onlookers towards the prone body. "Let me help you, I've got first aid training."

Malcolm and Ben carefully stripped away the fabric partially covering Susan's face. Susan's lips moved, but no words formed. Her eyes glazed over, and she lapsed into unconsciousness. The slight movement caused a large blood clot to snake its way down from the mashed nose. Blood congealed in her dirty blonde hair.

Robert had to hide a secret smile from the others as he saw Ann vomit into the bushes beside the school entrance. *You go, girl. Could be your turn next if you're not careful.*

A few more teachers arrived, adding to the confusion that had erupted. The scrunching of tires on the gravel driveway announced the arrival of a pickup truck carrying the first responders.

"Let us through! Let us get through!" ordered a burly man still dressed in his barn clothes. "Stand back and let us do our job."

As the responders took over, everyone else stood off to one side talking in muffled voices. Contributing to the conversation wherever possible, Robert tried to blend in seamlessly.

"Glad Ben and Malcolm had some idea what to do. We should let these guys do their thing now. Amy, move over a bit more. Let's make sure they have lots of room," he said, struggling to keep his voice normal as adrenaline coursed through his system. He eased the worried teachers farther away from the immediate scene. If his plan was to succeed, he had to keep it together. Now was not the time to tip his hand or let his guard down.

After what seemed like an eternity, the distressed onlookers were relieved to hear the keening whine of approaching sirens. Mesmerized, they watched the paramedics take over from the Melville Creek personnel. Susan was carefully immobilized, placed on a stretcher, and lifted into the waiting ambulance. Her bloodstained coat remained discarded on the steps.

As the wailing emergency vehicle turned the corner onto the highway and headed towards town, a shocked and sombre group watched Robert unlock the school door. Everyone filed inside.

"Do you think she'll make it? Looked pretty bad to me. Who in hell did she piss off?" Robert asked quietly.

Malcolm's pale face reflected his distress as he nervously touched his hand to his mouth. He shrugged. "I've no idea. Susan keeps to herself. Perhaps an old boyfriend caught up with her. You never know."

"Maybe. I think she was married before coming here to Wolfsburg. He could've been abusive. Could've ended badly. Maybe she was on the run," he said, adding to Malcolm's speculation. Once again, he was rewarded as he saw a flash of concern leap into the pale blue-gray eyes of his colleague.

Malcolm raised his shoulders again. "Like I said I don't really know. Susan kept pretty much to herself."

"Best we call Carolyn and let her know what's gone down. She's at Halverston this morning and isn't due out here until after lunch, but since she's the so-called boss, let her deal with it," Robert said loudly as he surveyed the other teachers standing in the entrance foyer.

He cleared his throat. "We'll have to call in a substitute for Susan's class. I'll do it," he said as he strode officiously out of the room and into Carolyn's office closing the door behind him.

"It's Susan's duty this morning," said Amy. "I'll go out with the kids. Suppose we should delay the bell until the sub makes it here? It's probably better than having her class upset and unsupervised."

"Thanks, Amy, I'll come out in a minute and help you," offered Colleen.

She could see Robert as he spoke into the phone on Carolyn's desk. "Do you think we should call the police or leave it up to Carolyn?"

Malcolm sitting slumped over at the table, raised his head from his arms. "I called the cops just after the ambulance left. The paramedics said I should. A unit's coming from town, but it shouldn't be too long now."

He rested his head again. He was feeling nauseous, and an aura of light was edging around his peripheral vision. Stress induced his migraines. Luckily he was able to handle emergencies, but after the initial incident he was usually incapacitated by these nasty headaches. *Poor Susan. God she looked a mess. What had she been trying to say?*

Colleen gazed sympathetically at Malcolm who was hunched over the long rectangular table that took up most of the staffroom. For once, her plump bustling figure was still. This was a dreadful shock for them all.

"See you out there," Amy said as she left to supervise the children on the playground.

Colleen pulled out one of the grey metal chairs and sat down heavily across from Malcolm, her eyes drifting over the bland beige-toned staffroom. A couple of worn sofas and three soft chairs made up a small seating area at the far end of the room below the large windows that overlooked the school grounds. She could see the two teacherages and the surrounding woods easily from where she sat. She was thankful to live in one of those small houses. Last year she had driven daily to and from town. It wasn't so bad in the spring and fall but when winter came roads were often dangerous. Drifting snow and black ice were common. The wildlife was a constant concern, especially when the moose and deer were attracted to the paved road seeking the chemicals spread by the highways department to control the slippery conditions.

Reluctant to think of the recent events, she distracted herself by examining the features of the room. Aside from the usual microwave, coffee pot, refrigerator and stove, the room was devoid of any character. The bulletin boards she had so carefully decorated with borders and captions did little to alleviate the boring bleakness of their staffroom.

Sighing, she noticed the cups and plates from yesterday were still piled in the sink unwashed. It was a real bone of contention that Robert and some of the others left their dirty dishes for others to clean up. Irritated, she got up and slammed the fridge to stop its noisy gurgling.

Malcolm's head rose sharply at the sound of her hand.

"Sorry, Malcolm. Didn't think," she said suddenly contrite. "I'd best get on outside. You okay?"

"Yes, I'll be fine. Just a slight headache," Malcolm replied, trying to be casual about his pounding head.

Joining Amy on the playground, she reached over and hugged her friend.

"How's it out here? Kids behaving?"

"Yeah, they're good."

The two women circled the school grounds together passing through the primary section with its slide, swings, tire obstacle course, paved hopscotch area and wooden benches.

"Better check on the older kids. Yesterday there was a bit of an argument over the hockey nets," Amy commented brushing her dark curls away from her face.

Today the children were playing peacefully. Both hockey teams seemed to be a good balance of strong and weaker players. It was amazing how 'hockey mad' these students were. In the summer it was street hockey giving way to ice hockey as soon as the weather turned cold enough.

Chapter Two

Robert speaking in a controlled, dispassionate voice calmly informed Carolyn of the situation.

"Ms. Myers… There has been an unfortunate incident at the school. Susan Lloyd was found unconscious on the school steps. I have everything under control but the situation is very grave. Paramedics have taken her to hospital and the police have been called… Yes… it appears she was attacked."

As he spoke to Carolyn Myers, he took care to appear to be in charge of the situation. He had little respect for this principal who had been parachuted in to supervise the rural schools after the previous principal's quick exit. He seethed with resentment; by rights the job should be his, as he was next senior in the school. His superiors had obviously felt otherwise. It was just a matter of time before Carolyn would screw up. She had little administrative experience and was a woman. No self-respecting man liked being bossed by a female, especially a sharp-faced bitch.

Although Carolyn, in her mid-forties, was reasonably attractive, she certainly wasn't his type. She was reserved and seemed to have an air of superiority about her. He also didn't appreciate women who failed to notice his considerable charms. He had yet to discover any dirty little secrets about Ms. Meyers, but he would. The last guy hadn't been so hard to get rid of.

"Yes, Ms. Myers," he continued. "Everything is under control. The police haven't arrived, but I'll fill them in if they get here before you do…. Well no, I wasn't the first one to find Susan; Malcolm was… Fine, let him have his day. He can't even remember what day it is when he's sober… What? No he's not drunk, just inept… Okay, see you when you get here. I'll ask the police to stay until you arrive." He hung up the phone just as two policemen walked in the front door.

Rising as he heard their footsteps echoing in the hall, he went to greet the uniformed officers.

As he extended his hand he said, "Hello, I'm Robert Doyle, head teacher. Thanks for coming so quickly." He gestured towards Carolyn's office.

"Please come in, make yourselves comfortable. I'm in charge as our part-time principal has to come in from one of her other schools."

The taller cop nodded. "Can you bring the children in another door? We don't want the crime scene to be contaminated any further. Who was the first on scene?" asked Sgt. Bates.

"Sure thing, it's time to ring the bell anyway. Malcolm, Malcolm McDermitt was first to find Susan. I'll send him in." With that, he left the office and went to find his colleague.

As Robert passed by an open window that looked out onto the playground he caught sight of Amy and Colleen making their rounds.

"Amy, bring the kids in through the gym door," he ordered. "The police don't want the scene contaminated."

Amy moved to stand in front of the school steps while Colleen dashed through the gym doors and strode swiftly down the hall to the office. There, she punched the outside bell three times. Startled by the unusual signal, the children gathered around Amy.

"Please go in through the gym door and then right to your class-rooms," she told the students. "Don't worry about changing into your inside shoes. We can do that later."

Finding Malcolm still slumped at the staff room table, Robert gave him a rough shove.

"Get your sorry ass to the office. The police want to interrogate you."

Malcolm raised his head slowly and stared at his rude co-worker. He shook his head slightly and squinted. "What? Why me?"

"You were the one that found her. They obviously want to rule you out as a suspect." Robert saw the glimmer of concern grow in Malcolm's eyes.

"Okay, sure." After getting up shakily from his chair, Malcolm made his way to the office.

Sgt. Bates and his fellow officer observed a pale, overweight man in his late forties coming towards them. It was clear that the man was feeling ill.

He rose quickly and held out his hand. "Patrick Bates. You must be Malcolm McDermitt, the one who discovered the victim? Must have been an awful shock. We need to get as many details as possible while it's still fresh in your mind. Do you think you can manage?" Bates said sympathetically, his years of investigative work kicking in. This man looked ready to cave in with stress.

"Yeah, okay," said Malcolm softly. "Whatever I can do to help. Susan's a friend of mine. Will she make it?"

"Don't have any word on the victim's condition yet," answered Sgt. Bates carefully. "The ambulance crew radioed headquarters that her heart stopped and that she had to be revived. Should have an update soon. Let's get down to it, Malcolm. Follow me to the front door."

Malcolm visibly pulled himself together. He owed it to Susan to get the facts straight. Although she wasn't a close friend, she took the time to include him in conversations and had often been kind. He had considered asking her to meet him for dinner when they were both in Belmont on the weekend, but had never found the courage. Now it might be too late.

As he approached the open doorway, Malcolm relived the horrible vision of the bruised and battered woman. He joined the two policemen standing at the top of the steps.

"Where was the victim when you found her?" quizzed Sgt. Bates.

"Lying in a heap on the steps, right where that big blood stain is," Malcolm stated flatly. "I moved her a bit to see what I ... we could do to help," he added. "She tried to say something before she passed out, but I didn't catch it properly. Something like, 'Watch out for Ro ... Ru ...' I don't know. Do you think she's going to die?" He began to shake and stutter with concern.

"Now calm down, Mr. McDermitt, calm down. No point in getting all upset. We simply don't know. The best you can do for her right now is to remember the details. Is there anything that you noticed? A car nearby? Someone watching or running away? Some sound, smell, anything that seemed out of the ordinary?"

"No, nothing. I didn't expect to stumble upon her like that. This is a quiet farming community. Nothing ever happens here. I was just heading into the school as usual. I always come at this time of the morning and am usually the first to arrive. Like to get an early start to my day. Susan's usually one of the last to pull in. Oh no," he gasped as his pallor whitened. "She must have been out here all night! Where's her car? It's a blue Ford something. Focus or something like that, I think."

"Light or dark blue?" questioned Sgt. Bates as his junior officer, a thin, wiry man, scribbled furiously in his notebook.

"Light blue, sort of metallic finish to it. Sometimes she walks to school. She only lives a couple kilometres down the road," Malcolm replied.

"Oh? Where's her place?"

"In that small block of apartments beside the general store. Number 3 is her unit. Had to drop some books off there the other day. It's a nice little place."

"Hmm. You and Susan, Susan Lloyd, good friends?"

Malcolm coloured as he responded. "No, just colleagues in the same school. This is my first year at Riverside. I haven't gotten to know very many people yet."

Sgt. Bates smiled. "Early days yet. It's only the end of September. How long has Susan taught here?"

Sgt. Bates liked this quiet, unassuming man. Not that he could rule out him as a suspect at this point, but his gut was telling him that Malcolm had nothing to do with this incident. Someone well-known to the victim was probably responsible. This crime had all the markings of being very personal. Revenge or jealousy was usually the motive behind such beatings.

"She's been here for three years and has always taught the third grade. Seems to be very respected by the other teachers and the community," Malcolm offered.

"Did anyone pick up her keys, cell phone, or anything from the scene?"

"No, I don't remember seeing anything other than Susan and the coat that was covering her. She always has a small, green backpack with her, but I don't think it was there." Malcolm looked at the policemen. "Poor girl. Was she suffering out here all night?"

"Looks like it. Listen, I'm done for now. If you remember anything else, give me a call. Here, take this card with my cell phone number. Not much point in calling the office in town because I'll be out here until we get to the bottom of this."

"Excuse me." Sgt. Bates turned away to answer his mobile phone. "Right, okay."

"Best we head inside, Malcolm. Can you gather the others in the staff room?"

Five minutes later, Sgt. Bates glanced around at the teachers that Malcolm had quickly summoned. Concern was etched on their faces as they waited for his update.

"I'm sorry to have to tell you that your friend and co-worker died in the emergency room. They did everything they could, but her injuries were too extensive. She died without having regained consciousness. This has now become a murder investigation."

Robert dipped his head quickly. Relief flooded him as he realized that he might get away with what he had done. Not that he had actually meant to kill her. That was an unfortunate development; but these things happen. Thank God she died before she put the finger on who had attacked her. All that was left now was to keep a low profile and pretend to grieve along with the rest of these morons.

In a quiet voice, Amy asked the group of teachers whether they should tell the children or wait for Carolyn to get there.

"They already know that the ambulance was here, and they've probably guessed it might be Susan. But perhaps we should delay telling them as long as we can," Colleen said.

As they began to discuss the logistics of informing the children, they heard the distinctive sound of high-heeled shoes coming down the hall. Carolyn Myers entered the room. One look at the assembled teachers confirmed the worst had happened.

Her navy suit, softened by the soft draping of her silk cream coloured shirt gave her an air of quiet professionalism. As she looked sympathetically from one staff member to the other, she paused to gather her thoughts.

Nodding to the police officers she introduced herself. "I'm Ms. Myers, Carolyn Myers. Can you fill me in on what's happened?"

As she sat listening to Sgt. Bates relay the information, she took off her glasses and laid them on the table. Without her eyewear, she seemed vulnerable. The lines around her eyes seemed to deepen as she took in the horror of the events. Her stylishly cut, dark hair fell forward as she covered her eyes.

When Sgt. Bates finished, she raised her head and thanked him.

"This is truly dreadful. Please let us know what you need from us. I'm sure I speak for all of us… we'll do anything we can to bring Susan's killer to justice. Susan was our friend."

After talking with each member of her staff and giving them a few more minutes to absorb the shocking events, she started to deal with the situation.

"Each of you return to your classes and supervise the children. Have them do some silent reading or other seatwork until I get to you. I'll come in and tell them that Ms. Lloyd died this morning. Since we don't really have any answers, I won't go into any details. Try to occupy the children with plain work and comfort them. Don't be afraid to show that you're upset, but do try to hold it together. I know this is rough on all of us. Susan was a good friend as well as a colleague. I'll take Susan's class after I get through speaking to the other grades."

She glanced at the teacher on call. "Mrs. Newberry, you go into Susan's class for now, and when I take over, you can rotate throughout the school giving the teachers a break if they need it. Don't tell Susan's kids. It's best if it comes from me. School will close today at 11:00.

Buses will be here at 10:45. I'll call the grief counsellor to come out this afternoon and help us plan the next few days. Right now, we just have to get through the next few hours."

Gray-faced teachers quickly dispersed to their rooms to settle the unattended children. Brushing aside the curious questions, they started in on the daily routine.

Malcolm's head pounded as he sat weakly at his desk.

"What's wrong, Mr. McDermitt?" nine-year-old Cindy asked. "You look real sick. Got one of your headaches again?"

"Umm. Yes. It's a doozy. Can you all just get out a book and read for a few minutes? The migraine pills will kick in soon." With that he laid his head down on his desk and shut his eyes. The children, used to his sudden headaches, chatted quietly amongst themselves and dragged out their silent-reading books.

Carolyn opened the door and glanced into Mr. McDermitt's room. Seeing him resting at his desk, she went over and put her arm around his shoulders. "Bad one, eh?" she said softly.

"I'll be okay. Getting a little better. These kids are so great. Quiet as mice!"

"Yes, you have a really good class, but they're going to need you. Are you able to cope?" Carolyn squeezed his shoulder.

"Sure, let's get it over with." Malcolm rose to his feet. "Class, please, put down your reading materials. Ms. Myers has something important to tell you."

Quiet gasps of disbelief rose as Ms. Myers told the children that the teacher who had taught them last year had died. Susan had been popular with her students. She had managed to control her classes with firm expectations and a keen sense of humour. The children, valuing her boundaries, had worked hard, learning a lot. Trying to grapple with the horrible reality, students sat immobile in their seats. A hand reached tentatively into the air.

"How'd she die, Ms. Myers? Was that her in the ambulance heading to town?"

"Yes, Holden, that was Ms. Lloyd. We don't know how she died, but we do know that the doctors tried their very best to save her."

"It's not fair. She's one of the good ones. She didn't get after you like Mr. Doyle does," whimpered Doug.

Carolyn frowned at Doug. She knew he had a problem with Mr. Doyle, but she couldn't allow him to be disrespectful. "I know you thought highly of Ms. Lloyd. We're all going to miss her a lot."

Then speaking quietly to Malcolm and his class, she told them that school would be over for the day at 11:00.

"There isn't much we can do today, but tomorrow we'll have people you can talk to if you need to. It's best you're at home with your family's support this afternoon. We'll be having a memorial service here at the school before the end of the week." She paused and then added, "I have to go to Ms. Lloyd's class now."

She moved towards the exit. As she reached the door, she turned back to the class with tears in her eyes. "I'm really sorry that Ms. Lloyd has died," she whispered.

The children, shocked at such raw emotion, looked at their teacher and saw tears running down his face. Muffled sobs erupted as the children gave way to their feelings. Realizing he had to do something, Malcolm cleared his throat.

"I'm going to put on some quiet music, and you can draw or write. It might help to write down some thoughts you have about Ms. Lloyd or how you're feeling. Or you can just sit and visit quietly." He crossed over to the CD player and selected a disc by Enya, his favourite relaxing music.

Carolyn delivered the shocking news to each class. As expected, the classes all handled the news differently. The kindergarten students, having no real concept of death yet, knew something had gone terribly wrong. However, with no outward show of emotion, they quietly went on with their play centers.

The grade one class reacted more to their teacher's distress than to Ms. Lloyd's death. They were upset to see Amy pale, trembling, and weeping.

Mrs. Newberry, sent to relieve Amy, gathered the children in the reading corner and began to read story after story to calm them. As she read *The Kissing Hand* by Audrey Penn, she could feel them settle and relax. Later she let them play Matho and use some of the "special" art supplies.

Naturally, it was Susan's class that was most affected by the news. Their parents, summoned by Mrs. Brown, the school secretary, had come quickly. Together the parents and Carolyn comforted the children. Most of the parents took their children home well before the dismissal time.

After the last child had been picked up by parents or neighbours or had boarded the school bus, Carolyn called her staff over the intercom.

"Could all school personnel please come to the staff room?"

The teachers gathered around the long table, talking quietly among themselves. Carolyn entered, followed closely behind by Sgt. Bates and his partner. They watched the slim man take a seat. His blue-gray eyes steadily examined them.

Carolyn began the meeting.

"For those who don't already know him, I would like to introduce Sgt. Bates from the RCMP detachment in Belmont. He's leading the investigation into Susan's death. This is his partner Ray Witmore."

Sgt. Bates cleared his throat and waited for everyone to look at him.

"Thank you for being here at this difficult time. I have some questions for each of you, so I'll be interviewing everyone individually in the Learning Assistance room. I'm afraid you can't leave the building until I've had a chance to talk to you. Is there anyone who has to leave at a certain time for child care or other such reasons? Mr. Witmore or I will speak to you first."

"I have a doctor's appointment in town at 4:30," Barb, the young kindergarten teacher said quietly. "I could cancel if I have to, but if I could go first, I'd appreciate it."

"My wife needs me to be home by 3:30," Robert stated emphatically. "Not sure what we can tell you anyway. Malcolm was the one who found her, and you've already talked to him. I'm very busy and have a lot of marking to do. I don't know what I could add to what you already know."

"I understand that you're all very busy, but this is now a homicide. In order to eliminate you as a suspect, we have to determine the whereabouts of each of you last night and early this morning. Besides, someone might have information that will help bring this to a speedy conclusion."

Sgt. Bates glanced at Robert. He didn't like this arrogant man. "Okay, I'll speak with you after I interview the young lady with the doctor's appointment. As for the rest of you, please stay in your classrooms and avoid talking to your fellow staff members about what happened this morning. I'll call you when it's your turn to be interviewed."

"Mr. Bram, the grief counsellor, is on his way out here to help us plan for the children. Can my staff and I meet with him while you're doing the interviews?" Ms. Myers asked.

"I suppose that would be okay as long as you make sure no one discusses the crime."

Throughout the long afternoon as Sgt. Bates questioned the teachers, Mr. Bram helped develop a plan to meet the needs of the children and the staff. The children all identified well with Mr. Bram. He was from the community and was of their faith. This kindly older gentleman was a good choice for the councellor for Riverside Elementary.

The children in Wolfburg, coming from a farming background, understood death but this death was violent and untimely. To soften the horror and circumstances, it was decided that a celebration of

Susan's life would be held at the school to be followed later by a more traditional service in the church.

It was well past six o'clock before the final interview had been conducted and the last teacher had been allowed to go home. Wednesday promised to be a hard day. Friday could be even more difficult. The celebration of Susan's life was scheduled for Friday afternoon.

Chapter Three

Quarter to bloody four, fumed Robert as he made his way out of the school and over to the teacherage. He quickly crossed the parking lot and climbed the steps to one of the squat buildings that bordered the school grounds. He and his wife Betsy were lucky to have this accommodation as there were only two such accommodations on the Riverside Elementary school grounds. There was also one old trailer, which the school board rented, located on Kies Road. Naturally, this rundown, very secluded trailer was not a popular choice among the established staff. The other teachers had to find their own living arrangements. Some even commuted from town on a daily basis. The trip took an hour and a half each way, longer in the winter.

The teacherages were given out according to seniority at the school. Since he had been at Riverside for nearly six years now, he had become the most senior last year and they had moved into the first teacherage during the summer. Colleen, the learning assistant teacher, and her two children occupied the other one.

Although the accommodations were small, there were three bedrooms and quite a bit of storage. His four-year-old son, Timmy, had the bedroom farthest away from the kitchen. He and Betsy slept in the biggest bedroom, and the third was his private sanctuary that no one was ever allowed to enter. He kept the door locked at all times. The combined living and dining room with its sparse furniture was plain but comfortable and overlooked the school grounds.

Yes, considering the cheap subsidized rent, it was a good deal. He also saved a lot of time as well as gas money, not having to go back and forth to town all the time. Money was important to Robert.

The little black and white Border collie received a vicious kick as it came out from under the steps to greet him.

"Get away, I've got my good pants on," he snarled. It slunk back under the steps as Robert continued to climb, his feet stomping angrily.

Betsy and Timmy glanced up from the picture book they were looking at, as he came in.

"You're late today. You have a meeting or something? I left your beer in the fridge," Betsy, his tired, thin-faced wife, said tentatively.

Robert strode into the bedroom without answering her.

"Put Timmy in his room, lock the door, and then get your ass in here," he ordered.

Betsy quickly led the fearful little boy to his room and then nervously went to join her husband.

"You had a bad day? What's this I heard about Susan?"

His closed fist caught her on the side of her head. Reeling around, she fell across the bed.

"Shut the fuck up! It was a great day. The best. Nothing for you to be concerned about, you nosy bitch," said Robert as he yanked off her black, cotton pants. His breath coming in sharp gasps as he was so excited. Over and over in his mind, he was reliving the beating he'd hung on Susan. Again he heard the sounds of his fists hitting her flesh; again he heard her muffled groans as she lay inert on the school steps. She had initially fought back but then had quickly given way in hopeless submission.

Much to Betsy's relief, he climaxed quickly. If he had trouble, he often resorted to more hitting and punching. He rolled off her.

"Supper had better be on the table in ten minutes," he said in a deadly quiet voice. "Ten minutes or else." He left the room and headed to his sanctuary.

Betsy struggled up off the bed and crossed over to the shabby dressing table. Their furniture was old and had often been purchased in second hand stores. Robert was very frugal and seldom spent money on anything but the bare necessities.

As she stared at her reflection in the mirror, she could see the start of yet another bruise that she would have to explain away. Through dull, dead eyes, she saw a stranger looking back at her. How had it come to this? There was nowhere to go. She had no money of her own, and of course there was little Timmy to think about. They could never survive without Robert. Thank God he didn't beat Timmy. He did lock him in his room and deny him food, but he had never beaten him. Timmy was careful not to give his father any reason to hit him. Keeping out of his father's way, he hardly ever uttered a word. Yes, Timmy was a good boy. He was her sole reason for living.

Chapter Four

Ben sat quietly beside his students. Since they were grade seven, the oldest grade in the school, traditionally they got to sit on the benches while the junior grades were relegated to the gym mats on the floor.

Ben had no difficulty controlling his students. Most of the girls were hopelessly infatuated with their teacher, and the boys respected his athletic abilities. At six feet four, Ben Smith cut a dashing picture. His medium-length, blond hair was carefully styled.

Ben abhorred junk food and exercised frequently; the results were obvious. His well-toned body looked good in slim jeans and body-hugging shirts that young men can wear with confidence. With his clothes reflecting the latest fashions straight out of Vancouver, he gave Robert a run for his money.

He was somewhat of a mystery to the students and the staff of Riverside Elementary. Most weeks, he left straight after school on Friday afternoon, heading to Belmont or to the more distant town of Clearville, returning late on Sunday night. On the other nights, after school hours, one could usually find Ben in his classroom prepping the next day's lessons or on the playground shooting hoops with the teenagers. If he wasn't at the school, he was in his tiny house beside the community hall, a short distance from the school.

Ben kept to himself in this tight-knit community, and few people really knew him even though this was his second year at the school. Since he was well respected as a competent teacher, the parents left him alone. Several of the unattached females in the community and a few of the women teachers were interested in this cute thirty-year-old, but no serious relationships had developed. He and Anita, the grade five teacher, had been linked at one time last year, but it seemed to be more of a friendship than a romance.

Before he took his class to the memorial service in the gym, Ben outlined his expectations. He didn't have to worry; realizing the gravity of the situation, the students were more than happy to cooperate.

Several of them had written tributes to Susan and were anxiously waiting to participate in the program.

"Make me proud," he said before leading his students out of the classroom. "I know Ms. Lloyd enjoyed teaching you all, and I'm sure you liked her as a teacher and mentor. You're the senior class. It is up to this class to set an example for the rest of the students."

"No problem, sir," replied Margaret dressed in her Sunday best. "We're used to going to church every Sunday. We know how to behave. Besides, it's only right. We're all really gutted about Ms. Lloyd. You don't have to worry. I just hope we can get through it without falling apart."

As he supervised his class seated in the gym, Ben reflected on the good nature of these country kids. Being brought up in this rural community was both a blessing and a curse. While they learned the values of family, friends, and the simple life, the children were often unprepared for the harsher realities that faced them in the more urban setting of Belmont.

The nearest high school was in Belmont. After grade seven, those going on to further education had to board in town during the school week. Fear of urban influences, in particular drugs and alcohol, led some parents in the deeply religious community to keep their children home either to work on the farm or to be home schooled.

He thought of his own childhood. His parents had loved him dearly when he was a little boy. He and his brother had been provided with all the comforts and opportunities available in their small town. However, when he felt he could no longer hide his sexual orientation from his parents, they had become estranged. Being gay was not accepted in Tremont. He left town shortly after coming out to his family, wanting to spare them any embarrassment and ridicule. Now, he kept to himself in this tiny farming village that was over three thousand miles away from where he grew up. He was concerned that the school board or the parents might turn against him if they knew he was different. There was no need for anyone to know his business. He liked it here, and besides, teaching jobs were few and far between.

His thoughts then turned to Susan. *What had she done to deserve such a violent death?* As far as he knew, she had had no enemies.

He had seen her shy away from Robert, but then again no one was comfortable around that man. Robert tried to give the impression that women found him irresistible, often making inappropriate comments and innuendoes. Also, his quick temper and abrasive manner alienated him from most of the staff. It was surprising, though, how much charm he could exude around the "right people." *Just check him out now.* While they waited for the rest of students and parents to find their seats, Robert was hobnobbing and chatting with the school board chairperson as if they were best of pals.

Soft music started playing over the speakers drawing Ben's thoughts towards the reason why they were gathered together. It was hard for Ben to imagine someone from around here committing such a despicable crime. Sgt. Bates was still investigating and had led them to believe it must have been someone who knew Susan. Perhaps the rumours were correct that Susan may have been the victim of a jealous ex-husband.

His thoughts were interrupted by the sounds of Carolyn calling the assembly to order.

***

Malcolm had abandoned his usual sweater and grey pants in favour of a smart dark blue suit. As he sat rigid in his seat, he dabbed at his forehead with his handkerchief, mopping the beads of sweat that formed and slowly trickled towards his eyebrows. He needed a drink. Some days were worse than others. He could feel his gut twist as the cravings took over. It had been four months, seven days, and three hours since his last drink of alcohol.

His students were seated on the blue mats in front of him. Every once in a while, one of the students coughed or sniffled. He was worn out from trying to comfort them; nothing was going to take this pain away, not for a very long time. Hopefully this memorial service would start the healing process. This was their chance to say good-bye. He left his seat and went to sit with his students on the mats. Perhaps being nearer to them might help them all.

***

Ann, conservatively dressed in a white blouse, straight black skirt and a soft blue cardigan that complimented her Latin colouring, looked up when Carolyn began to speak. As she listened to Ms. Myers eulogize Susan, reviewing her many virtues and accomplishments, she wondered if anyone would ever think that way about her. If they knew what she had been accused of doing, she would be shunned not eulogized.

The young woman sat remembering that dreadful day her world had fallen apart. The accusation, that she had molested Sean ... that she had taken advantage of a fourteen-year-old boy, was as raw now as when it was first uttered.

Sean had been trouble since the first day he set foot in her class. He had a huge chip on his shoulder because of having to repeat the grade. He was ready to make her life miserable. Try as she might, she wasn't able to break through his tough shell. She had offered to listen to his problems; ignored his rude outbursts and had made allowances for his poor behaviour. Although his parents had been grateful when she had suggested giving him additional help after school, Sean was more interested in joining his friends at the skateboard park. He resented having to stay behind for the extra tutoring.

Eventually he made up the story that she had "come on to him." He told his parents that she touched him and tried to seduce him. Naturally, they believed their son and went straight to the principal. Shocked and duty bound, the principal had reported the accusations to the school board.

Nothing had ever been proven, as Sean never pressed charges. He had gotten what he wanted; he was free to join his friends skateboarding.

All of Ann's family, with the exception of her younger sister, Evett, turned away from her in shame. Unable to face the turmoil without support, Ann had resigned from the district the following week.

Over the summer months, she applied to at least twenty postings. When this job for Riverview was offered, she accepted quickly. It was a combined grade one and two class, but she was trained in early elementary school methods, and the younger children would be a welcome change from the hormonal upper-grade students. Thanks to her father calling in some favours, her references would not reveal her troubles. Since charges had not been made, the College of Teachers would have no record of the incident. It helped that the posting was in such an isolated outlying area and as such was very unattractive to most young, fun-loving teachers. The principal seemed only too glad to fill the position.

She desperately missed her family and friends. When she left Alton, her hometown several hundred kilometers away, Ann cut all ties to her former life. She lived in fear that someone would discover her secret, so she was now known as Ann Santos. Maria Santos no longer existed. Family and friends would not be able to find her easily. Sitting in her chair beside her row of students, she sobbed softly as she thought of her estranged family. They would have been a great comfort to her this past week.

She and Susan had become quite close in the short time they had known each other. Susan had made her laugh and had begun to bring her out of the misery she felt. Now Susan was gone.

Thinking about Susan, Ann realized that she had known very little about her friend. They usually chatted about teaching, their classes, and the latest gossip in the staff room. Perhaps the lack of in-depth conversation was partly her fault. Ann never talked about her family and took care to avoid situations where the topic might come up.

There had been no warning. On Sunday they had been making plans to head to Clearville for a girls' weekend with Amy and Barb. The very next day, Susan had been discovered nearly dead. She had given no hint of being troubled by anyone or that she was concerned for her safety. Try as she might, Ann could think of nothing that would help bring Susan's killer to justice.

***

Robert glared at his class. The students were becoming restless on the mats. *Christ, can't they behave for five minutes?* Excusing himself, he left the chairperson and strode importantly over to the class. One look from Mr. Doyle and the group fell silent. Taking care to appear compassionate, Robert squeezed Steven's shoulder. Steven reminded him of a former acquaintance from high school and was Robert's least favourite student. Only Steven knew the nails digging into his back were a firm warning. He wrenched his shoulder away and moved over closer to his pals.

Robert sat down in his chair. *Give me a break. What's Malcolm doing sitting on the floor with his kids?* He couldn't deny that it looked good, but it was too late for him to follow suit. *Damn.*

***

Betsy looked towards her husband from the visitor's section. Timmy sat quietly on her lap, subdued by the atmosphere and crowd. She had spent ages in front of the mirror this morning applying a heavy base of makeup to hide the purple bruise along her jaw line. By wearing her hair down and over her ears, she was able to camouflage most of the bruising. Still, she felt self-conscious and wondered if anyone had seen her injuries. She would have stayed home, but Robert was afraid that her absence would be noticed.

Carolyn led the very simple service that had been designed with the children in mind. This was the students' time to reflect on their memories of Ms. Lloyd. The gym had been decorated with streamers and balloons in various hues of green and silver. Several photographs of Susan had been placed on a table in front. Susan was shown with her beloved dog Rascal, with her students tobogganing down the hill beside the church, and at her family home. The central picture was a simple portrait that highlighted her wonderful smile. Quiet music continued to play in the background.

After telling the students about Ms. Lloyd's career, Carolyn went on to relate several humorous events featuring the children of Riverview and their beloved teacher. Many of the anecdotes were silly, and the children were soon laughing and smiling. Everyone remembered the day Susan wore a regal gown and a tiara to school. She had explained it was her birthday and she declared she was a princess for a day.

One by one, the older students read the messages they had composed. Tears flowed as Doug, who had made great progress in her class, haltingly recited Ms. Lloyd's favourite poem. The mood had gradually lightened by the time the children filed out into the sunshine, each carrying a green or silver balloon. Ms. Myers counted quietly to three, and then the balloons lifted skyward, drifting in the slight autumn breeze.

Chapter Five

Two weeks later, Carolyn looked at the teachers seated in front of her at the large staff room table. The late afternoon sun streamed in the large windows but no one wanted to close the vertical blinds. Winter would be here soon enough bringing with it early darkness.

She had called a staff meeting to discuss finding a replacement for Susan. Mrs. Newberry had been only a temporary measure. With a ranch to run and several children of her own, she was not interested in continuing to teach the grade three class.

"Mrs. Newberry has asked that we try to find a replacement teacher for Susan's class as soon as possible. It'll be difficult because there aren't many teachers on the substitute list that are willing to commute to Riverside daily. We have no accommodation to offer them and all the apartments by the general store are filled. Susan's old place was snapped up by an oil rig worker the week after she died. Also, not many people are keen on taking over a class after the teacher's been murdered."

"Has the district advertised the position?" Ben wanted to know.

"Yes, on the National Teacher Employment website. So far we have three candidates, two from the substitute list and one from Upper John, District 54. I'll need a committee to review their qualifications and help me select a suitable candidate for the board to approve," Carolyn said as she glanced around. "Are there any volunteers?"

Robert stood up quickly. "Since I'm most senior here, I'm in the best position to look after Riverside's needs. I'll chair the committee. I know more about this school than you do," he said, his voice dripping with sarcasm.

"Sit down, Robert. You have a hard time working on committees, and I dread the thought of you guiding a group to an agreement. As teacher in charge, you should be on the panel, but we don't need a chair for this one-time committee."

Flushing with anger, Robert muttered, "You bitch."

"What was that? I didn't hear you," Carolyn said.

"Nothing. I said it was fine with me," he replied, knowing full well that Carolyn held the power for now. He strengthened his resolve to find out something, anything that would give him an edge over this domineering woman.

Ms. Myers appealed once more to the teachers. "I need two others to work on this committee." No one volunteered.

"Sorry, then I have to appoint two of you. Ben and Amy, you'll make up the rest of the committee. There'll be a half-day release on Tuesday. You'll review the CVs and make a decision."

Ben and Amy looked at each other. The last thing they wanted was to be on a committee with Robert, but they had no choice. Amy looked back at Carolyn, shrugged her shoulders, and smiled. "Well okay. I'll try my best to find someone to fill Susan's shoes. It won't be easy though."

"We all finished here? I've got work to do," stated Robert. Rising once again to his feet, he strode out of the room without waiting for Carolyn's response.

"I'm having a potluck on Saturday. I'll put up a note on the bulletin board as to the time, and you can list the food you'd like to bring. Sure hope you can make it. We need to have some fun," Carolyn said. "Spouses and significant others are most welcome to come."

Chapter Six

Sgt. Bates was getting nowhere. After spending several days at the scene and interviewing teachers, support personnel, and members of the community, he was no closer to solving the first murder in the living memory of this tiny northern community of Wolfsburg.

The lack of physical evidence where the victim had been discovered made him think the crime had been committed elsewhere. Her car had been found dumped in a slough, and water had destroyed any biologicals and possible fingerprints. There were tracks near the slough, but someone, probably kids, had contaminated the evidence by driving a four-wheeler over them.

Some burnt clothing found near to where the car had entered the slough hadn't been helpful either. It had consisted of painter's overalls and some leather gloves. The overalls could have been bought at any of the hardware stores in town. The gloves were almost completely destroyed, void of any incriminating evidence whatsoever.

Sgt. Bates had yet to identify any possible suspects. It appeared that Susan had been loved by the staff and students and was well respected by the friendly folks in Wolfsburg. His inquiries in her hometown revealed an ex-husband, but it appeared that the split had been on friendly terms.

It was now time to lay low and wait. Sooner or later, someone would slip up. First, he had to plant some seeds of doubt to get people thinking and watching their neighbours.

He called a meeting at the general store. Curious to see who attended, he watched carefully as people filed in. Most of the teachers were there, except for two of the ones who lived in Belmont. Farmers and oil patch workers quietly stood at the back near the produce. A couple of teenage girls leaned casually on the ice cream freezer. The wife of one of the local farmers came bustling in but left quickly when her baby started squalling. He noticed Robert standing near the front of the crowd with his hand on Betsy's shoulder. Timmy pressed up against her legs, leaning away from his father. Malcolm and Ben spoke quietly while they waited for the meeting to start. Mostly everyone from the small community was there.

"Thank you all for coming," said Sgt. Bates. "I'm sure you all know who I am by now … Sgt. Bates … please call me Patrick. I'm pleased to report that we've made significant progress in our investigation. Several key pieces of evidence have been uncovered, and we're waiting on lab results. In the meantime, contact me if you see or hear anything suspicious. You never know what information could connect all the dots and secure a conviction. We're trying our best, but I'm sure you'll all rest easier when the murderer is behind bars. The RCMP is stepping up its presence in Wolfsburg, and I'll be stationed here until the case is solved. Don't hesitate to contact me or to call 911 or the tip line 656 897 8477 if you have information for us."

Robert blanched. *What key pieces of evidence?* He had been sure he had left no traces or clues of any kind. Going over and over the events in his mind, Robert became increasingly uneasy. *What key pieces of evidence?*

Shifting his feet restlessly, he glanced at Betsy. "Come on, it's junior's bedtime." They turned and squeezed through the crowd. As they left the store, Robert held his wife's arm tightly. Oblivious to the stares from several people, they hurried up the street towards the teacherage.

Patrick Bates noted Robert's hasty departure with interest. The man was certainly a weird individual. Very few people around here liked him. He was glad none of his nieces and nephews had a teacher like Mr. Doyle. It would be hard to put up with sarcasm and arrogance all day.

"Once again, thank you for coming," said Sgt. Bates.

He started circulating through the crowd as everyone began talking and catching up with their neighbours. On easy terms with most of his audience, he chatted amiably with them.

Half an hour later, the small crowd had dispersed. There were chores and milking still to be done before bed.

***

Meanwhile, Betsy lay moaning on the bathroom floor. Robert delivered one more kick and then left the tiny space. As the door slammed, she took her arms down, no longer needing to shield her head. She rolled over and heaved herself up over the rim of the toilet. Hanging onto the cold, white porcelain, she vomited the remains of her supper. Staggering to her feet, she inspected the latest damage. Ugly welts were forming on her stomach, and pain radiated from her wrist. Grabbing a facecloth, she held it under the cold water and then bound the material around the injured joint.

"Mom ... Mom," a tiny voice came from the other side of the door. "Mom, are you okay?"

Betsy rushed to open the door, knelt and then gathered her son in her arms.

"Mommy's all right. I shouldn't have made him mad. Promise me you'll never make him mad!" Timmy buried his head in her shoulder, making her wince from the pain that leapt from her wrist. "Mommy's all right. Don't you worry. Come on let's make some hot chocolate. It'll make us feel better."

Using her uninjured hand, she put the kettle on and made hot chocolate for Timmy. They were safe for now. Once Robert had done his worst, he always holed himself up in his sanctuary, watching graphic bondage porn on the Net until morning.

Gazing at her son blowing gently to cool the hot liquid, she knew they couldn't take much more. However, escape seemed impossible. Robert always took the keys to the truck to school with him. It had been a long time since she had even been allowed to drive the vehicle. Besides, how would they manage on their own? How would she buy food and find a place to live? All the bank accounts were in Robert's name. Besides, Robert would discover them in no time. He had warned her that if she ever left him, they were as good as dead.

She couldn't go home to the farm. Her parents had died several years ago, and her brother had sold the farm to pay off the outstanding debts. Later, her brother Earl had taken a job overseas. She hadn't heard from him in more than three years.

She had no real friends. Robert made sure of that. He never let her go anywhere by herself, and he monitored any comings and goings at the teacherage from his classroom window. At social gatherings, he kept a close eye on her and was always within earshot. Robert seldom allowed her to go to the staff functions, always coming up with varied excuses to explain her absences. If anything ever happened to her and Timmy, no one would miss them for a very long time. She was trapped, well and truly trapped in a spiralling world of despair.

*****

Robert flicked on the computer screen and went directly to his favourite site. As he watched the whip come down on the creamy white buttocks, he felt himself grow hard. Tension increased as the hapless victim pleaded for mercy. His climax came quickly.

His thoughts then turned to what Sgt. Bates had said. *What key evidence?* He had been so careful to clean up. It was a brilliant idea to dump the car in Fred's slough. Even the hardware store couldn't identify him. When he purchased the coveralls and gloves, he had been wearing his disguise that he used to sneak into the casino. That stupid bouncer was fooled every time. Banning him from the premises had lasted all of two weeks. Bates must be blowing smoke. He had been too careful. Thank God Susan never regained consciousness. She should have died on the steps where he left her instead of hanging on all night.

Then an image of Carolyn, looking down her nose at him and speaking in that superior tone of hers, appeared. *Hard time working on committees... dread the thought of you guiding a group...* He remembered every detail of her put-down. That bitch deserved to be whipped like a dog.

Another picture, one of his emasculating mother standing over him with the wooden spoon clutched tightly in her hand, crowded into his mind. He could still hear her strident voice berating him. "You'll never amount to anything. You're such a loser. You haven't got it in you to become a successful man. Stop snivelling, you little shit, you good for nothing pansy. Mark my words; you'll never amount to anything." Her blows rained down with each scalding phrase.

He had proven her wrong. By sheer determination and smarts, he had won the head teacher position. He and Betsy had produced a fine son, and they had money in the bank.

True, his head teacher position was only temporary for this year. The renewal of that part of the contract depended on Carolyn's unlikely recommendation. Other candidates for the job included Ben, who had the senior class, and Malcolm, who was for some reason quite favoured, especially by Ms. Myers. Still, Robert was the most senior. Barring anyone else rising to attention of the board, he should be okay. He'd have to make sure they were discredited or would refuse the opportunity. That shouldn't be hard. He could scare anyone.

As he thought about the possible threats to his position, he was reminded of Ann. He was quite attracted to the lovely Latino girl. Latinos have a reputation for being hot-blooded. He could have some fun with her.

Chapter Seven

Ann chose a day when her family had gone to the lake, leaving the house empty. After packing her clothes, books, a few mementos, and the rocking chair that she had inherited from her grandmother into the car, she went back inside and looked around her childhood home. Sunlight streamed through the windows, illuminating the cheerful living room filled with comfortable overstuffed beige sofas and chocolate brown chairs. *Chatelaine*, *Yatchsman* and *Shape* magazines littered the coffee table indicative of her family's diverse tastes. The cat was stretched out, sunning itself on the window seat.

Sadly, there was nothing left here for her anymore. Her sister, Evett, would miss her, but she knew the rest of them would be relieved to be rid of the dark cloud of suspicion that enveloped her.

Alton was a small town where her well-known parents enjoyed a certain social status... In spite of her father calling in a favour and the board not publicly giving any reason for her unexpected departure, the rumour mill was working overtime. Since the accusation had come near the end of the school year, she had been able to keep a low profile for a while. Now in the late summer, the rumours had begun to fade in people's memories, but she realized that once the school year started, there would be renewed speculation.

Desperate to get away, she accepted the first job offer. It was a grade one class in a small school servicing the deeply religious community of Wolfsburg. Ms. Myers, the principal of several of the rural schools, had seemed pleasant enough on the phone. She had offered her a small, already-furnished trailer belonging to the district as accommodation.

Now, the only thing left to do was to leave her farewell note. Knowing that Evett would be devastated, Ann had not told her that she was going. This was going to be a huge shock. She ended up leaving two notes. The one for her family stated that she was sorry to have caused them such shame and distress. The other note simply contained the words *I love you, Evett*, a post box number in Belmont, and strict instructions for Evett to make contact only in an emergency. She had made arrangements for the post office in Belmont to forward any mail to Riverside School in Wolfsburg.

After sealing and addressing the envelopes, she took one last look around, reached over to give Snookie, the cat, a final pat on her sleek head, and then left quickly.

A short half-hour later she was forced to pull over to the side of the road. Ann sat weeping in her little, blue car. Never had she felt so alone. Never had she felt so unsure of herself. She visualized a bleak, empty future stretching out in front of her. *Damn that kid.* What had been a simple lie for him had ruined her reputation. Nothing would ever be the same again.

She remained so long in her parked car that the owner of the service station on the other side of the road came over to see what was wrong. He tapped on her window. Reluctantly, she pressed the button to lower her window.

"Something wrong with your car, lady?"

"Umm, no. It's okay, just taking a bit of a breather," replied Ann.

"Looks like you're more than a little upset, girl. Boyfriend troubles? No man is worth that many tears. You need a coffee?" the man offered.

"No thanks. It's very kind of you, but I best be getting along. I have a long road ahead of me. Hoping to make the border before night. Thanks again." She smiled and started the car. With a wave of her hand, she pulled out onto the highway. *Suck it up, princess,* she chastised herself. Then, all cried out, she laughed as she recalled Evett's favourite phrase: "Put on your big-girl panties and deal with it."

With one hand on the wheel, she pushed a CD into the player and set the volume of the music as loud as she could stand it. Willing her mind to go with the music and focus only on the road ahead, she left the town of Alton behind her.

Just after two in the afternoon, she stopped outside a small diner. Noticing two eighteen-wheelers parked beside the entrance, Ann took that as a sign the food was good. She had heard that truckers were very particular as to where they chow down. Maybe it was time to check out this theory. She climbed out of the car, stretched her back, and then entered the squeaky screen door of the diner.

Pausing for a couple of seconds, she let her eyes adjust to the dim lights. The place looked clean enough. She smiled at the waitress and then went to wash up in the ladies' room. Thank goodness she had chosen to go in there first. She burst out laughing when she discovered that her tears had left ragged tracks of mascara down her face. What a sight she was! No wonder the service station attendant had been so concerned.

After cleaning up and reapplying her makeup, Ann ventured out into the diner.

"Sit anywheres you want!" called the young waitress wearing a short-skirted uniform with a stain on the front. "Be with you in a sec."

The diner wasn't crowded so she had her choice of tables. Ann chose one next to the window and pulled out her crossword puzzle book. She loved crosswords and Sudoku.

"Menu?"

"Yes, please, and a coffee," answered Ann. "What's the special today?"

"It's all gone. Still lots of soup … split pea. I'll give you a couple of minutes to decide."

Ann chose a toasted bacon and tomato sandwich with fries. As she ate, she began to relax her tense shoulders. She watched the truckers finish their meal and head out to their rigs.

When a family of four came barrelling in, the place became a zoo. It never ceased to amaze Ann how little control some parents had over their children. The two-year-old left to his own devices played with his knife and spoon dropping them several times on the floor with shrieks of glee. His six-year-old sister loudly commanded her parents' undivided attention. She clearly ruled the family with her demands and pouting.

Before the children's bad behaviour could get to her, Ann got up and crossed over to the counter to pay the bill.

"Sorry about that," murmured the waitress as she rang in the sale. "Some people sure have them!"

"No worries. I was ready to leave anyway. Try not to kill them," she said with a chuckle and then went out into the brilliant sunshine.

The remainder of the afternoon passed by quickly. She stopped for the night in Richelieu, a pleasant settlement in the foothills of the Rocky Mountains. A strip of motels and fast-food restaurants welcomed visitors to the sleepy little town. After veering off the highway and into the main section of town, Ann pulled into the parking lot of Knight's Inn. The white stucco walls, a red painted door, and some ancient wrought iron railings gave it an olden-day atmosphere. Several cars and a couple of pickups were parked outside the entrance. She went inside.

The lobby seemed okay, but Ann was leery about staying in an unfamiliar place.

"Can I see the room first?" asked Ann.

The harried middle-aged clerk looked surprised. "I guess so, sure. You'll be perfectly safe here—I can tell you that. We actually have a convention of police chiefs staying here over the next few days." He led her down the hall and showed her the room.

The simple room was well furnished with a large double bed, dresser, desk and a television. The ensuite bathroom was adequate. It was nice enough but the room had a strong odour of cigarette smoke.

"Oh, no. I should have said a non-smoking room. Do you have any available?"

The clerk pursed his lips and looked slightly annoyed. "All our rooms are non-smoking. We'll have to have this one cleaned. You can be sure the previous guest will have to foot the bill. Here let's try this one." He opened the door to another room. "How's this?"

After a quick look in the bathroom and out the window, Ann nodded. "This is just fine. Thanks. Can you recommend a good place to eat?"

"Pizza Palace isn't bad if you like Italian. Then there's the new sushi place just down the next block."

"Great, thanks. I'll sign in and come back with my bags," Ann said.

After giving her credit card number, she wondered if it was a good idea to charge the room—considering she didn't want to be traced. She decided she would pay cash the next morning so that the charge wouldn't show up. As soon as she was settled in her new job, she intended to get new cards in her new name ... Ann Santos.

Choosing to eat at the sushi place turned out to be a good idea. The light meal of miso soup, a California roll, and vegetable tempura went down easily after her long drive. She sat off to one side of the main dining area observing the other patrons. There were three groups of tourists, a couple who had eyes only for each other, several uniformed policemen, and a man eating alone.

He raised his eyes as she glanced his way. Seeing that she was looking at him, he smiled and raised his glass of Japanese beer. Ann quickly smiled and looked away. She certainly didn't want him to think she wanted company, but she knew it was too late when she saw him get to his feet and come somewhat unsteadily over to her table.

"Do we know each other?" the tall, rather largely built man asked.

"No, I don't think so," replied Ann hastily. "I'm not from around here."

"Well, we could get to know one another," he said in a quiet voice.

"No, no thank you. I would rather be alone right now," Ann offered, hoping not to offend him.

"Suit yourself," he muttered and returned to his table.

Luckily her food arrived quickly, and she busied herself with the well-prepared meal. While she ate, she noticed the man get up, pay his bill, and leave the restaurant. Ann hated confrontation and was glad to see him leave.

"Care for some more green tea?" asked the server.

"No. I'd like a nightcap. Do you serve any of those special coffees here?"

"Just regular coffee, but we do have some excellent liqueurs. I recommend the plum liqueur called Umeshu," suggested the waiter.

"Okay, that and a cup of coffee, please."

Sipping the Umeshu, she relaxed and let her thoughts drift. The restaurant was quite busy, but they still had empty tables. She was in no hurry to leave and go back to the empty, impersonal motel room.

Twenty minutes later she realized it was getting late. She needed to get a good start in the morning. Reluctantly, she rose and went to the counter. Several of the officers were also waiting to settle their bills.

After paying with cash and leaving a generous tip on the table, she stepped out into the night.

A quick movement from beside the door caught her eye. Instantly aware, she turned and stared into the face of the guy who had troubled her in the restaurant. He must have been waiting for her.

"You changed your mind and want some company?" he slurred, his breath reeking of beer.

"No, no. I'm heading back to my room. It's late and I have to get up in the morning. Good night," she said, hoping to diffuse the situation.

"Come on, lady, we're both on our own. Let's make a twosome."

"You heard the lady, bugger off." One of the policemen stepped out from the shadows beside the restaurant entrance.

"Fuck you," growled the drunk as he turned and lurched down the street.

Ann let out the breath she had been holding. "Thanks, I'm glad you were out here. Guess I shouldn't let my guard down when I'm in a strange town."

"No problem," declared the young cop. "I had an idea in the restaurant that he wasn't going to take no for an answer. Come on, I'll walk you back to your room. Noticed you registering at the motel this afternoon. We're staying at the same place."

They walked back to the motel talking companionably. He certainly appeared to be a very nice, friendly, man. She smiled as she reached her door.

"Thank you very much for coming to my rescue. Good night," Ann said as she put the card in her door and opened it. "Thanks again."

The policeman raised his hand to his forehead in a brief salute and carried on down the hall.

After enjoying a soothing bath, Ann settled in for the night. She remembered that her old, soft pillow was in the car but decided she would do without it. She didn't want to run the risk of meeting anyone. So after setting her travel alarm for six o'clock and checking the chain on the door for the last time, she beat the over-stuffed pillow into submission. It took her some time to fall asleep, but when she did, she slept surprisingly well.

The persistent bleeping of her alarm roused her out of uneasy dreams, and it took several moments to orient herself to the unfamiliar surroundings. As her eyes became adjusted to the dim light, she saw the desk and television adjacent to the bed. She became aware of the sound of a shower running in the bathroom next door. A man's deep voice resonated as he sang in the cascading water.

Stumbling over her discarded shoes, she made her way into her bathroom and set about getting ready for the next part of her journey. A simple pair of jeans and a light sweater pulled over her T-shirt would be enough. It was cool outside right now, but the weather forecast had been for temperatures rising into the teens.

After quickly making sure she had left nothing behind, Ann left her room. She entered the lobby and settled her bill with the clerk on duty. Tugging her rolling suitcase behind her, she crossed over to her car.

"Here, let me help you with that," offered her saviour from the night before.

"Oh, hi." Ann smiled as she let him lift the case into the back of her little SUV. "You're up early." She noticed he was dressed in a light track-suit and was a bit out of breath. "Can I buy you breakfast? I really did appreciate your help last night."

"No thanks necessary. It was my pleasure. I'd love to grab breakfast with you, but we have a breakfast meeting in the conference room at seven. Have a safe trip. Take care." Once again, he did his funny little half-salute and jogged away to the lobby.

After getting breakfast at the McDonald's drive-in down the street, she hauled out onto the highway and continued east into the mountainous pass that separated the two provinces. The sun was shining and traffic was light.

Unfortunately, her mood did not mirror the perfect day. Distracting thoughts swept through her mind. She recalled the day when she had found out Sean had accused her of touching him. The repercussions had been swift and merciless. No one even considered that he might have been making up his story.

She second-guessed herself as she drove along the increasingly winding road. *Should she have stayed and cleared her name?* She wondered. Her running away had probably confirmed her guilt in most people's minds.

She shook her head ruefully. It was too late now. She had left and there was no turning back.

As the road conditions worsened, she forced these unwelcome reflections from her mind. There was no point in dwelling on what might have been. In times of trouble, she often divorced herself from her problems and lived in the here and now. Shelving her concerns, she made herself look around at the wonderful sunlit day.

Soon, it was taking all her concentration to navigate the winding road through the pass. Several times, she was forced to brake for a bear, a moose, or some deer that decided to cross the road. Wildlife was everywhere. Occasionally, she saw glimpses of deer feeding in the ditches. Once she was fortunate enough to see two coyotes hunting for mice in a small meadow.

At mid-day, she stopped at a small roadside rest stop. Walking down a small trail, Ann came to an icy cold stream sending up fine mist as it tumbled over a rocky ledge. Looking through the sunlit spray, she watched the water refract into colourful prisms. She relaxed her stiff shoulders while she listened to the rushing water somersault its way down a small gorge. Several birds with bright blue feathers rested in the nearby trees, chittering cheerfully to each other.

Thirsty, she knelt down at the stream's edge and scooped handfuls of the icy cold water into her mouth. It was delicious. Resting on her heels, she continued to soak in the sights, sounds, and mossy aroma of this peaceful setting.

"Be careful, don't you girls get too close to the edge," warned a woman's voice as two little girls and a young couple came into view.

"Oh, look at the birds, Mum," exclaimed the oldest girl. "What kind are they?"

"I don't know, Katy. We can look them up in Dad's bird book when we get back to the camper."

Her reverie disturbed, Ann got to her feet and reluctantly headed back over the trail to the parking lot. Checking the map, she realized that it would take over five hours to reach Belmont. There was another town, Clearville, just an hour away from this rest stop. She thought she might get some lunch there. Buckling her seat belt, she started the vehicle and carried on her way.

Descending into a valley, she could see the thriving town of Clearville spread out beside the Rouge River. The town had a pleasant look about it, with lots of green spaces and well-kept buildings. As usual, the industrial area consisted mainly of car dealerships and logging companies. Off in the distance, she could see the tell-tale plume of smoke coming from a pulp mill.

She stopped at the first nice-looking restaurant that she saw. Hungry, she made her way quickly into the café and sat down in one of the booths.

"Sorry, ma'am. We're just about ready to close for the afternoon," a large-bosomed waitress announced. "If you're looking for lunch, try the Thatch Roof, a diner about three blocks further down the street. They got good food there. Sorry."

"Darn, I guess I'm pretty late for lunch. This place looked good," murmured Ann. She gathered her stuff and made her way back out to the car.

Driving quickly, she almost missed the turn-off to the Thatch Roof. Entering the air-conditioned restaurant, she sat at the counter and ordered lunch. The clubhouse sandwich was delicious, and she devoured every crispy French fry.

It was well past ten o'clock when she arrived in Belmont. She was dismayed to see that Belmont with its air of quiet desperation appeared to be a much seedier town than Clearville. Several of the stores looked like they had gone out of business, and the streets were dirty.

As she made her way into the town center, the atmosphere changed radically. The place was jumping, especially around the two casinos perched opposite each other. Music blared from the casinos, and bright lights flooded the now dark streets. Cruising carefully, she managed to avoid the patrons spilling out into the evening. Male and female hookers could be seen plying their trade. Her heart sank. This was not somewhere to be on your own.

On the outskirts of town, she was able to find a Sandman hotel with a Denny's restaurant attached to it. This would have to do. She was exhausted. Anyway, she had to stay in Belmont. Her appointment with the principal for the rural schools was at ten the next morning.

Chapter Eight

Arriving at the low-squat building that housed the school board offices, Ann pushed open the glass entrance door and found herself in an impersonal lobby.

"I have an appointment with Ms. Myers," she told the pretty red-headed girl seated at the reception desk.

The girl smiled revealing her perfect white teeth. "I'll ring through."

A few minutes later, she was ushered into Carolyn Myer's office. Ann smiled and shook hands with the dark-haired, well-dressed woman seated behind the desk. "I'm so pleased to finally meet you in person. I'm looking forward to working in this district."

"Welcome to Belmont, and more particularly, welcome to your new position at Riverside. As you know, we had you slated for the grade one position, but I'm afraid it has now become a split grade one and two. Is that a problem for you?" asked Ms. Myers.

"No, not really. I would prefer a straight grade as it's harder to deliver two curriculums, but I'm sure I can manage," replied Ann. "How many children in the class? Are there any students with special needs?"

"No students with diagnosed special needs, but there is one child that we suspect has Asperger's Syndrome. He'll have an aide with him for part of the day." Carolyn was quite impressed with this young lady. She seemed to have a good head on her shoulders and certainly asked the right questions.

"Now here's the telephone number of the teacher in charge, Mr. Doyle. He has the keys to your trailer and your keys to the school. I've told him to expect you around three this afternoon. That will give you time to pick up some groceries before you head out. The general store out there has some items, but everything is very expensive. Be sure to gas up your car before you leave as well. There are no service stations between here and Wolfsburg."

"Fine," Ann said. She instantly liked Ms. Myers. From first impressions, Carolyn appeared to be friendly and professional. She seemed to know all about Riverside School and was aware of the makeup of the class. "When will I see you next? I understand you look after several schools."

"Oh, I won't be out to Riverside before school starts on Tuesday. Give me a call on Monday and let me know how everything's going. I'll see you Tuesday afternoon. And by the way, Tuesday is only a half-day attendance for the students." She stood up. "Best of luck to you and again, welcome."

Ann left the school board office feeling rather pleased. Things certainly seemed to be working out well. After her first impression of Belmont last night, she had been concerned that she had made a mistake accepting this position. Now, she began thinking that it might not be so bad after all. She called in at the post office to give them her new address in Wolfsburg. Then she bought some groceries at the supermarket near the town swimming pool.

It wasn't hard to find Riverside Elementary. The community, Wolfsburg, was not very big. It had a general store, three churches, a community hall, the school, one-storey apartment complex, and not much else.

As she had driven the seventy-five kilometers of gravel road from Belmont, she had passed by several large, sprawling ranches and what appeared to be three oil patch compounds. She guessed that most of the students were either driven or bussed to school.

Climbing the steps to the teacherage, she paused to scratch the ears of a small black and white dog that welcomed her. It was friendly enough and hadn't barked. She raised her hand and knocked loudly on the door. A small boy around five years old answered.

"Hi. Is your dad home?"

"Yes, just a minute. I'll get him." The door shut quickly before she could glimpse inside.

Ann could hear the little boy calling for his dad. Instinctively, she stepped back a bit as a tall, well-built man opened the door. His frame and personality filled the space.

"Oh, hello. You must be Ann Santos. Ms. Myers called to say you were on your way. Did you have any trouble finding our quaint hamlet?" Robert asked as he ushered her inside his small home.

"No, no trouble at all. You must be Mr. Doyle, the head teacher," replied Ann, taking in the neat space with its plain, comfortable furnishings. "You must enjoy family nights," she said, referring to the games piled on the coffee table.

"Yes, we play a lot of games. I don't allow my son or my wife to watch television. Television is a sheer waste of time."

"Well, I won't keep you. I need the keys to the school and to the trailer. By the way, where is the trailer? I thought it would be on the school grounds."

Robert laughed. "You'll find the trailer on the other side of the road. Turn down Kies Road. You can't miss it. It's a long walk to school, but it can be done."

A small woman entered the room. "This here is Betsy, my wife." Ann could see Timmy shyly peeking out from behind this mere slip of a woman.

"Hello," Ann greeted her. "You sure have a cozy place here."

"Listen, why don't you drop by for supper tonight," offered Robert. "It would save you having to rustle up something when you're tired."

Betsy shot him a surprised look. Robert never invited anyone over to the house. He must be trying to make an impression.

"Lovely. That's so kind of you. Sure, if it's no trouble. What can I bring? I picked up some nice donuts in town."

"Okay. See you back here at six," Robert said as he gave her the keys.

Chapter Nine

Nothing could have prepared Ann for the state of the trailer. The door gaped inwards, squeaking as it swung on its hinges in the slight breeze. Flies buzzed in the garbage strewn around the small yard.

Opening the door wider, she stepped inside. Both human and animal footprints could be seen in the mud that had been tracked throughout the small unit. A pile of dog feces was beside the kitchen stove. Dishes sat unwashed in the sink, and various pots and pans littered the countertop. A foul odour drifted from the fridge that had been left open. An old couch and chair left over from the seventies, a rickety coffee table, and a Formica table with two dilapidated chairs were the only furnishings in the combined living and dining area.

She inspected the other rooms. First she looked in the only bedroom. The double bed gave her the creeps. It had obviously been well used by some amorous people. Apart from the bed, there was a small dresser and a nightstand. A good-sized closet occupied one corner, and a small built-in desk filled the rest of the space.

The bathroom was in deplorable condition. The toilet was almost overflowing with waste. A shower dripped incessantly into a tub that was permanently stained orange by rusty hard water. Reaching over to flush the filthy toilet, Ann was relieved to find that it worked and was not blocked up. The sink, however, was another matter. A huge tangle of dark brown hair clogged the drain.

Curtains, linens, and cleaning supplies were non-existent. Sickened, Ann went to sit on the stoop. Her hands shook and angry, defeated tears threatened to flow. Surely they couldn't expect her to live in this dump. What was she going to do? She knew there was nowhere else to rent in Wolfsburg. She was stuck. The promising day had just turned into a nightmare.

Steeling herself, Ann returned inside to see what would need to be done if she was going to stay here tonight. She'd have to clean the trailer the best she could until she was able to get to town tomorrow for proper disinfecting supplies. She needed a place to sleep, and this would have to do.

Then there was the matter of security and privacy. There was always the chance someone might come back to this isolated trailer. Off to the side of what seemed to be a seldom-traveled road, the trashed mobile made a perfect hiding place. Such seclusion was dangerous. No one would even know she would be living here.

Trying the key in the door, Ann found that the door could be locked. The same key fit the back door as well. The back door opened outwards onto a small landing and stairs leading to the unkempt space behind the trailer.

Then remembering the magazines in her car, she carefully took them apart. Using tape from her box of school supplies, she managed to cover the windows with the sheets of paper. Tonight she would ask Mr. Doyle how she could get some curtains from the school district. This place was supposed to be furnished.

Ann then dealt with the bed situation. Since it was getting on towards five o'clock, there was no time to see if there were any beds in the medical room in the school that she could use for the night. Struggling with the weight of the mattress, she flipped it over. It was relatively clean on the underside. She got her emergency/camping sleeping bag from the back of her car. Pushing aside thoughts of the previous visitors' activities, she tossed her sleeping bag on top of the bed.

The bathroom was next. Using some shampoo from her toiletry bag, she managed to scrub at the toilet and sink. She knew she had no hope of cleaning the tub and shower yet. Sighing, she went to tackle the fridge and dishes.

Halfway through the dishes, she realized she was due at the Doyles'. After giving her hair a quick brush and reapplying her lipstick, she rushed outside. She locked the front door and jumped into her car.

Arriving only a few minutes late, she apologised profusely.

"I'm so sorry. I lost track of time. I hope I haven't spoiled dinner," she said as Betsy led her into the living room.

Betsy had her dull blonde hair tied back with an elastic band. She gazed at Ann through vacant unresponsive eyes, unsure of how to respond to Ann's apologies.

"That's all right," replied Betsy. "Robert had to go over to the school for something. I'm expecting him back shortly. Sit down. Dinner won't be long."

Ann took a seat on the utilitarian couch. Looking around, she noticed that everything was obsessively tidy and arranged neatly. Even the boy's toys seemed to be carefully ordered.

"Hi," whispered a small voice.

Ann turned and smiled at the solemn little boy who had quietly entered the room.

"Hello, yourself," she said. "Come and show me your favourite game. How old are you?"

Timmy smiled timidly at the visitor. He liked her long, dark hair and warm smile.

"I'm four almost five. Next year I get to go to kindergarten if my dad lets me. What grade you going to teach?" he asked.

"I've got grade one and two this year. So, if I stay, I may teach you in two years' time," replied Ann in a friendly tone. The young boy smiled again shyly and pulled out his favourite game, checkers.

"Wow, you play checkers! That's a grown up game!" Ann said. This serious little boy intrigued her. He seemed so bright and articulate for his age.

Timmy and Ann were busy getting acquainted as Robert bustled in through the door.

"Oh, I see you made it," he said, nodding to Ann as he took off his jacket and hung it on the hook beside the door. "Supper ready yet, Betsy?"

Betsy bobbed her head silently, and they all took their places around the small table. She portioned out the food in the tiny kitchen and brought out the supper to everyone.

Ann smiled appreciatively at Betsy.

"This looks wonderful. I just love crispy chicken and rice. What kind of vegetables are these?"

Betsy looked relieved. Unused to company, she had been afraid that the dinner might not meet Robert's strict standards.

"They're just a frozen mix I get at the market in town," she replied.

"Did you have any trouble finding the trailer?" Robert asked. "Haven't been there this summer. I'm supposed to look after the property, but it's not high on my list. The four thousand a year extra for being head teacher is a mere pittance. What with all the paper work and the organizing I have to do, I don't have time for much else. Ms. Myers leaves a lot of the day-to-day running of the school up to me."

Betsy smiled inwardly. Robert was making the head teacher position out to be much more than it was. He didn't have to do any organizing and had no say over the duties and responsibilities of the other teachers. Ms. Myers came out at least once a week. If there were any emergencies or problems, it was her responsibility as the agent of the school board to deal with the parents and students. Besides, the job was usually rotated each year between the teachers who had expressed a willingness to take it on. While the title of head teacher looked good on a resume, most teachers also appreciated the extra money that came with the job. Robert had had the job for two years in a row now. She knew he would probably have a hard time giving it up next year if he had to. The title fed his ego.

"Well, I wish someone had checked on the place. It's in horrible condition. It's not fit for an animal to live in, let alone a tenant," Ann replied. She then went on to describe what she had found when she entered the trailer.

Betsy looked shocked and dismayed but Robert just sat there while she detailed the problems.

"That sounds pretty bad. Give me a list of what you need, and I'll see what I can do. The district is pretty tight right now. I don't imagine we'll get much out of them. Don't make too many waves. You should be thankful it's a roof over your head. They could easily give the trailer to another teacher. There's a line-up of people wanting to live in Wolfsburg," he warned.

"I *am* thankful for a place to live. I certainly don't want to drive that gravel road to town every day, especially in the winter. Still, something has to be done … it's dreadful."

Betsy glanced at her husband and took a chance. "Let me loan you a couple of old sheets to use as curtains for now. I can let you have some bleach to do over the sinks and toilet."

"Oh my goodness, that's kind of you," said Ann. "That makes me feel so much better." She missed the glare that Robert gave Betsy.

"Best you keep your door locked at all times out there," warned Robert, lowering his voice so that Timmy wouldn't hear. "We've had a bit of trouble at that trailer in the past. Just last year, the female teacher living there was raped and badly beaten sometime over the Christmas holidays. She ended up leaving the district in January. And rumours have it that before Betsy and I came to Riverside, that mobile was the local place to score drugs. You know how rough those guys can be." He was rewarded to see Ann's face go pale.

Betsy also noticed Ann blanch. Robert was playing his mind games again. She had never heard of the drug dealings, but she did know about the teacher leaving in January after she had been attacked.

"For God's sake, Robert, you're scaring her." She turned to Ann. "Still it's best you follow his advice. The police never did catch anyone, but most people think it was some stranger that had come in off the highway. Nothing had ever happened like that around here before."

Ann was thoroughly shaken by what Robert had said. Things were going from bad to worse. Still, it seemed to her that the state of the trailer had more the characteristics of teenagers playing around and using it for a place to hang out, than being used for gang activity. She had found no drug paraphernalia and nothing that would to lead her to believe that it was a drug distribution place. How many people would come all the way from town to buy drugs in Wolfsburg? Besides, the community appeared to be upstanding and had a reputation for being very religious. Drugs would not be tolerated here. No, she didn't have to worry about gangs, but the rape story was disturbing. It would be difficult to summon help from such an isolated location.

Over the dinner of chicken, rice, and vegetables, Ann discovered a lot about Riverside school and the small hamlet of Wolfsburg. Robert was more than happy to tell his version of life in this rural area. Betsy added very little to her husband's tales, and Timmy said nothing at all.

"Oh, I forgot. I brought some donuts for dessert. They're in the car. Do you like donuts, Timmy?" Ann asked.

When Ann brought the treats in from the car, Timmy's eyes lit up at the sight of the sugary sweets. She was glad she had brought the donuts to share for dessert. It was obvious that such treats were rare in his world.

"Sure, you can have one, Timmy," Robert encouraged his son, playing the role of doting father for his new audience. They seldom had company over for a meal.

Timmy tentatively reached out and took the most tempting of the donuts, one that was covered with sticky chocolate and sprinkles.

"Thanks," he whispered to Ann. "I love donuts."

Suddenly the long day caught up with her. Ann was hardly able to keep her eyes open.

"Oh my, I'm so tired. It's been a really long day. I'm afraid if I don't go soon, I'll fall asleep right here at your table. Here, let me help you with these dishes." Ann rose wearily and started to gather up some of the plates.

"No, no. It's fine. Leave the dishes. You've had enough to do with all that mess in the trailer. I'll leave them to soak and do them in the morning," Betsy lied, knowing full well that Robert would never tolerate the dishes being left undone. She rose and led Ann to the front door.

"Oh, wait just a minute," Betsy said as she hurried to the kitchen. From under the sink she gathered some bleach and a couple of old cloths. She went over to the linen closet next to the bathroom and found a pair of threadbare sheets.

"Here," said Betsy as she handed Ann a plastic bag of supplies. "Hope they help."

Putting on her jacket, Ann bid the family goodnight and quickly got into her car. As darkness began to fall, she drove along slowly, looking for the driveway to the trailer. She located the turn-off and pulled into the driveway, parking as close to the door as possible. Making sure she had the key in her hand, she strode purposefully up the steps, unlocked the door, and entered.

Dumping the sheets and the bottle of bleach that Betsy had loaned her beside the door, she looked around carefully. Everything seemed to be okay, so she locked the door behind her and went into the bathroom. She froze. All her cosmetics, soaps, shampoo, and such had been emptied into the tub. Someone had been in there while she was at the Doyles'. Nothing else appeared to have been disturbed. Her clothes and other personal things lay scattered about the bedroom as she had left them. Horrified, she realized that someone else had a key to the mobile.

Ann grabbed a broom standing in the corner of the kitchen and went to check the closets and under the bed. Relieved to find no one hiding, she put the broom back into the utility room next to the bathroom. Standing in the middle of the hall, shaking violently, she was convinced she wouldn't get a bit of sleep tonight unless she managed to secure the place. She tugged and pulled the heavy armchair until it was positioned firmly in front of the trailer door. Fortunately, she had brought most of her important belongings inside during the afternoon. All that was left in the car were some rubber boots and a few more boxes holding her books and teaching supplies.

Not trusting that the magazine pages covering the windows would be sufficient to shield her from prying eyes, Ann draped the old sheets over the bedroom and living room windows. Then she jostled the washing machine across the floor until its side was in the way if the back door was opened.

Exhausted from her efforts and stress, Ann filled the dented kettle and set it on the electric stove. She made herself a cup of tea. As she slowly sipped the hot liquid, her nerves began to calm. She still had to clean up the mess in the tub and bleach the toilet and sink. Slowly, she forced herself to her feet. Grabbing an old towel from under the kitchen sink and the bleach from beside the front door, she carried on into the tiny bathroom and set to work.

It was well after midnight when she finally climbed into her sleeping bag and fell into an uneasy sleep. Every time she heard the trailer creak or groan, her eyes flew open. Towards morning, exhaustion took over and she slept.

***

Robert closed his eyes and drifted off into satisfied dreams. All was right in his world. The look on her face when he mentioned the beating had been enough to tell him that this sweet, young thing would be an easy mark.

Chapter Ten

Ann startled awake. It took her a few seconds to realize where she was. As her breathing slowed and returned to normal, she lay there thinking about her next steps. She had so much to do. Her classroom had to be prepared. The students would be arriving in just four days. She needed to get this dump scrubbed and straightened. Obviously, she also had to go back into town for cleaning supplies, locks, and a new mattress. First things first, she had to call Ms. Myers to let her know the difficulties she was facing.

At nine o'clock, she dialled the school board office and was told that Ms. Myers was away from her office but could be reached on her cell phone. Dialling the number the secretary had given her, Ann waited for Ms. Myers to pick up. The call went to voicemail.

"Ms. Myers, Ann Santos calling. Sorry to bother you, but I have some serious concerns here in Riverside. I have to go back into town this morning, so please call me as soon as you get this message. My number is 435–567–7890."

While she waited for Carolyn to return her call, Ann made herself some coffee and a light breakfast of egg and toast.

Since she had so much to do in the few days before school was to open for the year, she decided to see if she could hire Betsy to help clean the trailer. She could drop over there on her way to town and ask her. The quiet ring of her cell phone alerted her to Carolyn Myers's call.

"Carolyn, here, I got your message. What's wrong, Ann?"

As Ann started to describe the situation to Carolyn, she became overwhelmed. With a voice thickened with tears, she said, "I'm so sorry to bother you, but I don't know what else to do. Mr. Doyle doesn't seem to be very concerned, but I can't live in these conditions."

"Hey, calm down, Ann. We can fix this. Tell me what you need. Don't concern yourself about Mr. Doyle. He's only the head teacher. I approve expenses and I'll call in the maintenance crew if we must, although they're pretty busy right now repairing some burst pipes at

Lakewood," Carolyn told her. *That lazy hide. Doyle should have checked the trailer and made sure it was ready for Ann,* she thought to herself.

"I thought perhaps I might ask Betsy if she knows someone who could help me clean the trailer. Maybe she'd like to do it," Ann said.

"Well, you could try, but she keeps to herself a lot. I'll go as high as $20 an hour if you can get someone. You'll need new locks, but that won't happen until Tuesday at the earliest. In the meantime, get yourself a couple of deadbolts for the doors. Is that bed a double? Can you manage to fit a double mattress in your vehicle?"

"Yes, it's a double and I think I could manage if I take the back seats out of the SUV."

"Good, get that and some curtains, and we'll see about other items later. Keep all your receipts and give them to Robert to send in for reimbursement."

"Thanks, Ms. Myers. I feel so much better now. I haven't been over to the school yet, but I'll get there tomorrow. I want the classroom to be ready and to feel welcoming," Ann said.

"No problem. I'm sorry your arrival in Wolfsburg has been so rough," Carolyn said apologetically. "I'll see you on Tuesday. Be sure to call me if you need anything else."

Energized, Ann got herself ready to go to town. Shaking her head ruefully as she locked the front door, she turned and made her way down the outside steps. Standing in the bright sunshine, she surveyed the litter-filled yard. The area would be nice if it wasn't so unkempt. Perhaps someone at the general store might know a couple of teenagers she could hire to pick up the trash and cut back the overgrown bushes.

She noticed a small building to the rear of the property. Upon inspection, she discovered it was an old outhouse. There was no odour, and it appeared that no one had used it for a very long time. The door latched, and the outhouse was reasonably clean if you didn't count the numerous spider webs. Still, she hoped she'd never have to use it. Thank goodness for indoor plumbing.

Ann folded the back seats of the SUV down. There might be enough room for the mattress, but it would be tight. Finally she set off towards the store, Riverside school, and the Doyles' teacherage.

After driving up to the entrance of the general store, she parked and entered the odd-looking building. Part of it had been expanded to create a small café or diner. A group of older men were chatting in one of the booths. The rest of the store was laid out with rows of shelves holding everything from laundry detergent to dog food. An upright cooler held milk, eggs, butter, and soft drinks. Magazines and candy were displayed near the till, ready to entice impulse buyers.

"What can I do you for?" boomed a voice. "Looks like you're new around here."

"Hi. Yes, I'm Ann Santos," she said with a smile to the friendly middle-aged man behind the till. His booming voice matched his size. A beefy man with shocking red hair grinned at her.

"I'm going to be working at Riverside this year. I'm renting the old trailer down Kies Road. Do you know of any young people that would be interested in helping me fix up my yard? I can pay $10 an hour."

"Shouldn't be too hard to find someone. Not many jobs for kids around here." He turned towards the men sitting in the coffee area. "Hey, Bert, your kid and his friend Joe would jump at the chance to make a few bucks, right? Any chance he'd do some yard work for this cute young lady? She is living in that old trailer on Kies Road. The one that belongs to the school board." he said, calling over to one of the coffee drinkers.

"Yeah, sure, Mike will do it. When do you need him by?"

"Tomorrow morning around ten would be good," replied Ann.

"No can do ... church. Would one o'clock suit? That would give him time to eat at the potluck and get over to your place."

Ann blushed. "Oh right, tomorrow's Sunday. I've lost track of what day it is. Let's make it Monday, and then he won't have to work on the Sabbath. I'd like to talk to him on Sunday though, as I have to work over at the school on Monday, but he and his friend can do the work anytime on Monday. Should take them four hours at the most. I'd like some bushes cut back as well. Is he allowed to use a brush cutter or something like that? I won't be there to supervise them."

"Don't worry your pretty little head, girl," Mike's dad said with a laugh. "These are farm kids ... can handle anything. He's been driving the tractor since he was twelve. I'll bring them over about one on Sunday, and we can see what you want doing."

"Super." Turning her attention back to the shopkeeper, she said, "Well, I have to get on into town. I'll just take this Coke for now. Thanks."

At the Robert's place, she found Betsy and Timmy on their own. It looked as though they were making cookies. Robert had gone into town. Betsy immediately agreed to help Ann clean the trailer.

"Can we keep it quiet about the money?" whispered Betsy. "I'd like to have a bit of money that I didn't have to account for. Robert won't much like me going over to your place, but I'll tell him it was Carolyn's idea. He won't want to go against her. I'll have to bring Timmy over with me if that's okay. Robert doesn't like having to look after him."

"No problem, bring Timmy with you. I have lots of books and games he'd be interested in," Ann assured her. "I'll ask Carolyn for cash to pay both you and the boys I'm hiring to do the yard." Betsy agreed to start cleaning Monday afternoon.

In town, Ann bought cleaning supplies, a new mop, scrub brushes, and paper to line the kitchen shelves. Over at the furniture store, she was able to purchase a double mattress that was on sale because it didn't match any of the box springs. The salesperson helped her wedge it into the back of the SUV. It was going to be a struggle to get it up the trailer steps when she got back, but she would have to manage.

At the hardware store, as she was buying the last two deadbolt locks they had on hand, she spotted a cabinet containing guns, ammo, and animal repellent.

"Can you tell me if this stuff works?" she asked the young man behind the counter.

"What stuff? The guns or the spray?" the handsome, blond-haired clerk asked jokingly.

"Spray ... I could never shoot a gun!" exclaimed Ann, laughing. "Does it really work? Do you need a permit or anything?"

"Depends what you want it for. Not sure I'd trust it to turn away a charging grizzly, but small animals and people would sure be incapacitated by it. You need protection?"

Ann was tempted to share her worries with this friendly guy but decided against it.

"First time I've lived on my own in a rural area. Is there any chance of running into a grizzly or cougar around here?"

"Always a chance of that, but they're usually more afraid of you than you are of them. Cougars keep to themselves. Mostly go after small dogs and cats. If they're around farms, they'll take the newborns or scavenge the placentas. Grizzlies are another story. Make lots of noise when you walk through the bush. They don't appreciate being surprised," said the young man. "You don't need a permit for either size of spray. If you go and use it on a person, you could be charged, but it's better than being attacked or worse."

"No worries about that," Ann said heartily. "Most people are really nice around here. I think I'm going to like Belmont ... but I'll take one of each. The small one for when I walk to school; I'm afraid of stray dogs. And the bigger one will be for when I go snowshoeing or cross-country skiing."

"Okay, that'll be $65.98, please," he said.

Ann gave him cash. The two thousand dollars she had withdrawn before leaving Alton was almost gone. Next week she'd have to apply for new credit cards and set up a bank account under her new name. She had less than five hundred dollars left to get her to payday. Still, having the animal repellent gave her peace of mind. Hopefully, she would never have to use it.

After stopping at the liquor store to buy whiskey and two bottles of red wine, she called in at a fast-food place for a hamburger and fries, and then Ann made her way back to the tiny village of Wolfsburg. In the late afternoon, she could see stands of waving wheat ready for harvest. Large herds of black cattle dotted the pastures. Occasionally, she spotted sheep and even some llamas. This appeared to be a prosperous farming community.

Three churches welcomed the faithful to Wolfsburg. She wondered if it might be a good idea to go to each church in rotation so as not to offend anyone. Not adhering to any one particular branch of Christianity gave her the freedom to choose her place of worship. Church was a great place to meet people. In Alton, she had many friends; here she knew no one. It was different now. If she did make friends, she must never let them discover her past troubles. Who would welcome a suspected child molester?

She almost missed the turn off to the mobile as tears threatened to make their way down her face. She was so lonely and overwhelmed with the prospect of starting over in a new place. Her throat ached with the effort it took not to give in to her emotions. Crying did no good, and she had already done enough of that. *Put on your big-girl panties*, she chastised herself.

If someone had been videoing her getting the mattress out of the car, up the steps, and through the narrow trailer door, they could have made a fortune on one of those comedy sites or on the internet. Once it was finally inside, she sank hot and sweaty into the easy chair. She still had to drag her awkward purchase down the hall and onto the bed.

After catching her breath, she bullied the awkward, overstuffed mattress through the bedroom doorway and then leaned it against the far wall. Next, she wrestled the filthy, old bed out of the trailer and tossed it over the stair railing. One, two, three, and her new bedding was in place. Tonight she might be able to sleep without thoughts of bedbugs and lice crawling all over her.

Chapter Eleven

As Ann joined the other teachers seated around the long table in the library, she took stock of the last few days.

It had been a struggle, but she and Betsy had managed to transform the disgusting excuse for a trailer into a sparkling clean home. After thoroughly scrubbing every inch of the place, they had hung crisp green curtains and rearranged the furniture to give her maximum space. Ann's grandmother's handmade quilt brightened the bedroom, and a silly shower curtain with yellow ducklings made her smile when she entered the bathroom. The tub would never be rid of its ugly orange rust stain, but keeping the shower curtain closed solved that problem.

Betsy had borrowed Robert's tools, and the two women cut the holes and set the deadbolts in place. School maintenance guys were coming out on Wednesday to change the locks. She also felt a lot more secure now that Mike and his friend Joe had trimmed back the bushes giving the yard a much lighter and more open feel.

The young men had done an excellent job. All the trash had been removed and the bushes trimmed in less than half a day. Grateful, she had paid them each sixty dollars. Now, she no longer felt there might be someone or something hiding in the bushes ready to pounce on her as she unlocked her door.

Her classroom had been a pleasant surprise. It was the largest in the school and had its own mudroom and a bathroom for the children. A battery of windows looked out over the parking lot. She was happy to find large tables instead of individual desks since she preferred group-seating arrangements for her young students. There was a comfortable reading corner furnished with two old couches and a cheerful blue mat decorated with leaping dolphins. Since she had a chalk allergy, she was relieved to find two white boards instead of those old fashion chalkboards.

It had taken her two full days to arrange the room to her satisfaction. Large sheets of white butcher paper lay waiting for the children to paint full-sized "models" of themselves during the first week of school. Picture books and cheerful, small, easy-reading books lined the tops of the shelves. All the common school supplies were ready and waiting for her students.

Her pupils would take some getting used to, as she was accustomed to teenage attitudes. On the first day, like the teenagers, they had come in chattering and eager to catch up with their friends but had then grown shy and quiet when they noticed her waiting in the reading corner. Smiling, she welcomed them and gathered them together to sit on the mat. She began to read one of her favourite children's books, *Rainbow Fish*. As she read the story, the students relaxed and seemed to feel more comfortable. Soon they were telling her all the details of their summer holidays, what pets they had, and the important facts of their short lives. One by one, the wary, hovering parents had waved to his or her child and had quietly stolen out of the room. Yes, Ann thought that it had all gone rather well. The little ones would be a challenge, but they were open, bright, and trusting.

***

The first day of school was always a half day in session. Everyone sat patiently waiting for the start of the afternoon's staff meeting. Carolyn Myers, glancing quickly over the teachers, noted that Robert had not yet shown up. She always enjoyed the start-up of a new school year. September seemed charged with possibilities.

"Let's get started, shall we? I know you're all anxious to get planning lessons for tomorrow, but we do have the usual yearly schedules to set and expectations to discuss."

Robert noisily entered the room, interrupting her.

"Excuse me for being late. Had to discuss something with a parent. Looks like they want me to coach the basketball team," he stated in a self-satisfied tone.

"Well, we should perhaps give others a chance to coach if they would like to. Let's discuss that after we set the gym, library, and prep schedules," Carolyn suggested hastily. Robert always wanted to make the other teachers think he was a favourite with the parents, but Carolyn was well aware that many parents were offended by his overbearing attitude.

Ms. Myers ran the staff meeting efficiently. She welcomed the new staff members, set the schedules, reviewed the roles of the support staff, and outlined the duties of the head teacher.

"Please let Mr. Doyle know when supplies are low and give him any receipts you have if you need reimbursement. Remember, since he's a member of the teachers' union, he cannot deal with staff issues. Refer all personnel matters, leaves of absence, and parent concerns to me. Students will have more respect for you if you deal with discipline problems yourself, but if the incident is severe, please call me. You all have my cell phone number, and I'll be out here regularly on Tuesdays and every third Friday. Now as a treat, I brought lunch. Please help yourself to the salads, sandwiches, and sweets in the staff room. Ann, if you have a moment, I'd like to speak to you in my office."

Ann's stomach lurched. What could the principal want with her? She followed Carolyn into her office and stood waiting.

"I just wanted to apologize once more for the unfortunate mess you found yourself in on Friday. Is everything under control now?"

"Yes, thank you," said a much-relieved Ann. "Betsy was a great help, and I managed to get my room done in time. Do you think you could give me a cheque now for the money I owe her? I'm almost out of cash, and I can deposit it in the bank tomorrow."

"Sure," Carolyn said and quickly wrote out a cheque.

"Thanks so much for your support," Ann said.

"You're more than welcome. Now let's go get some lunch before it's all gone."

Chapter Twelve

Carolyn had left the resumes of the three candidates for Susan's job neatly stacked on the conference table. Ben picked the first one from the pile and started to read it while he waited for Robert and Amy to join him. Robert was on the phone with Carolyn while Amy was busy talking to a parent who had dropped by for their sick kid's homework.

With his head bent reading the first resume, Ben was startled by the scrape of the chair legs on the linoleum flooring announcing Robert's arrival.

"Well let's see what we have for choices," Robert said as he sat down. "Don't suppose there's much at this time of the year. Most successful teachers are already in the classroom. Probably only the dregs of the dregs left here."

Ben frowned. "Lots of new teachers haven't been able to find a position this year, and several of the more-experienced teachers on the substitute list are in the same boat. It's not like when you and I got hired to the district several years ago. Jobs are scarce now."

Amy rushed in. "Sorry I'm late. I had to talk to Mrs. Gilmont. Trevor has the chicken pox and will be home for a while. That one can't afford to miss school. She said she'd work with him though."

"Okay, let's get started," Robert said. "I've prepared a checklist for each of the candidates. Each of us will read the resume and fill out the checklist. We will compare the results when we're finished," he stated emphatically.

Ben and Amy looked at each other. It sounded like a fair way to proceed, so they didn't argue. Besides, arguing with Robert was useless at the best of times. This way they might get some input into the decision. Carolyn would make the choice anyway.

Eventually, the candidates were ranked in order of preference.

Sharon Maki, a long-time substitute, was the lowest as she had indicated it would be hard for her to find transportation every day to Riverside. Someone would have to give up his or her seat on the van that was driven out daily. No one relished the thought of telling one of the van's passengers that they would have to give up their coveted seat. Still, there was the possibility they could all rotate and take turns bringing their own vehicle.

Next was the other substitute teacher. Karen was well known to the Riverside staff as she frequently filled in for absent teachers. She lived in the community and did not have to find transportation. Unfortunately, her qualifications were for teaching high school. As a fill-in teacher, she was just fine, but Susan's class would need a lot of support and compassion. Also, if they gave her the position, they would lose a very convenient and capable relief teacher.

The obvious first choice was a fellow by the name of Kyle Murphy. He was single and had received his Bachelor of Education three years ago. He had spent the last two years in Thailand teaching English as a second language. This year, he was on District 54's substitute list. His practicums and training had all been in the elementary school setting. Since he was male, Susan's class might find the transition a bit easier. There might be less comparison from both the students and their parents.

Ben wondered if Kyle was gay. It might be nice to have someone like that in the school. Although Ben kept to himself, he was constantly afraid that his sexuality would be discovered. By having another like-minded individual on staff, he would be even less obvious.

Ben took care to casually date some of the female teachers and a couple of the ladies in the community. He and Anita, the quiet, shy, grade five teacher had been very close for a while last year. Their relationship had cooled somewhat when she wanted to take it to a more intimate level. He had an idea she suspected he was gay, but she had never voiced her opinion. Now she was content to be just friends. They had a good time dining out in town, going to hockey games, and participating in outdoor winter activities such as skiing and ice fishing. Often they just hung out together at one of their places watching movies and reality TV. He liked Anita; she was a good companion.

His thoughts turned to his latest boyfriend. On one of his frequent trips to Clearville, he had met Jake, standing near the pool table in the Olde Lance. Ben was immediately drawn to the tall, dark-haired man. As usual, Ben's blond hair, blue eyes, and charming manner helped him interest Jake in a quick encounter.

Later over drinks at the bar, they discovered they had more in common than just sex. Jake had just begun his teaching career at the senior high school in Clearville this fall. He was not in a committed relationship and was looking for someone to share his life. There the similarities ended.

Jake didn't mind who knew about his gay lifestyle, whereas it was important to Ben that he remained very private. Ben had tried to explain the conservative, religious community of Wolfsburg to Jake. He spoke of his upbringing in Tremont and of leaving that town because of the intolerance. Since he enjoyed his job at Riverside, he did not want to risk jeopardizing it for such a new relationship. Although Jake attempted to understand, he found it difficult. He did agree, however, to keep a low profile while they figured out where their friendship was going. The two of them met in Clearville most weekends. Once in a while, they ventured into Belmont staying at a motel on the outskirts of town.

The three-day Thanksgiving weekend was coming up soon. Lately Jake had been hinting that he wanted to see Ben's tiny house in Wolfsburg. Ben could pass him off as a visiting friend or relative. It would be wonderful to have Jake see his home, wake up to his company in the morning, and even be able to cook him a homemade breakfast. Still, it was a huge risk and one that Ben was hesitant to take. Most of the staff was planning to travel that weekend, as it would be the last opportunity to do so before the winter set in. Yes, it might work, especially if they were careful not to openly display affection and Ben passed Jake off as his brother.

"Good God," grumbled Robert as he looked at the clock. "Are we done here yet?"

Ben jolted out of his reverie and brought his thoughts back to the task at hand. "Yes, let's recommend Kyle. I think he's the most suitable. Do you agree, Amy?"

"No one's going to take Susan's place, but I do think we should go with a man. It would be easier on all of us not to be reminded constantly of poor Susan. Also, a man might be safer here, given that the police haven't arrested anyone," replied Amy.

Robert frowned. "Well, I suppose Kyle might be the most suitable. I really don't care. It's not like we have the final say anyway. Carolyn's just being political having us sit on a committee. They already have their minds made up. I'm off to home." With that, he gathered the files and tucked them into his briefcase.

"Where are you going with the personnel files, Robert?" asked Amy. "They're confidential. Shouldn't you put them in the office?"

"Mind your own business. Carolyn asked me to bring them into town tonight," Robert lied. "I'm going to grab some supper before I head in. See you in the morning." He quickly left the room.

"No way," Amy whispered to Ben after Robert was gone. "Carolyn's out here tomorrow. He doesn't have to take them to town. I don't trust him. Probably just wants to have a good nose." She hated the way Robert was so dismissive and rude when he talked to her.

Chapter Thirteen

"Welcome, Ben, welcome. Your friend is already here. I've given you your usual table beside the fountain," said Ernesto, shaking Ben's hand as he arrived at Roma.

Ben smiled his thanks. Ernesto was discrete and had seated them in a secluded area where they would be able to interact more freely. Jake leaped to his feet and embraced Ben as he approached the table. "Hey, handsome. I sure missed you lots this week. Did you have a decent drive? I made it here in jig time. Don't have as far to go," he laughed.

"Not bad. It's difficult leaving straight after school, but at least it's still light outside. Hey, we have three whole days," Ben said, referring to the holiday weekend.

Deep in conversation, the pair didn't notice a man sit down at the table adjacent to them. He had come in quietly and had seated himself. The waiter was now pouring his water and asking if he wanted a drink.

"Rye and water will do. Don't give me any of that cheap crap. Make sure it's decent rye," demanded the customer.

Ben quickly let go of Jake's hand as he heard the sound of a familiar voice. Raising his head, he stared straight into Robert's eyes.

"Evening." Robert's dark, flinty eyes took in the scene before him. He had not missed the handholding and the way the two men were intimately engaged in quiet conversation. "You two come here often?"

Ben coloured deeply and tried to recover his poise.

"Oh, hello, Robert. I'm surprised to see you in Clearville on the long weekend. I thought your family was heading out to Entermine. Let me introduce you to my brother, Jake."

"Your *brother*, Jake? Hi. You don't look a bit like Ben," he stated with a smirk. "Pleased to meet you." He rose from his table and crossed over to theirs. Pulling out one of the empty chairs, he made himself comfortable, settling in for the evening. "No point in sitting alone. Let me buy you two a drink. What'll you have?"

An uncomfortable atmosphere descended over the threesome. Alarm bells rang in Ben's head. Jake, sensing Ben's agitation, tried to make small talk with this intrusive man.

Thoroughly enjoying Ben's discomfort, Robert began chatting amiably, telling amusing anecdotes of life in Wolfsburg. When Robert excused himself to go to the washroom, Ben frantically suggested to Jake that they leave as quickly as they could.

"For God sake, let's get out of here. I can't stand the man, and you're acting like he's our best friend!"

"Chill out," Jake retorted. "I'm making the best out of this crappy situation. He doesn't suspect a thing, but he might if we leave too soon. Anyway, I'm sick of all this pretence."

"Bloody hell, Jake. This is my job we are talking about. Robert is one weird son of a bitch. I don't trust him at all. Let's just get out of here," Ben pleaded. "Say you have a headache or something. We'll go back to the hotel."

Jake grew quiet, and Ben knew he was upset. He wished he had Jake's courage and felt free to live his life openly, but that just wasn't the case. Teaching positions were scarce, and Ben was tired of moving around. It would be different if he lived in Clearville or even Belmont, but Wolfsburg was old world. The predominant religion in Wolfsburg held the tenant that homosexuality was evil. They probably equated gays with pedophiles. The last thing a teacher would want to be associated with was child molestation.

Robert inadvertently saved the evening. He had been steadily downing rye and was feeling no pain. Weaving through the tables on his way back to his reluctant dinner partners, he stumbled against the waiter who was carrying a full tray. Lasagne crashed to the floor, spilling noodles and red sauce all over Robert's highly polished shoes.

"You clumsy bastard!" yelled Robert. "Now look at my shoes! These are two-hundred-dollar shoes, you imbecile. Fetch the manager."

Fortunately, the manager was able to calm Robert down by cancelling his tab and calling the inebriated man a taxi. Ernesto smiled at the relieved couple that was now free to go on with their evening.

"Come on, let's get out of here," said Jake. "Let's see what we can salvage of this evening."

Ben was more than happy to follow his friend out of the restaurant and over to the motel. However, the evening was ruined. He couldn't stop thinking about the possible repercussions of Robert showing up at dinner. Jake, on the other hand, was hurt and annoyed at Ben for trying to pass him off as his brother. A long night followed a hot-tempered argument. Both men were happy to sleep in separate beds, coming together only shortly before dawn.

The sun was shining and the weather was quite warm for this time of year. Jake and Ben left their motel room in a much happier frame of mind. Turning onto the boulevard, they jogged up towards the river front trail. As they rounded the corner, they could see the meandering river winding its way down the valley. The air was filled with the odours of rotting leaves and wood smoke. Several running trails stretched out before them. Taking the path closest to the river, the pair set off at a good rate. Both men enjoyed running, and this was a perfect day to indulge in the sport.

As they sat in the sunshine resting on a rustic bench, they discussed the previous night's argument.

"This is more than just a friendship for me, Ben," declared Jake. "I want more than the occasional fling in some seedy motel in Clearville. I need more."

Ben looked at his friend. "I want more too, but it's so hard. You're used to being out, but I moved to Wolfsburg because I'm not ready yet. It could mean the end of my job as well. I've worked too hard for my degree, and I owe tons in student loans." He put his arm around Jake's shoulder.

"Okay, best you don't do that if we're going to say I'm your brother. Save it for when we're alone," Jake said with a wry smile.

They worked out a compromise. Jake would now be spending some weekends and holidays in Wolfsburg as Ben's brother. They would have to be careful, but at least they would be together.

As they returned to the motel, hot and sweaty from their run, they saw Robert's truck parked beside the entrance. They watched as Robert started his truck and left the parking lot. He gave them a small nod as his truck passed by.

Chapter Fourteen

Malcolm left the general store shortly after 9:00 p.m. He had enjoyed sitting and chatting with Sgt. Bates and Roy Smythe, whose old converted barn he rented, but now it was time to get home to that barn and settle in for the night. He liked to be in bed by 10:30 since he rose early to get to school before the other teachers. In the quiet of the early morning hours, he got most of his prep work and marking done while he was still fresh.

The barn conversion was up the hill behind the store. He was able to get to most parts of the small hamlet on foot. In fact, most mornings he walked to work, enjoying the peaceful, still sleeping village.

He had left his old pickup truck at home this evening, as he hadn't been sure how much parking would be available at the store for the meeting. Most of the community had turned out to hear the latest developments in the murder case. He shook his head wondering about the new evidence that Bates had alluded to. In the gathering darkness, he pulled out his flashlight.

As he strode along the gravel road, his feet, scrunching on the loose surface, disturbed the silent evening. A rabbit startled him as it bolted into the undergrowth. Shining his light into the bushes, he searched for the elusive rabbit, but it was long gone.

Malcolm was usually home way before dark, so he was relieved to find his bear spray still in his jacket pocket. You needed to be careful around these parts. It was not uncommon to see deer, bears, or an occasional cougar wandering about. Drawing the canister out of his pocket and holding it ready in his hand, he trudged up the slight incline to his home. The flashlight, illuminating the area, cast dancing shadows as it reflected off the surrounding brush.

He was thankful when the motion detector triggered the porch light as he crossed over the small yard. With three bounds, he mounted the steps and inserted the key in the door.

Sassy greeted him, spinning like a dervish and yelping excitedly. Reaching down, he scooped up his feisty, little white dog. Sassy was such a joy and filled his lonely life with companionship and affection.

"Hey, Sassy girl! Need to go out for a minute?"

He set the small dog down on the patch of grass in front of the porch. Sassy carefully checked out all the bushes and the garbage can.

"Hurry up, Sas," he urged. "I've got to get to bed."

With a small woof, the dog did as she was told and shot past him into the house. Slurping noises could be heard as she lapped at the water in her dish. Sassy nosed her food bowl and looked expectantly at her master.

"Okay, just a few nummies. You're getting to be a little porker, you know."

Malcolm gave her a handful of dog treats and then crossed through the foyer into his kitchen. After pouring himself a cool drink of water, he sat down at the old wooden table and reflected on the events of the evening.

He had been happy to hear that the police had discovered some key evidence. This was news to him. It was hardly likely that he would have been informed. His only part in the whole affair had been to discover poor Susan. He shuddered now, remembering the horrible sight of her lying on the school steps. The officer's announcement intrigued him … what key evidence?

His thoughts turned inward, and he reviewed his own circumstances. He had been here in Wolfsburg for only a couple of months. Every day was a struggle as he battled with his demons and tried to remain sober.

A short six months ago, he had been teaching on the Tine Reserve in the northern part of Ontario. The reserve itself had been a dry community, but that hadn't stopped Malcolm from getting what he needed. Liquor was readily available from Jimmy Flat. He could also drive a scant five miles down the road to the Jack Casino where cheap booze flowed like water and he was able to indulge in his second vice … gambling. It was this vile combination that led to his downfall.

Allowing himself to sink deeper into his reflections, he relived those awful six months. He could still feel the pain and the anguish that turned his life around.

***

"Well, look who's coming 'round at last," murmured a gentle voice.

More sounds became evident. A soft hissing sound, footsteps, rustling of clothing, and other voices made their way into his ears.

Malcolm became aware of odours next—antiseptics, stale food, fresh linen, and a faint scent of baby powder. Shaking his head, he drifted out of consciousness again.

Then slowly he became aware of a reddish tinge. He opened his eyelids slightly and squinted as the harsh light flooded his vision. Moaning, he shut his eyes against the assault.

"Quick, kill the overhead light. It's too much for him," insisted the same soft voice.

Malcolm moaned again but reopened his eyes. *Where am I? What's going on?*

"Well, hello there. Just take it easy now. You've been out of it for quite a while. In fact, we've had you asleep for two weeks. Don't fight the tubes in your nose; it's oxygen. You still need it."

Sara, whose soft voice had roused him from his coma, carefully explained what had happened to the confused patient. He had been rushed to the hospital following a severe beating outside the Jack Casino. Witnesses told of him being in a drunken stupor as he left the casino; his pockets loaded with his winnings. He was found later in the back alley after having been kicked and punched into unconsciousness. His winnings were gone and he was barely clinging to life. Scarcely recognizable, his face had been a bloody mess. More alarming, though, were the contusions on the back of his head. It had been necessary to place him in an induced coma while the swelling went down.

"A drink, I need a drink," he muttered.

"Here you go, sip slowly." A straw was placed against his parched lips. He drew in the liquid and just as quickly spat it out.

"No! I need a drink," Malcolm insisted. "A proper drink."

"Yes, I know you do. This is going to be one rough ride. You're in detox."

The voice was no longer gentle and had a hard, uncompromising edge to it.

Malcolm closed his eyes and sank into oblivion. Every fibre of his body ached for alcohol. His veins screamed, and his pulse throbbed. For the past two weeks, he had been unconscious and blissfully unaware. He had been in withdrawal. The worst was over—or was it? The physical need for booze was dreadful, but nothing could prepare him for the mental turmoil that was to come. Day after day, he endured the physical pain that often accompanies severe mental stress and drug withdrawal. The doctors gave him drugs, but nothing could really take away the urgent need to drink.

At the worst of it, he could remember warm hands holding his and comforting arms around his shaking shoulders. His angel with the soft voice and the faint scent of baby powder remained by his bedside. She held out hope as he shrieked with terror and comforted him as he cursed the darkness that threatened to overwhelm him.

Sara pulled double shifts and stayed with him as much as she could. Her husband, John, took over when Sara was unavailable. Malcolm got to know both of them well. Steadfastly, they helped him through the worst. He was indebted to them. Their kindness knew no limits, and when he asked them why, they simply said. "Because we've been there. We've been to hell and back."

After being dismissed from the hospital, Malcolm discovered that he had nowhere to go. Trying to distance themselves from the whole mess, the Tine Reserve had quickly replaced him at the school. His belongings had been sent to a self-storage unit in Blaineford.

Sara and John, realizing that this was the most crucial time in Malcolm's recovery, quickly insisted he live with them. He stayed for four months as he got his wits about him and his addictions under control.

Since he was terrified to be out on his own and away from his support, John suggested he apply for a posting in Wolfsburg that had come up for the next school year. It was an isolated, religious community with no tolerance for booze and miles away from any casino. Temptation would be minimal. This was the fresh start he needed.

Thanking his benefactors with all his heart, he promised to make the best of this opportunity. Since he knew that he could never repay their kindness, he owed it to them and to himself to beat his demons and to pay it forward. Whatever good he could do in Wolfsburg would be the beginning of his recovery. He was an excellent teacher who enjoyed his job. There were children out there that needed him to open their eyes to the opportunities that awaited them in life. No one knew him in Wolfsburg, and no one would judge him. So long as he could keep his past a secret, he should have no problems with the community. Yes, Wolfsburg would be a new start.

Sighing deeply, Malcolm clapped his hands and Sassy looked up.

"Time for bed, girl," he called as he shut off the kitchen light and made his way down the hall. Sassy scooted along in front of him and up onto the bed. After turning around three times, she settled in her usual place beside his pillow.

Malcolm set his alarm clock and turned in for the night. Soon the trailer was filled with the sound of Malcolm's snoring and the occasional snuffle from Sassy.

Chapter Fifteen

They all piled into the mini-bus that would be taking them to Belmont. This weekend event was the first of a series of conferences on bullying to be held in the northern section of the province. Although Riverside had very few incidents of bullying, occasionally the students could be unkind and hurtful. Carolyn had decided to spend part of the school's Northern Allotment monies on attending these sessions. Believing strongly that it was important to lay the foundations for behaviour in a child's early years, she had elected to concentrate resources in the elementary school. As the nine teachers took their places in the van, Carolyn informed them that Kyle would be joining them in Belmont.

"Let's all make him welcome, shall we? It's going to be difficult for him to take over the class this late in the fall, so he'll need all the help he can get. I should imagine that the children might be resistant at first. It's only natural. They're still grieving for Susan."

"Oh, for God's sake," muttered Robert. "She wasn't a bloody saint."

"Pardon me!" exclaimed Carolyn, shocked by his callousness.

"I meant that we may be exaggerating the children's response. Kids are resilient and have short memories," Robert hastened to explain, realising he might have overstepped the mark.

"Whatever. I'm sure Kyle will soon find his way," assured Ms. Myers with a disparaging glance at Robert. He could be very trying at times. In fact, she found him to be a cruel, insensitive man.

After an hour and a half on the road, the bus finally pulled up in front of the Belmont Hotel. Although it wasn't in the best location, it was the only hotel large enough for the conference and to accommodate most of the attendees. Everyone was paired up with a roommate except for Ms. Myers and Robert. Malcolm and Ben breathed a collective sigh of relief when they discovered they shared a room and didn't have to contend with Robert. It was bad enough he would be in their sessions during the day.

The conference workshops ended around three in the afternoon, leaving plenty of time for shopping, unwinding, and socializing. Carolyn had reserved a table for the Riverside staff in the dining room for seven o'clock that evening. It was important that they debrief the meetings that they had attended. Carolyn also wanted her staff to mingle away from the bustle of the school. In the cozy atmosphere of the dining room, they might be able to relax and enjoy themselves.

It had been a tough time over the last few weeks. Susan's untimely death had shaken most of them to the core. However, she could not fault her staff's performance. Although she noticed that most of the joy and laughter that usually accompanied the lunch hour and after-school coffee time in the staff room was absent, she also observed that the classrooms were alive with activities and well-taught lessons. The Riverside staff was extremely professional, and the school year was proceeding nicely. Focussing on student behaviour and anti-bullying tactics, learned here at the conference, might encourage a new sense of purpose.

Her thoughts drifted to who may have committed such a despicable crime. She racked her brain trying to come up with any warning signs, any clues or evidence that she could offer to Sgt. Bates. There was nothing. Susan had been well liked and respected by the parents and the community. Most of the staff, with the exception of Robert, got along well.

Robert had difficulties with everyone. He needed to have control, to have the last word, and he was mainly concerned with looking good in the eyes of the school board. Yes, he wasn't the most pleasant individual, but she could hardly suspect him of such brutality. Still, it was strange that no one ever saw much of his family. His wife, Betsy, was quiet and unassuming. It was probably just her nature to be that way. Timmy was very shy and retiring, but that wasn't unusual for a four-year-old child, especially one with no siblings. Cross Robert off the list. He may be an arrogant man, but he was hardly a murderer.

"Hi," said Ann, taking a seat next to Carolyn at their reserved table in the dining room. "The others aren't here yet?"

"No," replied Carolyn, "I saw several in the bar as I walked by. They should be here any moment. Did you enjoy today?"

"Yes, but it was a lot to take in. I can use some of the ideas, but since the children are so well behaved at Riverside, most of the reward systems would be unnecessary. Their values and morals are already in place. Wolfsburg parents seem to do such a good job of raising their kids."

"You sound like you're going to stay with us for a while. That nasty mess at the trailer and Susan's unfortunate death haven't put you off?" asked Carolyn.

"I really like it here. What's not to like? The kids are great, and I'm saving a ton of money by not being close to town and shopping. A couple of years of saving and my student loans are history. I can see some possibilities for advancement as well. How many years university training do you have to have before you can apply for a head teacher or principal position in this district?" Ann asked.

They were interrupted by the arrival of the group from the bar. In high spirits, their voices drowned out Carolyn's reply.

"Did you guys order yet?" Ben wanted to know.

"No, we just got here too," answered Ann. "Pass the menus around. What's good here?"

Just then they were interrupted again. This time by a young man dressed in jeans, a light sweater and a smart leather jacket. He smiled shyly at Carolyn.

"Hi. Nice of you to join us. Everyone this is Kyle. He is coming on staff on Monday. Let's make him welcome."

A brief round of introductions followed and Kyle sat down next to Malcolm. The quiet man blended in seamlessly with the original staff. Malcolm, always a gentleman, offered up small talk and included him in the conversations.

As the Riverview staff studied their menus, Carolyn led the conversation around to the lectures they had attended. It seemed like most had appreciated the day.

"One big idea I came away with is to examine how we behave ourselves," observed Ann quietly. "If we act in a respectful manner, the children will have a positive role model."

"I agree with you," said Carolyn. "A positive tone and mutual respect in a classroom can go a long way in preventing unwanted behaviours. Studies have also shown that children respond well to fair expectations and firm guidelines."

Robert snorted. "I give them firm guidelines. What I say goes! Heaven help them if they think otherwise. Never have any trouble in my room."

He was well on his way to becoming drunk. He glared at the other teachers, daring them to contradict him. Kyle looked more than a little surprised at Robert's declaration.

"We're not all like that," whispered Malcolm to Kyle. "Don't be concerned, you're coming to a really good school for the most part."

Ben glanced at Carolyn and noted her mouth pursed at Robert's bold statement. It was well known that Robert ruled his classroom with sarcasm and his no-nonsense manner. In fact, one could even say that his style was bullying and that he ruled by fear. Over the last few years, several parents had made complaints about his shouting and his abrasive methods. He had been warned, but nothing seemed to change.

Choosing to calm rather than irritate the inebriated man, Carolyn simply said, "Everyone has their own methods. Hopefully our sessions today have given you all something to think about."

She beckoned to the waitress.

"Now, come on, what's everyone ordering? Remember, the school's paying for your food but not your drinks."

One by one, they gave their food orders, and then the conversation drifted on to other topics.

Robert sat quietly now, observing. He had little patience for his fellow teachers and even less tolerance for Madam Myers.

Once more, Ann asked Carolyn about the qualifications needed to become a head teacher or principal in this school district. "We had to have our master's degree and at least five years of service before they would consider anyone in my last district," Ann explained.

"It's similar here, except we don't worry about the years of service in this district. We consider the candidate's whole teaching career," replied Carolyn. "Oh, that reminds me; we got a memo from the school board on Friday. The position of head teacher will be posted this coming spring and anyone can apply for it. We won't be rotating the position, and it will no longer automatically go to the most senior teacher in the school but rather to the most suitable candidate. They would prefer that you hold a master's degree, but it's okay if you're working on obtaining it. Along with a substantial increase in the rate of pay, the successful teacher would hold the position indefinitely."

She looked around the table and was pleased to see a scowl from Robert and some interested looks from several teachers.

"I see there's some interest in this. Prepare a good resume and exhibit some leadership skills between now and when the job is posted. I would be willing to evaluate your teaching and to prepare a summary of my impressions of your performance if you want. Just let me know," she said with an encouraging smile.

Frustration and worry began to plague Robert as he ate his New York steak. *Bloody hell, that job should be mine.* He was well aware that the parents had made complaints about his classroom management, and he hadn't even started his courses towards his master's degree. No doubt several of the young upstarts had theirs already or were at least halfway through the program. Then there was the evidence that Sgt. Bates had mentioned finding. Robert ordered another scotch on the rocks.

As the evening wore on, the teachers gradually left the dining room and headed off to their assigned rooms.

"Kyle, would you like to join us for a nightcap?" Ann suggested.

"I would but I have my girlfriend waiting for me at my place. I'll take a rain check." He smiled and made his way out of the dining room. Ann, Ben, and Malcolm moved to the lounge for special coffees, leaving Robert sitting at the table alone with his thoughts.

As he pondered his situation, he began to see a way out. He would simply have to discredit or silence his competition. It had worked before. He had been successful in getting rid of the son of a bitch, Marty Freemont. Too bad Ms. Myers had replaced him. Freemont was easily controlled. He caved when Robert had threatened to tell the board his dirty little secret.

Robert sized up the staff and decided that Ann, Ben, and Malcolm were the biggest threats to his position of head teacher. He also would like to see Carolyn gone. He had no use for her, and she had a lot of influence with the board.

As for the evidence problem, Bates could be making things up. He searched his memory for any slip-up that he might have made. No, he had been very careful.

It had been late on Sunday evening. Susan was finishing up her photocopying in the workroom when he had approached her.

"Working late, are we? Or are you waiting for me?" he said with a smirk.

Susan looked up, startled. "You want to use the copier?" she asked.

"I want to use something but not the copier," he said as he stood blocking the door to the hall. Uneasy, she looked around for a way to make a quick exit.

"I have to go finish up my marking," she stammered. "I'm done with the photocopier. You might have to put more toner in. I think it's getting low." She edged around the machine towards the door.

Robert moved again, sealing off the possibility of escape. She panicked and let out a scream as he came towards her. Reaching out, he grabbed her arm, twisting it behind her back.

"No point in screaming. There's no one else in the school this late. You must have been waiting for me. Relax. You're gonna enjoy what I have in store for you," he breathed in her ear.

He quickly spun her around and grabbed her other arm. Holding her jammed up against the counter with one hand, he fumbled with his other hand for the roll of duct tape he had stashed in his jacket pocket. With one quick motion, he wrapped the silver tape tightly around her wrists, immobilizing her upper body. Jerking her shoulders, she struggled from his firm grip and wheeled around to face him.

"Let me go, you bastard!" Susan screamed while trying to knee him in the groin. Dashing for the doorway, she fell heavily to the floor as he tackled her like a football player. Bringing his fist down, he smashed it into her jaw. Straddling her, he held her legs together as he wrapped tape around her ankles. She screamed and screamed. He couldn't stand the racket she was making, so he found a filthy rag under the sink and stuffed it in her mouth, fastening it with the sticky tape. With terrified eyes, Susan begged silently for mercy. Lust shot through him as she was clearly helpless.

"I said relax. We're going somewhere more private," he chortled as he left her lying on the workroom floor.

After checking to make sure no one was in the school parking lot, he pulled his truck up beside the back exit and opened the tailgate. He reached for his coveralls and the rubber gloves that he kept in case he had to get his hands dirty. Standing in the vehicle's shadow, he carefully pulled on the clothing. Robert was always fastidious about keeping his garments clean. There was already some blood on his fist, but he knew he could easily wash that off.

By half-carrying and half-dragging Susan, he managed to load her into the truck bed where she lay like a sack of flour.

Robert re-entered the workroom and scanned the area. Picking up the papers and books that had been knocked over during the struggle, he straightened up the room and then went to the janitor's closet. After finding the wet floor mop and the squeeze bucket, he proceeded to rid the linoleum of the splotches of Susan's blood. Returning to the janitor's room, he carefully rinsed out the mop in the large sink until the water ran clear. Back in the workroom, he took the toner cartridge out of the copier and shook it hard. Black powder spewed out of one end and drifted over the damp floor. He reached down with some scrap paper and smeared it around in the black mess. It looked as though someone had unsuccessfully tried to clean up the spill.

During the short ride to the lake, he could hear Susan thrashing about on the bed of the pickup.

"Cut it out," he called through the sliding window that led to the canopied back. "You're wasting your time. There's no escaping what's in store for you. No one around in these woods. No one to help you now."

Edging his vehicle around a barrier the conservation officers had erected in an attempt to discourage off-roading, he found the four-wheeler track and followed it deeper into the bush. About eight clicks in, he turned up a small ridge. His tire tracks had blended in easily with the other tread marks.

As he got out of the truck, he pulled on his leather gloves. He was always careful to protect his hands. Scratches and bruising could be misinterpreted. Betsy had long given up trying to fight him off, but ... *you never know with this one.*

At first he had tried to be nice, giving her every opportunity to play along, but she resisted violently. As he unfastened her ankles so that he could drag off her slacks, she kicked him hard between his legs. He rolled off to one side clutching at himself.

Struggling to her feet, she had taken off through the bush as fast as she could manage. Luckily for him, she was no match for his surefooted pursuit. She tripped over a root, and he fell upon her. Enraged, he started methodically beating her into submission. Watching her reaction as she lay sprawled, slack-jawed on the ground, he drew a condom out of his wallet. *You never know where some of these whores have been.*

The next few hours passed in a blur, but he remembered thinking he'd killed her. It was impossible for anyone to survive such a beating. After stuffing the used condoms into the pocket of his coveralls, he bundled her body into the back of the truck and returned to the school as darkness fell. Glancing around to make sure he was alone, Robert backed his vehicle over the parking lot towards the school steps. Three tugs later, Susan was left in a heap on the steps.

He quickly went over to her car that was parked beside the gym. There he found her purse and coat that she had left tossed carelessly on the backseat. After partially covering her body with the coat, he started her car and left the school grounds.

It was a simple matter to dump the car in the slough. Pausing long enough to light a small fire, he stripped off the coveralls and then threw them, her purse, and his bloody gloves into the blaze. After scattering the ashes, he took a last look around. The tall grass was already springing back, obscuring the car's path. It took him well over an hour to walk back to the school along the dusty dirt access road.

After he parked his truck in front of his teacherage, he entered and went straight into the bathroom. Scrubbing furiously at his arms, he erased any trace of his crime. Then he glanced down and saw that his shoes were stained with blood.

Damn. "Bring me my other pair of sneakers!" he hollered to Betsy. "I hit a deer on the way back from town, and these are covered in blood. Protected my clothes with my coveralls but forgot about the damn shoes. Have to burn these ones now."

"Oh no. Are you okay? Any damage to the truck?" Betsy called through the bathroom door.

"I'm fine, and would you believe no dent in the truck? Had to finish the doe off though. Chucked her in the ditch for the coyotes. Too much bruising for the meat to be any good."

***

Robert shook his head, bringing himself out of his reverie. The booze had caught up with him. Weaving his way across the now-deserted dining room, he stumbled past the lounge and into the elevator. Just before he passed out on his bed, he once again reviewed his actions following that fateful night. He had washed the truck the next day. It was a stroke of genius for him to dump the body on the steps for Malcolm to find the next morning. He was able to feign surprise and concern when Susan's body had been discovered. Thank goodness she died before she could identify him. That was another stroke of luck. Satisfied that he had left nothing to chance, he closed his eyes and slept.

Chapter Sixteen

Malcolm attended Alcoholics Anonymous meetings in Belmont twice a month. He had promised Sara and John that he would go, and it also fulfilled a condition of his probation. Three years ago, he had been charged with driving under the influence. He might have lost his driver's license for five years, but since he was a respected teacher and needed his car for transportation to work, the judge had imposed conditions instead. He had to abstain from alcohol and drugs and prove that he was dealing with his addiction. Failing to satisfy the court would mean he would be prohibited from driving and perhaps would have to serve jail time.

Since Tine was a dry reserve, he had been able to get away with his drinking. No one checked up on him. The police had been too busy dealing with the bootleggers and drug dealers that plagued the community. The casino, with its gang and organized crime affiliations, kept them very busy as well. After his beating and hospitalization, he had been warned to comply with his probation orders.

The Tine Reserve had its own school; one that was not controlled by the public education system. As was typical there, he had not even been asked to sign a formal teaching contract with the reserve, and no personnel records were passed on to his present employers.

Although his present school board was unaware of his problem, there was always a possibility that they could find out. He worried about the community as well. Wolfsburg did not tolerate alcohol in any form.

He found a chapter of Alcoholics Anonymous in Belmont that held meetings every Saturday night at seven o'clock. Welcoming him warmly, the leaders devised a method of tracking his attendance. He kept a written journal of his recovery, which they signed after each meeting. So far, things were working out well. The journal helped him immensely, giving him an avenue to express his thoughts and frustrations. It also served as valid proof that he was attempting to remain sober.

Malcolm's bigger problem was his other addiction. The casinos in Belmont were located just two short blocks from his AA meetings. Unable to resist the siren call of lady luck, Malcolm gambled most Saturday nights. His preferred game was Black Jack. In the three months he had been in the area, he had accumulated over ten thousand dollars' worth of debt. He had been barred from one of the casinos, but the other one still allowed him to play. He hadn't used up all his chances there, yet. He frequently visited the cash advance stores and had maxed out his credit cards.

As his debts mounted, he struggled not to drink. Creditors began to call at all hours of the day. His frustrations and desperation grew as he rationalized his gambling. He had to play until his winnings covered his mounting debt. His luck had to change soon. At least he wasn't drinking.

***

Annoyed, Robert picked up the phone that was ringing incessantly in the office. This was not one of Carolyn's days at Riverside and everyone else appeared to be deaf around there. Of course, the part-time secretary had long since gone home.

"Robert Doyle here," he said, clipping the words off smartly. He waited as the caller paused and then asked to speak to Malcolm McDermitt.

"Sorry he's in class right now. Can I be of assistance? What does this concern?" Robert inquired. He was wondering if perhaps the police wanted to interview Malcolm again.

"No, this is a private matter. Please have him call Ace Collections as soon as he's available," said a young woman's voice. "I go off shift at three o'clock, so if he would call before then, I'd appreciate it. Thanks." She rang off.

Robert's interest had been piqued. He had never heard of Ace Collections. They were not a local firm. After leaving a quickly scrawled message stuck to the center of the staff room white board, he went to ring the bell for lunchtime. He was hungry. Betsy had better have something decent, on the table, for lunch.

It took him a few minutes to settle his class for their lunch break and then start towards the school's exit. As Robert crossed through the workroom into the hall, he was just in time to see Malcolm snatch the message from the bulletin board. Malcolm glanced around fearfully to see if anyone was watching. Seeing Robert in the doorway, he looked away.

"I see you got your message. Pleasant young thing, she seemed really anxious to hear from you. Some girlfriend we don't know about?" Robert asked.

Malcolm coloured deeply. "No, nothing like that," he muttered, turning swiftly to the fridge to retrieve his lunch kit. He sat down at the table and began pulling out his food.

"Well, best you call. Shouldn't have personal calls at work you know," added Robert officiously. "Where is Ace Collections anyway? I've never heard of them."

"I don't know who they are. I'll call them later," Malcolm stated flatly. He wasn't about to tell Robert anything.

Colleen and Barb came in chatting cheerfully. Instantly, their voices silenced as they entered the room. Robert had that effect on people. No one ever knew what kind of a mood he would be in.

"Mmm, sounded important. I'm off for lunch. I'm sure you all can manage for a few minutes by yourselves." Robert left for his teacherage.

"What sounded important?" Colleen asked as she sat down across from Malcolm.

"Don't you worry; it was just some phone call for me. You know how Robert can make anything sound important." Now the creditors were calling him at work. He'd have to get them off his back before they tried to garnishee his wages.

"Let the idiot have his power trip. You just have to learn how to ignore him and to keep your head down like I do," Barb suggested. "Hopefully he won't be head teacher next year."

"I sure as hell hope he's not," said Colleen. "Two years of him is enough. Maybe Ben will try for it. What about Ann? She sure was asking a lot of questions the other night. Neither one of us is interested. No one that has a family has enough time to spare. Mal, you should apply. You'd be good, and the kids sure like you."

Malcolm smiled. "Thanks for your vote of confidence. I think I'd have to wait a couple of years though. New kid on the block, you know."

"If you're interested, you should let Carolyn know. She said it would become a continuing position. Who knows when it would be vacant again," advised Barb as she bit into her sandwich.

***

Robert sat silently at the table shoving the remains of last night's stew into his mouth.

"Not bad. Stew always tastes better the second day. Got any more of those biscuits?

"No, Timmy had a couple for breakfast. There weren't very many left," Betsy answered as she warily watched her husband. He had been even more sour than usual.

For days he had holed up in his room hacking away on his computer or playing that stupid game. He was obsessed with the game, *Shoot Now Ask Later*. If he had something on his mind, he often retreated for days, only coming out of his sanctuary for meals or to go to work. Robert had been distant ever since the meeting at the store. A fleeting suspicion crossed her mind. Had Robert been involved in Susan's death? Did he know something and was keeping quiet?

***

Robert watched as Carolyn put on her sneakers and left her office to join the senior classes on the field. She enjoyed spending time with the students, thinking that the children would relate better to her if they saw her frequently.

Ben had organized team competitions for this afternoon. Robert and Ben's classes were responsible for setting up an obstacle course and getting out the equipment for the challenges. Two adults were plenty to supervise the students. Robert was free to do some snooping.

Making the most of this opportunity, he entered Carolyn's office and scanned the area. On the floor beside her chair was her briefcase holding her laptop and files. Robert looked out the window and saw that Carolyn was a distant figure on the playing field. He snubbed the lock on the office door and quickly ripped open the briefcase.

He took out Carolyn's pearl-coloured laptop and examined it carefully. Usually, people left a clue to their passwords somewhere on the machine. It was his lucky day. A small business card was tucked into a side pocket inside the briefcase. Three words were inscribed on the back: Invermere, jockey, and silver. After tucking the card back into the small pocket, Robert replaced the little laptop in the briefcase. There wasn't time to explore any further. The students had finished setting up the obstacle courses and Ben and Carolyn were making their way back across the field, returning to the school. He let himself out of the office and sauntered into the staff room.

"All set for this afternoon's fun and games, ladies?" he asked Barb, Ann and Colleen as he took his usual place at the head of the long table. "It better be good. My kids need to get down to their math pages rather than waste time playing *Survivor*."

"Hey, it should be fun," Ann said. "Besides, it's Friday afternoon and most of the kids have put in a good week. They deserve a few games. Plus, Ben put in a lot of time organizing this, and he's sure good at it. I think Carolyn considers him to be a great candidate for head teacher."

"Takes a man's man to run things properly. I think he's a bit too light in the loafers to be effective, if you know what I mean," said Robert with a smirk.

"What are you on about now?" asked Ann. The man was so strange. "What does light in the loafers even mean?"

"Airy fairy, rainbow child … light in the loafers!" Robert replied, laughing.

Just then, Ben and Carolyn walked in.

"Nice to hear some laughter around here," Carolyn said with a smile. "Let's get the children into their house teams and head out to the field. Ben's done a good job as usual. Should be a fun afternoon."

The whole school, students and staff included, did have an enjoyable afternoon. The activities cumulated in a water balloon toss that left most everyone at least a little bit damp.

***

In the privacy of his sanctuary, later that night, the flickering blue glow of the computer's screen revealed Robert as he tried out various combinations of Carolyn's name and passwords. He was a patient man and eventually was rewarded by typing C Myers and silver jockey. *Clever bitch to use a two-part password,* he thought.

A few simple clicks of his mouse and he had access to the personnel files of all the Riverside staff. Skipping over Barb's and Colleen's, he came to Malcolm's file.

Malcolm was thirty-six years old, a lot younger than he looked. Records showed that he had taught in two school districts in Ontario before moving to the northern part of this province. His assignments had been mainly as a classroom teacher for the upper elementary schools, most often a grade four or five class. Each of his moves had followed his resignation from a previous district, but no reasons had been given. Robert assumed that the man must have simply wanted a change. However, there was no trace of his teaching position for the year before he came to Wolfsburg.

There was even less information on Ben. At twenty-nine, he had only taught for three years in a town called Tremont before coming to this posting at Riverside. However, his glowing practicum reports practically leapt off the screen. It seemed as though his sponsor teachers and professors had been impressed with his performance. Several of his supervisors gave enthusiastic accounts of his organizational skills and his extensive after-school programs geared towards teenagers.

Ann had no records at all. Perhaps the district hadn't gotten around to forwarding her resume and history to Carolyn yet. It was also well known that this district, often so eager to fill the more isolated rural postings, seldom even bothered to check references and employment histories. Robert, himself, had flown in under the radar. His quick exit from Sunomo appeared nowhere in his files. The school board only knew what he had wanted them to know.

He rubbed his eyes, suddenly tired. He shut off his computer and sat looking about his private place. Thankfully, he had this room to himself. Betsy and Timmy never came in here. He simply didn't allow it. It had been a long day. Nothing in the files had looked very promising, but it was early days yet. Everyone had secrets. It was just a matter of ferreting them out.

***

The next day, he questioned Malcolm as they sat drinking coffee at recess time. They were the only two teachers in the staff room. Ann and Barb were out with the children, and Ben and the other staff seldom came in for the short break.

"Where were you teaching last year, Malcolm?" Robert casually asked.

Malcolm was startled but could think of no way to avoid the question without raising suspicion. Robert seemed to be trying to make conversation. Not wanting to look rude, Malcolm gave a vague answer. "Oh some Indian reserve in Manitoba. Didn't work out though. The accommodations were the pits, and pay was lousy."

"Which one was that?" Robert pressed for more detail.

"Redfern, I was at Redfern," Malcolm lied.

Just then, the bell signalled the end to the recess break. Both men got up, put their cups in the sink, and headed back to class.

Later that night in his sanctuary, Robert googled Redfern Reserve. There was one in Saskatchewan but none in Manitoba. Strange, he was sure Malcolm had said Manitoba. On a hunch, he typed in a search for First Nation reserves in Manitoba, and several came up on the screen. Working his way carefully, searching the reserves by name, he came across a newspaper article detailing a beating of a teacher outside the Tine Reserve.

Apparently the teacher had won big at the Jack Casino and had told all in sundry about his substantial winnings. He had been set upon and robbed by unknown persons in the alley behind the Jack. The beating had left him in a coma for two weeks. Further searches revealed that the band had quickly hired another teacher to take his position. Then the trail ran cold. No more details were forthcoming. Everything was adding up. Malcolm could easily be the victim of this beating.

It appears that our Malcolm may have a little gambling problem, thought Robert as he shut down his computer. Then he remembered that he had never seen Malcolm take a drink. At all the staff functions, he used the excuse he had to drive. Once, at the conference, he had even said he was on antibiotics for an abscessed tooth. The man appeared to avoid alcohol with steely determination. More investigation was needed. Robert felt he was close to solving Malcolm's riddle.

***

Tailing Malcolm had been easy. After parking his truck in the supermarket lot, Robert set off on foot half a block behind his quarry. The expensive black wig fit snuggly over his sandy coloured hair. With dark makeup giving him a Middle Eastern complexion, there was little chance of him being recognized. Still, he was taking no chances and followed Malcolm moving along at the same pace.

Malcolm turned into the church hall at the corner of Fifth and Broad Street. Robert lounged on a nearby bench until Malcolm reappeared an hour later. He was chatting with several other men as he strolled towards the downtown area.

"See you later!" Malcolm called to his companions. "I'm going to head over to my aunt's."

"Sure, same time next week," answered the thinner man with a wave of his hand.

Malcolm turned the corner and doubled back. Taking a sharp right, he moved quickly along, unaware that Robert was shadowing him. As he approached the casinos, Malcolm crossed the street and entered the Ace in the Hole. Music blared as he went through the door into the dingy, smoke-filled atmosphere.

Ten minutes later, Robert, still in his disguise, sat down at the roulette table. He could see Malcolm at the adjacent table sipping what looked like a Coke. Placing his chips in front of him, Robert signalled the dealer and began to play.

After a while, he casually gathered in his chips and strode past Malcolm's game.

"Looks like you're here for a while. Mind if I get in on your action?" he asked, lowering the tone of his voice in an effort to disguise it.

"No, I'll play with anyone. Need to hit the can though. Be back in a sec," Malcolm said as he got up and crossed over to the men's room.

Robert had no luck. He was bust in six hands.

"Well that's it for me. Be heading home now," he said as he reached up and scratched his hairline. The wig moved and Robert winked. "See you soon."

Malcolm stared at this dark haired fellow. There was something familiar about him, but he couldn't figure out what it was. "Sure, see you around sometime," Malcolm said as he turned back to the dealer. "Let's go. I'm still behind, but luck's turning. Let's play."

Chapter Seventeen

Three days later Robert was finishing up some paperwork in Carolyn's office. Gazing out of the window, he could see Ben shooting hoops in the playground with a few of the local high school boys. Immediately he was reminded of the wonderful testimonies that laced Ben's personnel file. The man was a big problem. He could easily take the head teacher position if the parents had any input into the selection. Ben was well liked around here.

The busy farmers appreciated Ben keeping the young guys occupied after school. It sure was preferable to their running the roads in their dads' old pickups or riding the trails on their quads. After supper, there was just enough time for homework or chores before they headed off to bed. Morning came quickly, and even children as young as seven were expected to complete the morning tasks before the school bus picked them up. Yes, Ben was a golden boy.

However, it should be easy to discredit Ben in such a small, isolated village. A few hints that Ben was a homosexual would be enough. In this fundamentalist community, the church elders sometimes equated being gay to being a pedophile and same sex unions were viewed as an abomination. The Bible was interpreted literally, and the church was against gay marriages. The charter of human rights and freedoms didn't really matter in this closed community. People here took the teachings of the church as the one and only truth. Who could blame them? Their society worked well for them and had existed for many years.

Thinking back to the night he had seen Ben at Ernesto's restaurant, Roma, he was quite certain that Jake was not Ben's brother. He recognized a guilty look when he saw one. That look and the quick letting go of hands had not escaped his keen observation. Then when he noticed them returning from their morning jog, it had all but sealed the situation in his mind. Their attention had been on each other, like that of couples in the first bloom of love. They had seen his truck nose out of the parking lot. Robert was certain they recognized him as he waved and pulled out onto the highway.

After school in the staff room, last Friday, Robert had made sure to congratulate Ben on the successful afternoon he organized for the students.

"Well done, Ben. Kids certainly seemed to enjoy themselves today. Don't you think so, Carolyn? Good idea of mine to take a break from all the slogging."

Ben raised his eyebrows in surprise. Robert had said nothing of the sort and had met the *Survivor Challenge* afternoon with nothing but negative comments. Still, since he didn't quite trust Robert, Ben decided not to say anything too confrontational. "I think Ann and Barb had quite a few ideas for the afternoon," Ben murmured. "Anyway, I'm glad the kids had fun."

Robert subtly changed the subject. "When are we going to meet your friend Jake?" he asked.

Ben's face coloured. "Who?"

"Jake, the fellow you were with at Roma on Saturday night," said Robert insistently. "He seemed like such a nice fellow."

"Oh, my brother Jake. He's away for a couple of weeks but he might make it out here just before the long weekend in October."

"Oh yeah, your brother Jake. I still don't think he looks anything like you. But you should know. No reason to think otherwise, I'm sure. No reason at all. " Robert let the statements hang in the air.

Carolyn looked up puzzled. She shook her head at Robert's remarks.

"What are you going on about now?" she asked Robert as she noticed Ben flush.

"Nothing, just a joke. No one can take a joke around here!"

Ben stammered that he had marking to do and left the staff room quickly. As he made his way towards his classroom, his thoughts raced. Robert clearly suspected that his and Jake's relationship was not platonic. Ben had been quite sure that the odious man had a good idea they were partners, and this seemed to confirm it. He needed to throw Robert off the trail. Turning on his heel, he retraced his steps to the staff room.

"Oh, Ann, can I speak to you a moment?" Ben asked quietly but loud enough for the others to hear.

"Sure, what's up, Ben?" Ann said as she stepped out into the hall with him.

"I'm heading into town later and was wondering if you'd like to catch a meal at that Italian place on the corner of George? Can't be a late night because I have to get started on my midterm reports, so I'd have you back by ten at the latest."

Ann was pleasantly surprised. She rather liked Ben. He had been very helpful to her as she attempted to settle into the routines around here. She wasn't looking for any kind of romantic relationship at the moment, but still, it would be nice to go out.

"Great, I'd like that. Shall we say you pick me up at six?" replied Ann. Ben agreed, and she returned to the staff room and back to the conversation.

"What was all that about?" inquired Robert, his curiosity getting the better of him.

"Nothing, Ben and I are just going out for dinner tonight," said Ann with a smile.

"That's great, Ann. It's wonderful to see you're settling in and making friends," Carolyn commented. "Well, I'm off to town. See you next Tuesday." Carolyn gathered up her briefcase and coat and left.

Ann quickly rinsed out her cup in the sink and grabbed her coat. She caught up to Carolyn as her principal reached the front door. Holding the door open for Carolyn, Ann smiled again.

"See you next week, Ms. Myers." Deciding to take a risk, she added, "Oh, Carolyn…I mean Ms. Myers, I was wondering if you had time to observe a couple of my lessons in the near future? I'm thinking I might apply for head teacher, and I would also appreciate some advice on planning. It would be good to know whether I'm on track with the grade one and two curriculum. It's still a bit difficult trying to meld the two of them."

"No problem. How about we meet after school next Tuesday and see where I can help you the most. Don't forget we have the math-helping teacher who could come out to give you some advice too. I always found that math was the most onerous to set up. Anyway, you can relax; so far I'm quite impressed with how you're coming along. It takes a while to find your footing in a new situation. And please call me Carolyn when were not in front of the students. I prefer to be infor-mal." Carolyn replied.

"Thanks, Ms. Myers…Carolyn. I sure like the way everyone is so friendly and helpful. My other school was so large that it was hard to make friends," said Ann with a smile.

"Looks like you're doing okay in that way," chuckled Carolyn. "So you're going out with Ben tonight?"

Ann blushed. "Oh my goodness. Yes, it should be a nice time. He's just being friendly."

"Handsome guy though," called Carolyn as she crossed over to her car.

***

Robert laughed to himself. He could see what Ben was trying to do. Let the kid have his due; it was rather clever to try to hide behind a woman. Most people would have been fooled. Ben was definitely gay but not the swishy, obvious kind.

Two down and two to go, Robert thought to himself. He mentally checked off his list.

Malcolm's story was pretty much a done deal. After a little more detective work, that milk toast's life would be like an open book. Ben would be easy to discredit given his sexual orientation.

It was just a matter of time before he'd uncover something about Ann. Then there was super-bitch. Carolyn must be hiding something. Everyone had something to hide.

Chapter Eighteen

The van sped along the gravel road heading to town. It had been a real rush to get everyone into the vehicle and away from the school. School dismissed at 2:15, and the only plane out of Belmont left at 5:20. Carolyn had arranged for them to be checked through security just after four, but that still cut it close.

Ann sat next to Ben thinking about the lovely dinner they had enjoyed last week. Both the food and company had been excellent. Now, this Friday they were heading to Saint Albert another conference on that new behavioural model Carolyn was so enthusiastic about. This conference was much bigger than the one last month and several well-known speakers were scheduled to present. That's if they could get there safely. Robert was driving too fast for this winding road.

"For Christ's sake, slow down around the corners," complained Ben. "I want to get there in one piece." He detested the way Robert drove.

"Relax. I drive this road all the time. We can make good time on this stretch before we have to slow down for the cops that hang out around the service station." To emphasize his point, Robert increased the pressure on the accelerator and the van careened around the next bend.

"Oh for goodness sake, slow down," Ben repeated.

"Yes, Robert, slow down. You're making me really nervous," added Ann as she tried to relax her grip on the hand rest.

Slamming his foot on the brake, Robert slowed to thirty kilometers an hour. "Okay, here you go. We can miss the plane if you like."

"Grow up," muttered Ben.

Thankfully, they were approaching the outskirts of Belmont. The traffic was stop-and-go all the way to the airport. Robert was forced to pay attention to the conditions and abandon his stupid games.

Malcolm's head began to throb as he anticipated the flight ahead. He was a nervous flier. In the past, he used to have several drinks before boarding, but of course this time he had to white-knuckle it.

Ann was not looking forward to the conference. Although she missed the hustle and bustle of city life, she worried that there might be someone from her old district attending the behavioural conference. Many districts would be sending delegates to this session that was being held in the prestigious Hotel DelMann. At the same time, she did think this might be a pleasant change from her quiet existence in Wolfsburg.

When they got to the airport pre-boarding had been called. They hurried into security and joined the lineup of last minute arrivals.

Flipping her suitcase open, she watched as the security personnel rifled through her clothes. Glancing off to one side, she saw Robert stiffen as the attendant asked him to open his wheeled suitcase.

"Bloody hell, okay, just don't mess up my stuff. I packed carefully so that there wouldn't be any wrinkles," he groused.

Eventually, the Riverside staff boarded the plane and took their assigned seats. Ben and Ann sat together, cheerfully chatting as the plane taxied for takeoff. Malcolm, who was sitting next to Colleen, relaxed as she patted his arm sympathetically. "It's okay. The worst part is almost over. You'll feel better once we're in the air," she said, smiling kindly. She liked Malcolm and could understand someone being scared to fly. She couldn't swim very well and was nervous to go boating. Everyone had his or her own fears. Barb hated spiders; in fact, she also hated anything with six legs and wings. There were many times she let out a scream at school. The older building was plagued with insects, especially during the warmer months. Colleen patted Malcolm's arm again and he smiled gratefully.

***

Throwing her handbag on the bed, Ann sat down and eased off her tight shoes. It had been a very long day. First, she had taught all day, and then she endured Robert's chaotic driving to the airport and the seemingly endless flight. She was glad to finally be alone and free to let down her guard. Needing her privacy, she was paying extra for this room. Most of the other teachers were sharing. She headed into the room's well-appointed bathroom.

A short while later, closing her eyes in pleasure; she submerged herself, luxuriating in the warm jasmine-scented water. Soft music from the bedside radio drifted under the door. As she sipped white wine she'd purchased from the mini-bar, Ann let her thoughts soar with the music.

Through half-closed eyes, she sighed and appreciated the huge off-white tub with its brushed chrome fixtures. She observed the plush towels carefully placed on the heated towel rack and the selection of soaps, bath gels, and lotions resting in a small wicker basket. This luxury was no comparison to the dingy, rust-stained tub that she had become accustomed to in the old trailer. She could easily get used to this, she mused.

A hammering at the door roused her from her reverie. Climbing out of the tub, she quickly threw on the soft robe and made her way to the door.

Seeing no one standing in front of the peephole, she called, "Who's there?"

Silence echoed. She peered through the small window again. She could see no one in the hallway. Shrugging to herself, she concluded that it must have been someone at the wrong room. Ann retraced her steps to the bathroom and began drying herself using the largest bath towel she had ever seen.

The loud knocking came again. This time she crossed swiftly to the door and stared through the peephole. She caught a glimpse of movement as a shadowy figure quickly ducked into a doorway. Uneasy, she checked to make sure she had fastened the security chain. Turning from the door, she entered the bathroom and quickly finished dressing. Her pleasant evening had turned sour.

***

Robert made his way into the hotel lobby and crossed over to the City View lounge. Although the lounge was aptly named as it showcased a splendid view of the city skyline, it was not that view that interested Robert.

Over by the plate glass windows, Malcolm and Ben were seated and engaged in quiet conversation. They looked up as he approached.

"Hi, Robert. Why don't you join us," Ben said politely.

"Don't mind if I do," replied Robert. "Just came down for a nightcap. It's been a long day." He signalled impatiently to the waiter.

"Yes, sir. What can I get for you?"

"Scotch with ice. Be sure it's good scotch," Robert ordered. "And whatever they're having." He glanced at Malcolm's glass. "What are you drinking tonight?"

"Just orange juice for me, thanks," Malcolm said quietly.

"What are you? A man or a mouse? Have a proper drink. He'll have a scotch like me and another beer for this guy." Robert waved his hand in Ben's direction.

"No, I'll just have another orange juice, please," Malcolm said to the waiter.

Robert seized the opportunity to confirm his suspicions about Malcolm's drinking problem. "I never see you with a real drink. You got a booze problem?" he asked Malcolm.

Malcolm's face went red, and he looked at Ben and then back to Robert.

"No, of course not. I just don't drink much. Alcohol brings on my migraine headaches if I'm not careful. Not that it's any of your business." Malcolm was furious. He could hardly look at Robert.

Ben watched the altercation cautiously. He didn't blame Malcolm for being annoyed, but they were both aware that Robert could turn nasty in a heartbeat. "Best we make this our last one," he said to Malcolm. "Breakfast is at seven, and we have a long day ahead of us tomorrow."

Malcolm smiled appreciatively. It was good of Ben to give him an out. He waited until the waiter had brought their drinks. "Matter of fact, I'm beat," he said. "Going to head for bed. I'll just take this up with me." He stood, picked up his drink, and left the lounge.

Ben and Robert sat silently sipping their drinks, looking out over the city lights. It was a relief when the bartender announced closing time.

"Best we call it a night as well," Robert said as he got to his feet. "See you in the morning."

Ben drained his beer and sat waiting until Robert entered the elevator. Then he made his way through the hotel's front doors and out to the street. Flipping open his cell phone, he punched in Jake's number.

"Hey. How's it going?" he said as Jake picked up on the first ring.

***

"Maria! Maria!" a shrill voice called from across the room. A tall woman with streaked blonde hair stood and squeezed past the people sitting in her row of seats, making her way towards Ann.

Ann swiftly ducked into the hallway and entered the ladies' room. *Oh my God. It's Sharon.* She quickly entered the first unoccupied stall. Her heart sank as she realized that Sharon had followed her into the restroom.

"Maria, are you in here?"

Flushing the toilet, Ann unfastened the door and came face-to-face with Sharon.

"Hi, fancy seeing you here at the conference. It's such a surprise to run into someone from Alton," Ann said as she washed her hands.

"Maria, we were all wondering where you took off to. It was as though you dropped off the face of the earth," Sharon declared as she reached out to hug her friend.

Ann burst into tears as she was engulfed in Sharon's warm embrace.

"Oh my God, what's wrong?" Sharon whispered.

"I had to leave. You know what happened."

"Yes, we heard about the accusations, but no one believed them. No one who knows you could believe such a horrible story," Sharon assured her friend. "Where did you end up going? Where are you teaching now?"

"I can't say. I want a fresh start. You remember Harold Caine. He was accused of having sex with that high school girl. I know the charges were dismissed, but suspicion always clings. Harold never got over it and ended up having to leave teaching. The people I work for don't know anything about my past. And I want to keep it that way," Ann said as tears streamed down her face.

Sharon's heart wrenched. She knew what Ann was saying was true. Not everyone who knew about Sean's ugly allegation believed that Maria Santos was totally blameless. Sharon once again embraced her friend.

"Okay, if that's what you want, I'll keep your secret. Can I at least tell Evett I saw you?"

"No, don't. It would be too hard on her. I made a clean break. She knows I love her and knows how to get in touch with me if there's an emergency. Best we leave it that way." Ann smiled ruefully. Her face saddened as she remembered her beloved sister.

"Please don't tell anyone here that you know me. You know that those kinds of accusations are so hard to disprove. No one would hire a teacher with a suspicious past, and this is one of those rare school districts that didn't check. I like my new job and don't want to have to try to find another one. I've even changed my name to Ann. Please, please don't let on," she begged.

Sharon gazed at Ann and saw how desperately Ann needed her to keep quiet. She nodded and reached out her hand, touching Ann lightly on the shoulder. "You can count on me, Maria. You have to know that all your friends would have stood by you. You didn't have to run." She reluctantly turned to leave. "Take care of yourself, Maria."

Ann waited a good five minutes before leaving the washroom. As she did, she saw Robert strolling down the hallway. Quickly, she went back to the Riverside staff in the conference room. Ben looked at her with some concern.

"Hey, what's up? You look upset," he observed kindly.

"No, I'm fine. I just had an allergy attack. I'll be all right as soon as the meds kick in." She sniffled and blew her nose.

Robert watched the exchange with interest. He had heard the tall blonde call out "Maria" and follow Ann of the room. He was sure he had seen this woman exit the washroom followed shortly by Ann. Now, here Ann was all red faced and teary eyed. He didn't believe the allergy story for a minute. Something strange was going on. He'd get to the bottom of this. All he had to do was to get the blonde to talk.

***

"Well, hello there," Robert said as he sat down beside Sharon at the bar. "I sure enjoyed what you had to say about your school's success with the Respect Program."

Sharon glanced at Robert in surprise. She didn't recall meeting him before in any of the workshops, but she might have. It had been crowded, and lots of people had been noisily debating the topics.

"Thanks. There are so many of those kinds of programs, but I think it's one of the better ones," she said, shifting slightly in her seat.

"Can I buy you another drink?" Robert asked, looking around. "That is unless your boyfriend has something to say about it," he joked, knowing full well she was alone. He had been observing her for the last fifteen minutes.

"Ha ... I'm by myself tonight. The girlfriends went shopping at the mall on the corner. It's open late…until nine, I think. I'm beat so I chose to stay behind. Now I'm holding up the bar."

"Great, what are you having?" Robert raised his index finger at the bartender. "I'll have a double scotch on the rocks, and the lady will have whatever her heart desires."

After a couple more drinks, Sharon and Robert moved into the dining room and settled down at one of the more secluded tables. The alcohol was starting to affect Sharon, and she welcomed the idea of food.

Gradually, Robert worked the conversation around to teaching and where each of them had been employed. He discovered that she had taught all of her ten years in the Alton school district.

"That's interesting. I thought one of the teachers at Riverside, Ann Santos, said she had taught in Alton. Do you know her?" Robert fished.

Sharon's alarm bells rang. She wasn't that drunk, and something didn't seem quite right.

"No, I don't know an Ann Santos. It's a large school district. I don't know half the teachers there."

She picked at her dessert. Usually she loved cheesecake, but this wasn't going down very well. Yawning, she declared, "Gosh. I'm awfully tired. Think I'll head up to my room before I fall asleep at the table. Thanks for the company tonight. I enjoyed getting to know you."

Unable to leave well enough alone, Robert couldn't resist trying to score. "You could get to know me a whole lot better if you're interested."

Sharon laughed. "Don't think so." She smiled, tapped his wedding ring, and swiftly she got to her feet. "Here, this is towards the bill," she said as she deposited two twenties on the table. "Maybe I'll see you in one of the workshops tomorrow."

She made her way out of the dining room and disappeared into the elevator.

Damn, Robert thought to himself. He knew he should have taken off the bloody ring. Far from being tired, Robert was almost vibrating with excitement. He stopped by the hotel desk and asked about their Internet service. After leaving his room number and credit card imprint with the concierge, he entered the Internet café and punched in the access code the clerk had given him.

The blue screen flickered, and he was soon searching Alton's newspapers' Web pages and the school district site. Towards two o'clock in the morning, his efforts were rewarded. Buried in the back pages of the *Alton Gazette* was a police report. Maria Santos had been accused of molesting a seventeen-year-old student. The report went on to say the police were investigating but no charges had yet been laid in the case. Then the trail ran cold. He could find no further reports.

Pumping his fist in the air, he closed down his computer. He had what he needed on Ann. This was his currency. Who knew what favours he could purchase?

***

After the Sunday sessions were over, Ben, Ann, and Malcolm sat quietly at the table nearest the window. From their small table they could see the lights of the city below them, stretching out over the valley. They watched the stream of traffic making its way onto the access ramp to the highway.

LIN WEICH

"Not sure I'd want to live here with all this crowding. It's real quiet in Wolfsburg, but at least you can breathe," observed Malcolm. "I, for one, will be glad to get back tomorrow."

"I know what you mean," Ann said. "I do miss the city though. There are no restaurants in Wolfsburg, and I get really tried of cooking for one. You guys will have to come over for supper soon. I can cook a mean chili."

"Be great," agreed Ben.

Malcolm nodded. He enjoyed Ann and Ben's company. It didn't seem to matter to them that they were several years his junior.

"We should head upstairs. That plane takes off awfully early tomorrow. Seven-thirty, isn't it?" Ben asked.

"Yup, taxi leaves the hotel at six," Malcolm said as he rose to his feet. "Lucky there's no school on Monday. I'm worn out. Good conference though. Let me get this." He grabbed the bill and headed over to the bartender.

"Thanks," Ann called. She turned to Ben. "I sure enjoyed our dinner last weekend. What are you doing next weekend?"

"Oh, good news. My brother Jake is coming for the weekend," Ben said with a smile. "It's been a long time since we had some time just to hang out together. He teaches in Belmont, but with the end of semester he's been busy. The computers crashed at the high school, and everyone had to redo their marks and reports. Someone said it was sabotage, but you know how rumours get started. Probably just an overloaded system."

"Probably, but what do I know! Computers are not my friends. If anyone's going to lose data, it would be me," laughed Ann. "Listen, you two come over to my place on Saturday night and I'll cook. I'll invite Malcolm as well."

"Great. I'm taking Jake fishing at Robin Lake in the morning, but we should be back in plenty of time. What can I bring?"

"Okay, let's say six o'clock. You can bring some wine ... red, please," Ann said.

Chapter Nineteen

Patrick Bates stirred his coffee. He gazed listlessly out the window at the beautiful late fall day. He was mind-numbingly bored.

His eyes took in the tidy shelves and harsh overhead fluorescent lights. Packets of hard candy hung in neat rows enticing customers as they paid for their purchases. Herb, the storeowner, was out back helping to unload the supply truck. Pushing away from the small table, Patrick went through to the back of the store.

"Can I give you guys a hand?" he asked as he reached for a box of apples.

"Sure, if you want," grunted Herb. "Not much to do today? Guess the teachers are all at the conference down south. Can't even keep your eye on that Santos chick." He had noticed that Bates appeared to be interested in the pretty young thing. "You should ask her out sometime."

"Might do that," agreed Patrick as he stacked the crate of apples beside the cooler. "Would beat watching the only two channels available on TV."

"Wouldn't know about that. We don't watch the television at my house. Some Mennonites can watch some of the programs, but I belong to the group that frowns upon any kind of outside influences."

Bates worked silently for a while and then collected his coat from the diner. "Be seeing you," he called as he swung through the door and out into the crisp autumn day.

In a few minutes, he was on the gravel road heading towards Robin Lake. It was there that he did his best thinking. The lake reminded him of a lake back home where his dad used to take him fishing. Many carefree days had been spent there dangling his fishing line and occasionally catching a keeper. His dad had been dead several years now, but his mom was still alive.

She lived in a small independent living apartment over in Clearville. Not that he got to see her much lately; this assignment was taking a lot longer than anyone had anticipated. Thankfully, she had agreed to look after his two cats while he was in Wolfsburg. With no family of his own, Patrick depended on his mother's good will as far as Greta and Monty were concerned. She loved those cats, spoiled them with numerous treats, and smothered them with constant affection.

Bates smiled. Things were getting pretty desperate if he was dreaming about his cats. Yes, he thought, he was lonesome. He might ask Ann out. He needed a contact within the staff, and Ann would also be good company. She was attractive and seemed friendly whenever their paths crossed.

Sitting down beside the boat launch, he began to review his progress on the Susan Lloyd case. So far he had nothing but a few suspicions. Surveillance of the school grounds so far had yielded little out of the ordinary. The teachers came and went in rhythm with the school day. At three o'clock, the janitor, an older man from the Grant commune, arrived to start his shift. This custodian usually left by six o'clock. Robert Doyle and Colleen Brownmiller, who lived in the teacherages adjacent to the school, kept less than predictable hours.

The only other traffic into the school had been school district personnel, maintenance workers fixing the roof, and the principal, Carolyn Myers. No strangers hung around before or after school. No one seemed to be out of place.

It was quiet around the teacherages. Robert came and went at all hours, but his wife, Betsy, and their little boy were seldom seen. The child didn't play outside, and the Doyles had very few visitors.

Patrick had interviewed the staff and was able to rule out most of them as suspects.

Malcolm McDermitt had been the first on scene, but his story checked out. The mild-mannered teacher appeared to be genuine enough. He had been really upset at discovering the body. Still, there was something odd about Malcolm. The man was quite a loner and kept to himself for the most part. The heavy lines around his eyes and his pasty complexion hinted at a hard life. He may be, or might have been, addicted to booze or drugs. The haunted look that sometime invaded Malcolm's eyes also hinted at troubles. Perhaps he had money or gambling problems. Years on the force gave Bates an edge when it came to reading people. There was no evidence that his possible addiction interfered with his job. Perhaps he was in recovery. It was no one else's business. Good luck to the guy.

Ben Smith, the young, blond teacher, was another unlikely suspect. Susan Lloyd had been repeatedly raped as well as beaten. Although Ben took care to date several female teachers and even a couple of ladies from the community, it was a front. Patrick had seen him several times in Clearville and Belmont with a dark-haired man. The friendship appeared to be very close. A homosexual would not fare well in this tight-knit religious community. It was little wonder that Ben took great care to keep his private life under wraps. Susan may have discovered his secret, but the evidence did not implicate Ben. If he had killed her, he certainly would not have raped her.

Ann, the newest teacher at the school, could also be ruled out. The crime was one of rage and passion. It was almost certainly committed by a man—likely a strong, enraged male that had been rejected and needed validation through violence.

Nothing stood out about any of the staff for that matter. The janitor had gone off shift around six that evening, well before Susan's body had been dumped on the steps. He was an upstanding member of his church who spent his nights cleaning the school, and driving the school bus during the day. According to his wife and son, he was in bed by ten that night.

Malcolm had mentioned that Susan might have had an ex-husband, but that lead turned cold. She indeed had been married, but the ex had died in a car accident three years ago. His investigations had shown she had not been involved with anyone else since then.

Colleen, Barb and Carolyn were all non-starters as well. For one thing they were women and none of them seemed to have a shred of motive. By all accounts Susan had gotten along very well with the staff.

At present, there were only three persons of interest.

Jim Cove's boy, Terrance, who loved fast cars and fast women and certainly thought a lot of himself, might have resented Susan if she had spurned him.

Shane, the old hermit, lived down by the slough where Susan's car had been located. No evidence there, really. The community rarely saw this recluse. When Patrick had interviewed him, he had found a doddering old man who was barely able to look after himself, let alone subdue a panicked woman fighting for her life.

Then there was Robert. That sarcastic odd-ball didn't get along with anyone. His wife had that haunted look of a victim of violence. She often appeared to have bruises and had sported a black eye at the memorial. When she came into the store on Friday, he'd seen that her arm was in a sling. The kid was pretty timid as well.

Robert was a possibility, but there was simply no tangible evidence to link him to the crime. Furthermore, Bates couldn't find motive or opportunity. Still, he bore watching. Perhaps another chat with Betsy was in order.

With a last look at the peaceful lake, Patrick returned to his vehicle and headed towards the school. The school van was not in the parking lot, and several of the teachers' cars and trucks were still parked outside the school. Good, the teachers had not yet returned from their weekend trip.

As Patrick walked over to Doyle's teacherage, he saw Timmy outside playing with a little girl about seven years old.

"Hi, Tim. Who's your friend?" he asked in a friendly voice.

"Oh, hi, Mr. ... Mr. Bates. This here is Angela. Her mom's at the teacher's conference, and we're looking after her. She just lives next door," Timmy said importantly.

"Hey there, Angela. Say, Tim, is your mom home?"

"Sure she is. I'll get her," Tim said and ran into the house.

"Mom, Mr. Bates is here."

Betsy dried her hands slowly on the tea towel. She could feel the blood drain from her face. *What did he want?* She anxiously scanned the parking lot for the white van. Relieved that the teachers had not returned from the airport, she hurried to the front door.

"Hello. Robert's not home yet. He'll be back around supper time, I think."

"Not Robert that I came to see. I was just in the neighbourhood and thought I'd drop by. You busy, or do you have time for coffee? That coffee over at the store wears pretty thin. Do you have a few minutes?" Patrick smiled.

Betsy thought quickly. She couldn't turn the officer away without seeming rude. The teachers weren't due back for at least a couple of hours, and it would be nice to have some company.

"Sure. I'll put the coffee pot on. Let's sit outside in the sunshine," agreed Betsy. "Timmy. Would you and Angela like to have some juice?"

Patrick sat down on the steps and waited for Betsy to return with the drinks. Tim and Angela went back to their building site, a few feet away. They were busy constructing roads in the dirt beside the other teacherage's porch. As cheerful children's voices filled the autumn air, Patrick could already feel the promise of colder weather. So far, this fall had been quite mild. Knowing this part of the country, he was aware that it was only a matter of time before the snows came.

"Thanks," Patrick said as Betsy handed him a mug of coffee. She took some juice boxes over to the children.

"How's the arm feeling?" he asked casually. "How again was it that you hurt yourself?"

Betsy felt a warm flush creep over her face.

"Oh, I fell over Charlie, our dog," she replied, pointing to the collie that lay in a patch of sun. "It's getting better. Just a sprain. The doctor said I'd be able to use it soon. Just in time for canning."

"Didn't know you had a garden," Patrick observed.

"No, we don't. Robert always buys beets and cucumbers from the Grant commune. Sometimes he gets beans, but he was too late this year. They sell their extra produce real cheap."

"Nothing like pickled beets. My mom used to make them every year before she went into the independent living place," Patrick said.

Betsy startled as she heard a vehicle on the road. Furtively, she glanced at her watch. The last thing she wanted was for Robert to see her chatting with Sgt. Bates.

Patrick observed Betsy's distress. The woman was terrified of her husband. The story of tripping over the dog was not what Robert had told him. According to him, she had fallen when she tripped over a toy Timmy had left on the step. Not wanting to cause her any more anxiety, Patrick got to his feet.

"Thanks for the coffee, Betsy. Take care of yourself. If you ever need anything or want to chat, I can usually be found over at the store. They've rented me the back room until the investigation comes to a close. Not that there are many leads though. No one's doing much talking. Oh well, I'll get a break soon. Let's hope it's before the snow flies."

As he pulled out of the school grounds, he saw Betsy go over to the children and shepherd them inside. *Poor woman*, he thought to himself. There wasn't much he could do for her if she wasn't willing to confide in him. If he witnessed Robert abusing her, he could charge him, but the son of a bitch was much too careful for that.

***

Later that evening as Patrick sat devouring meatloaf with cream gravy, Ann came into the store. She had on a light blue jacket and track pants. After picking up a loaf of bread and some milk, she strode swiftly to the counter.

"I'll just take these. Got to get some supper on. It's getting really late," Ann said as she paid for her purchases.

"You should do what I do," laughed Patrick from his seat in the diner. "The meatloaf is really good tonight."

Ann looked at the friendly cop and smiled. "It sure would beat cooking. Is it really good?"

"Yup, come join me, and we'll get Herb to rustle up a plate," he encouraged her, motioning to the seat opposite him. Herb grinned and hustled through to the kitchen area to serve up yet another plate of meatloaf.

As Ann and Patrick chatted over their food, she told him about the conference, and he told her about his life in the police force. They discussed hobbies, favourite movies and other safe topics. Conversation flowed easily. Realizing they had quite a few interests in common, they easily spent the next hour laughing and sipping coffee.

"Oh goodness, look at the time. Herb must be ready to close up and I have to get to bed. I'm on duty tomorrow morning. Got to arrive at school by seven-thirty. Great suggestion of yours, that meatloaf was delicious. How much do I owe you, Herb?"

"Three dollars and fifty cents."

Ann put a five on the table, picked up her groceries, and waved as she headed out the door.

Patrick took a chance and hurried out the door, catching up to her as she climbed into her car.

"How about dinner in town on Saturday night. I'm due for some down time and need to get out of here for a bit. I could pick you up about four."

Ann considered this pleasant man. They had just spent a lovely evening in lively conversation. She had enjoyed herself, but he was a cop. Still, what were the chances he would find out about her past? He had no real idea where she came from or what led her to Wolfsburg and Riverside Elementary. She'd just have to make darn sure she didn't let any details slip.

"Sure, sounds great but Saturday's not good. Wednesday okay or are you still on duty? I'll have to get some groceries, so could we hit the supermarket first? That way I won't have to go into town on Friday."

"Okay, I'll make Wednesday work. Pick you up at four," replied Patrick as he gently closed her door.

Ann smiled as she drove to the isolated trailer. Bates appeared to be pretty sociable, and she was lonely. It would be good to have some male company. Not that Ben wasn't fun, but she had a good idea that their friendship would remain just that—friendship. It occurred to her that Ben might be gay. There seemed to be no sexual attraction between them.

Chapter Twenty

Robert sat in his sanctuary and stared out the window, his eyes failing to register the brilliant autumn day. The swirling leaves and scudding white clouds did nothing to lift his black mood. Not even the delicious aromas from the slow cooker permeating the small house could rouse him from his sombre reflections.

To hell with that witch, Carolyn. To hell with them all, he thought as he realized the head teacher position was slipping further and further from his grasp. He knew he would have to either discredit or drive away the competition.

Snickering quietly to himself, he decided it would be much more fun to drive them away. He could easily make those sorry sons of bitches wish they'd never set foot in Riverside Elementary. By making their lives a misery, he could force them to apply for a transfer or even to resign from the district. Inflicting pain and suffering gave him such a thrill.

Life was getting pretty dull around here. Betsy was less than exciting. She couldn't even arouse him unless he beat her first. Besides, he had to lay off her for a while; people were getting too nosey. They were always asking questions. The whores in town all recognized him now and wouldn't even get in the truck. Clearville was too far to go in the winter. Yes, he decided. He would stick closer to home. Malcolm, Ben, and Ann would become his new playthings.

***

Friday, Jake arrived in Wolfsburg around six and effortlessly found Ben's house. While he stood waiting for Ben to answer his knock, he checked out the surroundings. The older, blue building next door was low and quite large. It appeared to be a community hall or some kind of church. A sign above the entrance simply said Wolfsburg. Two women were busy unloading some boxes out of the back of a station wagon; they looked up and smiled.

Ben opened the door and then stopped short of hugging Jake when he noticed the women in the hall's parking lot.

"Hi there, Jake. Come on in," he said, waving to the ladies. "Hi, Mrs. Barnes! Setting up for your nephew's wedding?"

"Yes, we're getting a head start on the food prep. There'll be over a hundred guests!"

"Come on in," Ben repeated. After pulling Jake into his small home and then closing the door, he eagerly engulfed him in a warm embrace. "I'm so glad you finally made it here. I can't wait to show you around Wolfsburg, the school, and of course my favourite fishing hole, Robin Lake."

"Hold on, hold on. Catch your breath, man," Jake said as he laughed at his partner's enthusiasm. He had looked forward all week to this weekend. It would be wonderful to just relax, eat at home, and hang out. The city got tiresome, and even the restaurants became too much bother.

"We're invited for supper over at my friend Ann's. She's the one I told you about. I've taken her out to dinner and she and I get together to watch the odd movie. The other day we went for a hike after school. You'll like her she's good fun."

"Does she know about us?" asked Jake, suddenly serious. "Who exactly does know about us?" He was still annoyed at having to pretend that he was Ben's brother.

"No, she doesn't know for sure, but I think she has a pretty good idea that I'm not into women. She's very attractive, and I haven't made any advances towards her. Saw her out with the cop, Bates, the other day. No, she's becoming a good friend. If she suspects anything, she'll keep her mouth shut." He shot a guilty look at his lover. "You'll see what I'm up against when I show you around. Please, please understand," he implored Jake.

"Relax, it's okay for now. I'll play your game," grumbled Jake. He felt sorry for Ben. Still, he felt frustrated. Why his friend couldn't be comfortable with his sexuality was beyond him. Surely, this place wasn't *that* archaic. This was the twenty-first century.

"Here, open this," said Jake, pulling a bottle of champagne out of his suitcase. "Time for celebration."

***

Saturday morning, Ben boiled up some potatoes and eggs. Setting them aside to cool, he called to Jake who was shaving in the tiny bathroom.

"Hurry up in there. Let's go over to the school, and you can see my classroom before we take off for the lake. These can cool off, and we can throw tonight's potato salad together later."

"I'm almost ready. Think we'll need a jacket?"

"Not a bad idea. It gets windy up by the lake."

Jake and Ben drove over to Riverside Elementary. It was unlikely they would run into anyone this early on a Saturday morning. After unlocking the main door, they meandered down the hall as Ben detailed the various rooms and described the activities that were important to the school. Jake was impressed by the huge emphasis the staff and students placed on the anti-bullying program they had been implementing.

"Thought you said these kids didn't have much of a bullying problem here," said Jake.

"No, they don't. Occasionally, students who come in from the outside will bully. Usually they do it to appear cool or to fit in. It doesn't take long for the newcomers to get, as we say, 'Riversided.' They learn pretty quickly that these kids stick up for each other."

"So why the program?"

"Carolyn Myers, the principal, says the kids from Wolfsburg get set upon when they go to high school. We're trying to give them tools so they don't get bullied. Another problem is that these kids have such a high respect for any kind of authority figure hammered into them by the church that it sometimes clouds their judgement. It can be dangerous. And between you and me, there's one teacher here that rules his class by intimidation. In fact, he pretty much rules the staff as well. We all try to stay out of his way. It doesn't help that he's head teacher to boot."

They turned as they heard the front door being opened.

"Speak of the devil," murmured Ben.

"Hi, Robert. Meet my brother Jake. Oh, yes, you two have already met, haven't you … at Roma, the restaurant in town."

"Right, your brother Jake," scoffed Robert as he looked at the pair. "What are you up to today?"

"Ben's going to show me Robin Lake," offered Jake. "According to him, there's lots of fish in there."

"Going to take a boat out or do you fish from shore?" Robert asked.

"I don't have a boat," Ben replied. "We'll have to cast out from the boat launch."

"Old man Samuel has aluminum fourteen footer. You could rent it off of him," suggested Robert, knowing full well that old Samuel would never loan or rent anything of value. "Well, I have to pick up those files Carolyn wants me to go over. See you later."

Ben shook his head. Part of the charm of the lake was the boat launch. You could sit comfortably and cast out almost to the middle of the lake. Boats were too much trouble for one person to handle. Most of the time, he went fishing by himself. Often after fishing for a while, he would end up sitting quietly in the evening, watching the sun go down over the lake. He was looking forward to sharing this special place with Jake.

They finished touring the school and headed over to the store to pick up some sandwiches and coffee for a picnic lunch.

They reached the lake just after ten, then set their lines and settled in to wait for a bite. It seemed as though the fish had disappeared. Neither Jake nor Ben got a single nibble.

"Damn, you'll never believe that this lake is the local hot spot," Ben lamented.

"No worries. It's just great being out here with you. Let's have those sandwiches. It was nice of that guy... Herb was it? ... to put the coffee in a thermos. I'm getting a little chilled, and hot coffee will go down a treat."

They spread the car blanket at the base of the cedar tree and sat eating their picnic. Birds twittered in the bushes, and a loon could be heard trilling over by the opposite bank. Ben reached over and squeezed Jake's shoulder. "Come here, you," he said, pulling Jake closer.

Suddenly the air went still. An audible click of a camera punctuated the quiet.

***

Ann worked quickly, putting the finishing touches on her dessert. The raspberry cheesecake looked perfect. Her chilli was simmering in the slow cooker. Cooking was one of her favourite pastimes, and it had been a long time since she cooked for anyone but herself. She was eagerly anticipating tonight's company.

Casting a practiced eye around the table, she mentally checked off what everyone was bringing. Ben was making potato salad, and Malcolm had said something about a Caesar salad. Patrick was picking up some crusty buns from the bakery in town.

She had invited him on the spur of the moment. Hopefully, the others wouldn't mind. Patrick could be funny and certainly didn't talk shop when he was off duty.

As she uncorked the red wine, she heard the doorbell ring. The first of her guests had arrived bringing potato salad and a fancy bottle of brandy.

"Welcome. You must be Jake," Ann enthused, giving him a friendly hug. "It's so nice to finally meet you. Ben talks about you all the time."

Leading her visitors into the combined kitchen, dining, and living room, her laughter filled the room.

"This is it, my humble abode. Not much, but you should have seen it when I first got here." Ann then proceeded to regale them with the story of her first night in Wolfsburg.

Jake listened, horrified. It would have been enough to send anyone screaming out of the community.

"Oh, my God!" he exclaimed. "It's a wonder you stayed."

"Not really." Ann shrugged. "I had nowhere to go, and school started in two days. I had a contract, and those are so hard to get these days. Besides, it all worked out. I've met some wonderful people, including your brother." Ann smiled at Ben.

"Oh, I invited Patrick Bates to dinner tonight. Hope you don't mind. I've started to get to know him, and he's good company. He's bored to death over at the store. They're renting him the back room while he works on the murder investigation. He's so stir crazy that we even went bowling in town the other night, after dinner. We had a ball."

"I don't mind at all," Ben said, "but Malcolm still gets a bit gloomy whenever he thinks about Susan. We'll just have to try to keep from mentioning her too much."

"Didn't think of that," Ann said tentatively. "It'll probably be all right, Patrick doesn't seem like a cop when he's off duty."

Malcolm arrived, followed shortly by Patrick Bates. Ann flew into hostess mode getting drinks for all. She poured wine for Jake, Ben, and herself. Patrick accepted a beer, and Malcolm stuck to orange juice with a splash of club soda.

A lively evening followed, filled with interesting conversation, a few bawdy jokes, and ripples of laughter. Ann relaxed and took pleasure in her newfound friends. Little did she know this was to be one of the last enjoyable evenings in this trailer.

***

From his hiding place behind Ben's truck, Robert could see into the brightly-lit space. As he watched, Ann stood up, crossed over to the window, and drew the curtains against the oncoming night. Music began to drift out into the chilled air.

He took his keys from his pocket and then held them firmly in his hand as he drew several lines down the side of each vehicle. A satisfying scrunch of metal against metal accompanied each stroke. Darkness hid all evidence of his handiwork. Each victim would have an unpleasant surprise in the morning.

***

The next day, each target reacted differently to the damage done to their vehicle.

Patrick immediately thought that some teenager had keyed his car while it was parked outside the back door of the store. He asked Herb if he could park in the front during the evenings.

Ben was mortified when they noticed the damage to Jake's vehicle. They had taken Jake's car to Ann's because Ben's truck had been covered in mud from that morning's trip to Robin Lake.

"I'm so sorry, Jake. I'll pay for it to be fixed. Damn, you came out for a nice weekend and now look what's happened."

"Let's try giving it a good polish and wax job. Most of the marks seem to be shallow. It might work," suggested Jake. The guys spent the rest of the day working turtle wax into the pale gray car. Happy with the results, Ben and Jake went for an evening jog.

Passing by Ann's trailer, they decided to call in to thank her for the lovely evening. She was sitting on her steps with a buffing cloth in her hands.

"Hi, you two. Come and look what someone did to my car," she said as they got nearer. "Kids must have keyed it while I was at the school."

"No, I don't think so. Jake's car has been done as well. Right down the passenger side," Ben told her. "Must have happened while we were eating dinner last night. We didn't notice until this morning."

"Really? Someone was here last night?" Ann said as she glanced uneasily towards the bushes that bordered her yard. "That just plain creeps me out. I'm going to call Patrick and Malcolm to see if their cars were scratched as well."

A few minutes later, she joined the men on the steps.

"Well that beats all," she said, ruefully shaking her head. "Both Malcolm and Patrick's vehicles were keyed as well."

"Come on in for coffee," Ann offered. "Patrick's heading over here to see if he can find any clues as to who did it."

True to his word, Patrick drove in the driveway five minutes later.

An examination of Ann's yard yielded nothing of value. It had rained lightly overnight, and any footprints had been either softened, smudging any identifiable ridges, or were confused with the other footprints from her guests.

"Sorry guys can't find a thing." Patrick looked at Ann. "Be sure to always lock your door. This place is far too isolated for you to be careless. You do have a cell phone, don't you?"

"Yes, doesn't everyone have a cell these days?" she replied.

"Well, put me in your directory. I can be here in five minutes ... less if I have to."

"I'll be okay. It was probably teenagers with nothing better to do. I'll keep the yard light on for a couple of nights. That should let them know I'm watching."

***

First thing on Monday, as Ben entered his classroom, he was surprised to see his screen saver scrolling over the monitor. He crossed over to his computer desk. He was puzzled; he always closed down the computer when he was finished using it. Touching the mouse lightly, he was jolted into awareness. Vivid, garish colours of a gay-porn website illuminated the screen.

Startled, he looked around the room and towards the hall. Thankfully, no one was in sight. Strobe lights and flashing images of young, semi-clad men leered at him as he stared mesmerized by what he saw.

A cough sounded beside the classroom door. In a flash, he reached over and exited the site.

"Doing a little research?" Robert asked quietly. "Best you be careful what you look up on the school district server. They have a filter, you know. Still, that didn't stop my class from enjoying an interesting 'kittens for sale' site the other day. Just type in the word *gay* and see what you get."

"Mr. Doyle," the secretary's voice came over the intercom. "Mr. Doyle, please come to the office."

"Got to go, duty calls," Robert said, turning on his heel and striding off down the corridor.

Ben sat immobilized in his chair. His mind raced as he thought of the consequences if anyone found such incriminating data on his computer. He never visited porn sites. It simply wasn't his style. Reaching over to the computer, he fired it up again. Carefully, he clicked the mouse, erasing the history and dumping the trash file. Still shaking, he shut off the machine. He then hurried to the staff room to join the others. By the time he had taken his seat, Carolyn had already started the staff meeting.

Robert stared at Ben. "Hey, what's wrong? Looks like you've seen a ghost," he said, trying to appear concerned. "You okay?"

The other teachers glanced at Ben. He did appear to be shaken.

"Something wrong?" asked Carolyn.

"No, I'm fine," Ben muttered, struggling to regain his composure. He bent his head and began studying the agenda.

***

As Ben walked into the staff room after school, he could see Robert already sitting at the table. He crossed over to the coffee machine and poured himself a cup of the stale brew. Taking a sip, he winced at the bitterness.

"Awful stuff at this time of day," he said companionably, his eyes coming to rest on a newspaper clipping left on the table. It described a recent gay bashing in Vancouver, BC.

Watching Ben stiffen, Robert enjoyed warm feelings of satisfaction spreading through his veins.

"Nasty goings on," Robert said, jabbing the scrap of newsprint with his fingertips. "Still, can't say I blame the attackers. Scum of the earth, those fags. Imagine what would happen around here. I hear its zero tolerance for homos as far as the church is concerned. In fact, Pastor Isaac is preaching on the evils of gay marriage this coming Sunday."

"That right?" murmured Ben. He sipped his coffee and pulled over the remains of the *Province,* studiously ignoring Robert as he skimmed the headlines.

Robert looked up as Ann came bustling in. Ben carefully reached out and slid the offensive clipping under the newspaper.

"Hey, guys. How was your afternoon?" she said as she sat down. "Mine wasn't so good. Kendal threw up all over her desk, and I couldn't find a clean-up kit. Robert, do we have anymore or do you need to order some?"

Robert looked at her disdainfully. "Did you look in the janitor's room or is that beyond you? Those kits are bloody expensive. If there's none left, you'll just have to use soap and water. Think about it … its copy paper or the extras. We have no money." He stood up and strode out of the room.

"Well, I just asked," Ann said in an exasperated tone. "Forgive me for asking."

"Just ignore the man," Ben said. "He's nothing but a pain in the ass. I've got a couple of kits under my classroom sink. You can have one. He probably gets his kids to clean up any vomit. Can't picture Robert in his fancy clothes cleaning up puke. Can you?"

Ann laughed. Ben always put things in perspective. She looked at her friend, noticing he still looked pale.

"You okay? Is something bothering you?" Reaching over to pat his hand, she added, "I've been told I'm a good listener, so if you ever need one ..."

"I'm fine. Just a long day," Ben replied. "Feel like grabbing a burger at the store?"

"Great. Give me five minutes to pack up my stuff. Shall we walk over? Do us good to get some air."

Patrick waved as Ann and Ben entered the store.

"Hey you two; come and join me."

Ann glanced at Ben. "Do you mind?"

Ben shrugged and smiled. "No, it's fine. He was good company the other night. Besides, I think he's interested in you," he teased.

As the three of them sat chatting and laughing over their coffees, Robert came in the door. They fell silent at the sight of him.

Robert wondered what they had been laughing about. It could have been about him given the way they shut up as he came in. He'd fix their wagon. It was just a matter of time. Edging over to the magazine rack, he chose two tabloids.

***

The next morning, the tabloids were lying in the middle of the staff room table. Both were open to the same story, a speculative article on who was gay and who was not in the Hollywood elite. Ben quickly scooped the trashy magazines into the garbage can under the sink.

"Where are those magazines?" asked Robert as he came in for his coat at lunchtime. "Looks like someone's easily offended or maybe just wants to read in private." He chuckled as he left for lunch at his teacherage.

***

Friday night, Patrick phoned Ann as he pulled into the parking lot outside the store.

"I picked up a bottle of Triggs and some Chinese food in town. I don't want to eat alone in my room. Feel like sharing?" It had been a long week, and he welcomed a chance for some female companionship.

"Have to wash my hair," she joked. "No seriously. Come on over. I'll set the table."

They spent a very pleasant evening. Once the food was reheated, it was quite good, and the wine was even better.

Ann carefully kept the conversation casual or centered on Patrick's experiences. Though she was mindful about not revealing too much of her background, the wine worked its magic and she found herself responding warmly to this intriguing man.

Patrick could feel her reluctance to talk about her past. Letting it go for now, he concentrated on her lively personality and the increasing temptations. As they sat side by side on the couch, he slipped his arm around her shoulders drawing her in for a light kiss.

As their lips met, they both realized that their relationship had changed.

***

Ann snuggled deeper into the warm bed. It was getting late.

"I best be going. Tongues might wag if I stay much later. Sun will be up in a couple of hours." Patrick leaned over the bed and ruffled her hair. "Back to that cold little room behind the store."

Ann smiled at Patrick. For the first time since coming to Wolfsburg, Ann felt content. Her job was going well, and she had several new friends, one of whom had just become her lover.

During her conversations with Patrick last night, she realized that he wasn't looking for a serious relationship right now. He was married to his job. There was also a good chance that he would be reassigned or transferred to another province after this stint in Wolfsburg was finished.

The situation suited her well. She couldn't afford to get too close to anyone. This was destined to be a "sing in the sunshine" affair. When he left, she would be sorry, but she was determined to make the best of things for now.

"Toasty in here," she teased. "See you soon." She closed her eyes, sank further down into the soft bed, drifting back to sleep.

Patrick dressed quietly, watching her sleep. As he left, he snubbed the lock, pulling the door shut behind him. He was uneasy that she lived in such an isolated location, but she seemed quite capable of looking after herself. Ann was beautiful, but she was also a strong woman. She could stand on her own two feet. That was one of the things he admired about her.

His thoughts turned to what secrets she might be hiding. He knew when someone was being evasive, and Ann was certainly concealing her past. Let her keep her own council. He didn't want to get serious anyway. He had put in for a transfer up north. The lure of the Arctic was strong. It was truly the last frontier. So long as she didn't have a boyfriend or husband lurking in the bushes, he'd go along for now.

Smiling, he buckled his seat belt and pulled out of the driveway. A black truck, without its lights on, drove slowly behind him, shadowing his every move.

***

On Monday morning, Ben wasn't surprised to see a church bulletin containing Rev Isaac's sermon pinned to the staff notice board. He had almost expected it. Robert was up to his usual nastiness.

He had begun to realize that it was very likely that Robert suspected he was gay. He had seen them at Roma, Robert didn't seem to believe Jake was Ben's brother, and he hinted at Ben's sexuality at every opportunity.

Ben couldn't shake the notion that he was being followed. They had seen Robert in the motel parking lot, and while he and Jake had been at Robin Lake, he had a feeling they were being watched. They had both been startled by what might have been a click of a camera's shutter.

Luckily, it was early in the morning and none of the other teachers except Malcolm were in the school. Ben ripped the bulletin off the board and stuffed it in his pants pocket.

Several hours later, Robert walked into the staff room at recess time and looked at the notice board. His missive was gone. Ben was carefully stirring his coffee and studying the newspaper. Malcolm stood looking out the window at the children playing by the swings. Colleen, Amy, Ann and Barb were casually chatting as they sipped their morning brew.

"Morning, all. Carolyn's off sick today, so there won't be any prep time. She told me to tell you she'll make it up next week," Robert reported officiously.

"Good, I depend on my prep time," grumbled Amy. "Besides it's in the contract that we get an hour and a half preparation time each week. Do you know in the high school they get an hour *every day*?" She was finding it particularly hard to manage this year. She had a difficult class and seldom found the time to come into the staff room.

"Yah, they claim it's because of all the marking. I think it's because they bitched louder," Ben said.

"Suits me fine," said Malcolm. "I wouldn't want to put up with all those teenage hormones every day."

"Every now and then I miss the teenagers a bit," declared Ann. "I taught middle school a while back. Still, the little ones steal your heart. A combination grade one and two class is a lot of work though. Kids never leave you alone for a second."

"You should do what I do. If they ask for help more than twice in a session, they have to start the task over again. Sure cuts down on the interruptions," stated Robert. "You people are too soft on your kids. They have to learn to listen the first time."

No one said anything. Robert looked from one to the other. He could see by the looks on their faces that they felt superior to him. They didn't appreciate his discipline methods. Some of the parents didn't either, but that was their problem. His classroom ran like a clock, and he seldom heard a peep out of the students. These teachers could learn a thing or two from him.

Chapter Twenty-One

Betsy looked over at her husband sleeping beside her. His dark hair curled over the pillow as he lay snoring softly. His lips relaxed into a thin frown. It had been a long time since he'd raised his fists to her or had even demanded sex. That meant only one thing; Robert was up to something. He had been strange ever since he came back from the last conference.

She no longer knew where he went, especially at night. He came and went at will, often returning well after midnight. Sometimes his clothes were covered in mud or wet from the rain. He had uncharacteristically gone to church last Sunday. In fact, he had dragged the whole family along to hear Rev Isaac's sermon on gay marriages. It was hardly a suitable topic for Timmy, but he had insisted that they attend.

Last night, he had gone to town and returned with several bottles of vodka. When she asked him what they were for, he had shoved her against the cupboards and growled at her to mind her own business. She knew enough to stay out of it. Hopefully, he'd leave her alone.

***

Malcolm finished transposing his hastily scribbled notes onto the computer and then threw his scrap paper into the garbage can. A glint of light winked back at him. On top of the discarded papers and assorted trash lay an empty vodka bottle.

Shocked, he reached in and pulled it out. With a quick look around, he dropped the bottle back in, got up, and shut the classroom door. Once more, he retrieved the empty, smelling its mouth to see if the clear bottle had really contained booze. *What's going on? Why did someone use my garbage can to dispose of their bottle?* Thoughts whirled around his head. Then the dreaded idea, *What if someone thinks this was my booze?* Snatching up the garbage bag out of the waste can, he tied it securely and hurried out to his truck. On his way home, he pitched the offending trash into the community dumpster.

It was a little after six when he finally arrived home. Sassy, his little dog, leaped and twirled as he let her out of his home. Desperate to pee, she shot over to beside the lilac bushes and squatted. Finally, she allowed him to pick her up.

Carrying the dog in his arms, Malcolm mounted the stairs again and went inside. He sank gratefully into his easy chair and switched on the news. This was usually the hardest time of day for him to avoid drinking. Tonight it was especially difficult; he was tired and stressed.

It might have been one of the high school students getting rid of a weekend bottle, but why would they have used his garbage can at the school? It didn't make sense. They would have simply chucked the bottle into the bush. No, it appeared that someone had deliberately put it there for the janitor to find. Thankfully, he had discovered it before he went home.

***

Later that week, Doug, one of Malcolm's students, came across a six pack of beer as he searched for the geoboards in the math cupboard. "Hey, Mr. McDermitt, what's this doing here?" asked the surprised student.

"I have no idea, Doug. Best I have a word with Ms. Myers. Here, I'll put it in the staff room for now." Malcolm hurried off with the beer and set it on the staff room table.

In no time at all, news of a six pack of beer found in Mr. McDermitt's math cupboard spread like a rash all over the school grounds. Robert hurried in from the playground and called the staff together.

"What's going on?" he said, staring hard at Malcolm. "You all know the rules about bringing alcohol to school. It's against school policy and the law. I'm going to have to call Ms. Myers. Carolyn will be shocked at your behaviour."

"Well, it's not mine," stated Malcolm flatly. "I don't drink."

"Tell us another one," Robert sneered as he pointed at the offending beer.

"No, truthfully. I have no idea who owns it or how it got into my math cupboard," Malcolm protested. His head was beginning to throb violently. Lurching to his feet, he dashed in the direction of the staff washroom.

"Oh yeah, another one of his migraines. Probably a bloody hangover," Robert said to his captive audience. "I'm calling Carolyn." He turned and strode into the office; his hand was already reaching for the phone.

As he left the room, the shocked staff looked at one another. This was a side of Malcolm they had not expected.

"What gives?" asked Barb quietly.

"I don't know. Maybe someone was drinking in the school last night. Hopefully, it wasn't Malcolm," replied Colleen as she picked up the six pack of beer. "Doesn't look like there is any gone."

"Well let's not jump to any hasty conclusions," Ann said. "There's no proof the beer belongs to Malcolm. It could be anyone's. Besides, I've never seen him drink. Not even at the conferences."

Malcolm returned clutching at his temples.

"Can someone drive me home? This is a bad one. I can't drive."

"Sure, I'll just get my keys. Do you need me to get any of your stuff?" Ann replied.

"Just my packsack. Colleen, please call me a sub," whispered Malcolm as he staggered towards the washroom again.

"Ben, can you help me get him to my car?" Ann said as Malcolm weaved unsteadily out of the restroom. "In fact, maybe you better come with me so we can get him into bed. My mom used to get migraines. They're awful. Sometimes the only thing you can do is go to bed and take medication," she added as she gathered up Malcolm's packsack and her purse.

The three of them passed by Robert as he returned to the staff room after having called Carolyn Myers.

"Where in hell are you all going?" he asked.

"Malcolm's too sick to teach. We're taking him home. Colleen's calling in a sub for him," Ann said.

Robert leaned in towards Malcolm and grabbed his arm.

"Carolyn's real pissed off. She's on her way over now," he smirked.

Malcolm turned his head and vomited into the garbage can near the entrance. Ben held him up and then gently steered him towards Ann's car.

***

Two days later, Malcolm returned to his room after school to pick up some marking to take home. He was surprised to see Doug waiting for him. Doug was sitting in one of the student desks with his chin resting on his folded arms. One look at the boy and he could tell something was seriously wrong. Doug's shoulders slumped in misery.

"Something on your mind, Doug?" Malcolm asked quietly.

Doug raised his head and looked at his homeroom teacher. He stammered, "It's that Mr. Doyle. I can't stand him. He shouts at me every chance he gets. I can't even be with my friends on the playground without him calling me over and reaming me out. I don't do nothing, nothing at all. Seems like he's trying to get me for some reason."

"You sure you don't do anything? You know you can give attitude sometimes," Malcolm said calmly.

"No, I swear I don't do anything. He knows I like you and I'm glad I have you for homeroom. Maybe he just wants to get at you by picking on me," Doug said, shaking his head. "None of us think it was your beer, you know. Doyle probably set you up."

Malcolm was dismayed. Doug was certainly upset and could be right as far as Robert wanting to get at him. Carolyn had given no credence to Robert's allegations that the beer found in the math cupboard belonged to Malcolm or any one of his students. The matter had been dropped, and Robert had been furious.

"Now, Doug, we can't go accusing people of stuff because we don't like them. I'll have a word with Mr. Doyle and see what's up. In the meantime, keep a low profile and don't give him any lip," suggested Malcolm.

"Okay, sir. Trevor said I should talk to you, and he was right. Don't know how much more I can take though."

"Trevor's a good friend to you. You have lots of friends—and me. I'll see what I can do," promised Malcolm.

After Doug left, Malcolm walked quickly down the hall and into Robert's classroom. Robert was at his desk grading papers.

"Can we have a chat?" Malcolm asked. "I've just been talking to Doug Weibe and he's quite upset. Thinks you have it out for him."

"Who? Doug Weibe? Oh that little punk. Yeah, we've crossed paths lately."

"What's the problem with his behaviour?" pressed Malcolm. "Is there something I should know about?"

"Not really. He's just a pain in the ass. I like pushing his buttons. Thin-skinned, that one. So he wimped to you, did he? What a loser."

"Well, lay off him if he isn't doing anything wrong. The kid has a hard life with his dad out of work and his mom having had that cancer scare."

"Cry me a river. In fact, cry me a bleeding lake. If he can't take it, he had better stay out of my way," threatened Robert, getting up out of his chair. He crossed over to the doorway where Malcolm stood. Leaning in menacingly, he said, "Why don't you just get out of here before I lose my temper."

Malcolm took a step backwards. "Best you quit while you're ahead. Ms. Myers will hear about this and about Doug if you don't stop bullying him." He turned and walked briskly down the hallway.

Back in the staff room, Malcolm's hand shook as he poured a cup of coffee from the carafe. Digging in his briefcase, he extracted a large bottle of Tylenol and took two of the extra-strength capsules. He hated confrontation, but Doug didn't deserve that kind of treatment from Robert.

In his room, sitting at his desk again, Robert assessed the situation. He was surprised at the courage Malcolm had shown. As much as he enjoyed tormenting Doug, he decided he had better lay off for a while. He had several parents on his ass right now. They were complaining again about his discipline methods and his marking system. He might not be able to torment Doug, but Malcolm was free to take his place. The jerk had no right to talk to him that way.

He saw Malcolm's truck head out of the school grounds and turn onto the road leading to town. After hurriedly packing up his new calf-leather briefcase, he got his coat and headed over to his teacherage.

"Hi, you're home. You have a good day?" Betsy called as he entered.

Robert shucked off his boots and brushed past her on his way to his sanctuary. "Out of my way, woman. Got stuff to do."

Christ this is heavy; he thought as he lugged the case of vodka out the door and lifted it into his truck.

***

Later that night around ten, Malcolm parked his truck in front of his house. He could hear Sassy barking frantically.

"Okay, girl, I'm coming." He charged up the path towards the front door.

Clunk—his foot connected with the first glass bottle.

Several half-empty bottles of vodka sat on his steps and porch. The air reeked with the acrid smell of spilled booze. Some of the bottles had been smashed, leaving shards of glass strewn over the weathered decking. Sassy barked furiously.

"Okay, girl, okay." Malcolm opened the door slowly and scooped up his dog before she could trample in the broken glass. After putting her down gently on the lawn, he stood between Sassy and the steps.

"Finished?" he asked as he picked her up again. Looking around, he could see at least ten bottles in varying states of fullness displayed for the world to see.

Slowly, he began to clean up the mess. He hosed down the porch and stashed the garbage bags full of broken bottles beside the steps. By the time he was finished, he was shaking with fatigue, stress, and the very real need to empty one of those bottles.

***

The next day, to Malcolm's horror, he found an AA pamphlet stuffed in every teacher's internal mailbox. The bright blue and white cover cheerfully encouraged anyone with an alcohol problem to come to a meeting. It promised complete confidentiality.

Malcolm's creditors began to call with increasing frequency, and each time Robert took a message, he posted it in the center of the staff bulletin board. Malcolm made it a point, before each break, to rush down to the staff room before any of the other teachers could arrive. He would carefully scan the room looking for anything incriminating.

When he found a poster of the Twelve Steps to Recovery displayed on the union notice board, he knew he couldn't take much more. That night, he made a desperate phone call to Sara and John.

Although they were pleased to hear from him, there was little advice they could give him. They suggested that he acknowledge he was an alcoholic and was in treatment. However, this was an impossible task for such an intensely private man. More importantly, he was worried that the district would try to transfer him out of the straight-laced community. Wolfsburg was one of the best postings he had ever obtained. He was starting to make friends here and liked living in this agreeable community. The last thing he wanted was for anyone to find out about his drinking problem and that he owed a fortune to the casinos in town.

He was in a wretched position, unable to risk disclosure. The nights became unbearable. Slowly, he slid back into the old habit of having just one to settle his nerves.

Each time he would promise himself that tomorrow would be different, but somehow it never was. He spiralled deeper and deeper into depression. In the quiet of his lonely evenings, he would often find himself with his face buried in Sassy's wiry white hair, sobbing. She would lick his face, tasting the salty tears.

"Oh, girl, life sucks," he'd whisper as he held his beloved pet. "Life just plain sucks."

Chapter Twenty-Two

It had been over two months since Ann had given Mr. Doyle the receipt for the trailer expenses. Carolyn had given Ann cash to pay Betsy and the boys, but she still needed to be reimbursed for the curtains and the bed.

She walked into the office after school and waited for Robert to acknowledge her.

She inquired tentatively, "Remember the bills I submitted to you at the beginning of the year, the ones for the curtains and the bed I had to replace in the trailer? I was wondering if you had heard anything from the district finance department. I could really do with the money."

Robert gave her an impatient look. "You'll be lucky. They don't usually cover those kinds of expenses. I sent them off a while ago. If we haven't heard, it means they're not paying."

"Carolyn assured me there would be no problem. Perhaps I should ask her to look into it," Ann insisted.

"No, I'll send the requisition in again. You should know, though, they don't take kindly to you young people always expecting special favours. Maybe I could be talked into using my influence. Interested in persuading me?" he insinuated.

Ann was quite taken back by what she assumed was a poor joke. She quickly put on her game face and replied, "Not likely. How do I know you have any influence over the district's purse strings?" As she turned to leave, she looked back at him. "Seriously, please submit the paper work again. I need the money. Moving here was really expensive. It *is* one of your responsibilities as head teacher, isn't it?"

"Yeah, and it'll be one of my responsibilities again next year. I intend to keep the position. The money's good and I'm perfectly suited for the job. I don't rattle easy and I have the respect of the community. Unlike some people, there are no skeletons in my closet," said Robert as he watched her move towards the door.

He saw her pause as she took in his words. Serve the bitch right. Obviously, that nice piece of ass thought she was too good for him.

"I suppose you're going to try for the job along with those other two losers, Ben and Malcolm," he added.

"I haven't decided. I am interested. Head teacher looks good on a resume," Ann replied carefully. "Malcolm said he might, and Ben is definitely going to apply."

"Hmmph," snorted Robert as she made her escape out the door. His plans were already in place, and it was just a matter of time before they all had second thoughts about applying for his position.

***

Settling into her grandmother's rocking chair, Ann switched on the television and surfed through the channels on the satellite. It had been a long day, and she felt the need to unwind before turning in for the night.

Glancing up, she noticed that she had forgotten to draw the drapes. Light spilled out into the yard surrounding the isolated trailer. Although it was unlikely that anyone was out there, she quickly got up and drew the heavy material over the window. She checked the door and ensured the deadbolt was in place.

There was nothing that held her attention on the television, so she clicked off the machine and picked up her latest novel, a mystery set in the Deep South. It was not a very good book and after a few minutes, she gave up trying to read. Sighing wearily, Ann got to her feet and headed into the bathroom. She heard a heavy scratching noise as she passed the draped window.

Startled, she flinched away from the sound and stood still. Then shaking her head ruefully, she chided herself for letting her imagination get the better of her. She shouldn't read mysteries before bed.

After finishing up in the bathroom, she entered her bedroom, dragged her navy nightgown over her head, and climbed into the inviting bed. She checked to see if she set her alarm clock, then smacked her pillow a couple of times and settled down for the night.

Sleep came rapidly these days. She seemed to be always tired from her busy days teaching the little ones. The preparations took so much time. Also, charming as they were grade ones never left you alone for a minute. Unlike the teenagers she had taught before, they always seemed to need something. At least the marking for elementary grades wasn't as bad. Last year, there had been many times she had fallen asleep grading stories and essays.

An insistent tapping on the siding of the trailer woke her from a deep sleep. It took her several moments to figure out what had woken her up at three in the morning. The tapping came again, more relentless and louder.

Ann stole out of bed and crept to the bedroom window. Quickly she wrenched the curtains aside and peered out into the predawn light. Out of the corner of her eye, she glimpsed a shadowy figure moving through the bushes beside the driveway, heading towards the road. Then she saw the long tree branch lying just under the window. It was obvious that someone was trying to scare her.

Circling the inside of her trailer, she cautiously peered out of the windows, trying to catch sight of her unwelcome visitor. After seeing no movement and hearing no unusual sounds, she checked the doors and windows to making sure they were securely fastened.

It was impossible to get back to sleep. Starting at every little sound, she lay awake until the alarm went off at six. Bleary eyed from tension and lack of sleep, Ann forced herself out of bed.

She phoned Patrick at his room behind the store but only received his voicemail. Leaving a brief message, she asked him to phone her at the school.

Ann didn't really want to bother Patrick with her problems, but something was very wrong. She had definitely seen someone in the bushes, and someone had been under her bedroom window trying to wake her up. If it was neighbourhood kids having a lark, he could put a stop to it quickly. And if it was something more serious, he would know what to do. Still, she was reluctant. It was rather early in their relationship to start involving him in her concerns. She was quite capable of looking after herself.

***

Just before leaving town, Patrick checked his messages using his mobile phone. He was surprised to have a message from Ann. After listening to it again carefully and hearing the anxiety in her voice, he called the school and asked to speak to Ann, only to be informed she was in class and unable to take his call.

He mulled over the call. It was unlike Ann to phone for no reason, especially first thing in the morning. They had made a date for later in the week, so perhaps she was cancelling. Still, that wouldn't account for the uneasiness in her tone. No, something was wrong. He decided to go to the school and wait to see her.

"Hello, Sgt. Bates," the secretary said, smiling warmly. "To what do we owe the pleasure of your company? Got any new leads you're following up on?"

"No, nothing new I'm afraid. No, I'm here to see Ann. She left a message on my phone. She didn't sound too good, so I'm here to check up on her."

"She looked terrible this morning, like she hadn't slept much. Kept to herself all day, so I didn't get a chance to ask her if anything was wrong. School's out in half an hour. Do you want to wait in the staff room? There's a fresh pot of coffee."

"Okay, thanks."

As Patrick entered the staff room, he was pleased to see Carolyn Myers, helping herself to some coffee.

"Oh, hi there, Carolyn," he said. "How's everything going at Riverside?"

Carolyn glanced over in his direction. "Fine, just fine. Things seem to be getting back to normal around here. Any progress in the case?"

Patrick looked around the room. It was not the ideal place to review the investigation.

"Can we go into your office? We can go over what I have to date if you like. I have half an hour before I can see Ann. I'm a little worried about her. She left a message on my phone this morning, and she sounded upset."

He and Carolyn spent the next while in her office going over his progress—or rather, lack of progress. It was a frustrating situation, but he had hopes that something would break soon. Usually, his cases were solved by now. He had no evidence worth a darn and only a couple of suspects. Robert was his prime person of interest, but he knew very little about the man.

"Between you and me, Carolyn, what's Robert Doyle like? I personally don't enjoy the man, but I know very little about his background. Can you tell me about his last posting before he came to Wolfsburg? The school board records are skimpy to say the least. They indicate that he was up north but not why he resigned his position."

"Sorry, I don't know much about him. He was hired to Riverside before I became the principal of rural schools. In fact, he wanted the position of rural school principal after the previous principal left suddenly, but the board felt he lacked experience and people skills. Can't say I disagreed with their opinion. They gave me the job, and he got the job of head teacher instead. He answers to me, and since I'm a woman and younger than him, that's a major problem to him. However, I make it work," she said with a small grin.

"Oh, I can see how Robert might have trouble adjusting to that situation. He's an excellent example of a chauvinistic pig. How his wife puts up with him is a miracle. Have you noticed anything about Betsy that would cause you to be concerned?" asked Patrick.

"Oh, you mean the bruises. I did see she had her arm in a sling the other day. Yes, I do wonder about how she's treated. I've never had any worries about Timmy though."

"I was talking to Betsy the other day when you all were away at the behavioural conference. She seemed pretty jumpy. Always checking to see if the van was returning. Gave her my card. That's about all I can do without proof or her contacting the authorities for help. Victims are usually very reluctant to turn in their abusers," Patrick informed Carolyn. "I'd be happy to rattle his cage if you could give me a reason."

Just then the dismissal bell interrupted them.

"Sorry, I have to go supervise the children getting on the bus. Ann should be free in a couple of minutes. Go on down to her classroom if you like," Carolyn said and then left her office.

Patrick made his way down the hallway, conscious of the curious stares from the children as they made their way out to the school bus. He paused at Ann's classroom door. Her head was bent over her desk as she wrote. Once again, he was drawn to her dark beauty. He had enjoyed their last evening a lot. Although he wasn't interested in getting too serious, he wasn't adverse to some quality female time. He had gotten the distinct impression that she felt the same way about him.

"Ahem," he said softly as he stood waiting at the door. "I'm here to see Ms. Santos," he joked.

Ann's head shot up, and she gasped at the formal sound of her name. Quickly recovering her composure, she stood up and smiled in his direction. Patrick had noticed her reaction.

"Sorry, didn't mean to startle you," he said apologetically.

"Oh that's okay. I was just off in another world. I wasn't expecting to see you," she replied.

"You had me a little concerned with the phone call. Did you need to cancel our date on Friday?"

"No, nothing like that. I just had a bit of trouble at the trailer last night," Ann said as she glanced around the room. "Can we go for a drive? I really don't want to talk about it here at school."

Ann and Patrick drove in companionable silence down the dirt road that led to Robin Lake. The trees had almost finished shedding their leaves, and a distinct coolness clung to the air.

They got out of his vehicle, crossed over the greying grass, and settled on a log at the water's edge. Reflections of the almost bare trees, spiky evergreens, and the blue sky were etched in the still water. Patrick waited patiently for Ann to start talking.

Ann laughed ruefully. "I feel like such a baby. In this beautiful setting, my problem seems to be much less real. Last night, however, it was all too real." She went on to tell him about the previous night's unsettling events.

Patrick listened. He could tell that it had upset her and that she was still very much concerned. It could be kids, he speculated, or something much more sinister.

She was an attractive young woman and she did live in that isolated hovel called a trailer. Although she was trying to be strong, she must have realized that in the case of an emergency, help would be a long time coming if she were even able to summon it. He put his arm around her shoulder and drew her close.

"Listen, I know you can handle it, but I don't want you to be careless. It's more than likely some kids getting their kicks out of scaring you, but don't forget, there *was* a murder committed just a few weeks ago. I'll cruise by a couple of times during the next few nights and just have a look. Do you have me on speed dial on that cell phone of yours?"

Ann nodded.

"Good. Next time, call my cell, not the room phone, so there's no delay in me getting your message."

Already she was feeling better about telling Patrick. He was right; it was probably just kids. They would be scared off if they saw that he was keeping the trailer under surveillance.

"Can you skip rocks or are you a girly girl?" teased Patrick as he pulled her to her feet.

Ann's spirits lifted, and she laughed. This man had a knack for making her feel better.

"I grew up with only a sister, but we certainly were tomboys." She reached down, selected a perfect, flat, oval stone, and sent it leaping over the motionless water.

Patrick hooted with laughter and gathered her into his arms.

"You sure are something else," he whispered as he kissed her soundly. "Come on, let's get back. If you can stand the cuisine at the store diner again, I'll treat you to dinner."

***

After supper, Patrick followed Ann's car to the trailer. He looked around her yard for footprints or anything out of the ordinary and then checked the front and back doors to ensure they could be locked securely. He noticed that both doors had deadbolts, and the moulding around the back door appeared loose.

"Maybe you should get this fixed," Patrick commented, gesturing towards the back door. "Meantime, wedge the edge of the washing machine in front of it. You want to be able to get out in case of a fire or something, so don't block it much. Anyway, I'll swing by later tonight. Hopefully it's just kids and they'll be scared off or lose interest."

After Patrick left, Ann carefully locked the doors and closed all but the bedroom window. She enjoyed fresh air while she slept so she left it open a small crack. Several times over the course of the evening, she saw headlights approach and carry on down the side road. She peered out the window and cautiously scanned the yard before she ventured out to put her garbage into the bin at the side of the steps. It felt like she was always up out of her seat, checking out the windows. Every crack of the trailer roof, every whisper of wind encouraged her to investigate. Finally, unable to relax, she poured herself a bath.

Floating in the warmth, she closed her eyes. She opened them abruptly when her head sank underneath the tepid water. She had fallen asleep in the tub. Thoroughly chilled and with fingers resembling dried grapes, she climbed out and rubbed herself dry with one of her new Pacific blue towels. Towels were a weakness for her. She loved the subtle hues and the luxurious feel of quality bath linens.

Sleep once more evaded her. As soon as she rested her head on her pillow, her eyes refused to obey the siren call of sleep. Tossing and turning, fluffing pillows and throwing the covers on and off proved to be futile. She would look like a used dishcloth tomorrow if she didn't get to sleep. The more she fretted, the more the luminous clock face mocked her. Desperate, she searched among her medicines for some kind of sleep-inducing potion. Gulping two antihistamines, she crawled back into bed and covered her head with her pillow. She had to trust Patrick. He'd keep her safe.

***

After a week of drive-by surveillance, Patrick and Ann assumed it had been juveniles causing the disturbances. He decided to ease up on his patrols. Nothing out of the ordinary had surfaced.

Robert watched the road from his truck that he'd concealed beside the school dumpster. For the past week, he had observed Sgt. Bates going to and coming from Ann's place. Bates's trips had become less frequent, which only meant one thing; they thought everything was over, and Bates was giving up the surveillance.

Robert waited a comfortable three days and then set out once more for the secluded trailer. Driving slowly past, he went to the end of the road and turned around in Joe Engles's field. There wasn't a sign of Bates. Pulling a heavy black sweatshirt over his head, he yanked up the hood and got out of the truck. His face was covered with camouflage paint, revealing only the whites of his eyes.

Slowly he approached his target. Gripping the length of pipe in his fist, he took aim at the bedroom window. The sound of splintering glass shook the midnight calm. Robert was gratified to hear a muffled scream and to see Ann fearfully peaking from behind the curtains in the utility room.

He swiftly ran around to the front door and banged on it. The noise was deafening as the pipe struck the metal door over and over again.

Ann desperately punched in Patrick's number.

"He's here, he's here now," she whispered into the phone. "He just smashed the bedroom window, and now I hear someone at the front door. Oh God, listen to that! He'll break the door down!"

"Take a breath, Ann. He can't get in. It's a metal door. Does he have a ladder? He'd need a ladder to climb in your bedroom window."

Robert switched positions and waited quietly in front of the living room window, standing stock still.

"I can't hear him anymore. I'm going to look to see if he's gone. Don't hang up—for God's sake, don't hang up," Ann begged.

Robert's patience was rewarded as Ann unwittingly revealed herself peering from behind the living room drapes. He stood in plain view and brandished the pipe. Then he slowly turned and walked down the driveway towards the road. He had several minutes to make his escape before Bates would be able to respond.

Stifling a scream, Ann whispered into the phone, "He was just standing there holding a pipe! I could only see his eyes, but he knows I'm watching. He's gone down the driveway. Patrick, please come quickly!"

Patrick careened past the school and onto the dirt road leading to Ann's. He failed to see the dark truck sitting at the edge of Joe Engles's field. Robert waited until he was sure Bates had time to get up the stairs and into Ann's trailer. Then he drove out onto the rough road with his headlights off, blessing his quiet engine. He parked beside the teacherage, climbed the steps, and entered quietly. All was silent. His key turned in the lock of his sanctuary, and then he lay fully clothed on his lumpy couch.

Betsy's eyes fixed on the clock. What was he doing out at four in the morning?

Chapter Twenty-Three

Shortly after her window was smashed, Ann began receiving phone calls. At first they were simply hang-ups, but they soon progressed to heavy, raspy breathing and whistling.

Not needing to draw any more attention to herself than necessary, she was hesitant to mention them to Patrick. She could handle prank calls. He was still driving by her house, checking things out, but he came less and less frequently as the days went on.

They had set up a signal between their cell phones. One push of the pound key rang his phone with a special ringtone. At that signal, Patrick promised to come immediately. Since it was clear that the intruder was well aware of her movements and those of Sgt. Bates, speed was their only hope of catching her tormentor. She was supposed to activate the signal at the first hint of trouble. So far, the last couple of weeks, everything had been quiet. With the exception of the annoying phone calls, everything appeared to be getting back to normal.

***

Ann woke up and stretched luxuriously. Today was Saturday, and she had been looking forward to sleeping in. Warm blankets hugged her shoulders, and the weak autumn sunlight streaming in the window promised a good day.

Tonight she was having dinner with Patrick at that fancy Italian restaurant, Roma. She had only been there twice before, and each time she found the food deliciously prepared. When she ate out on her own, she tended to stick to fast-food places, so Roma and interesting company would be a treat.

First, however, she had to go over to the school and prepare the lessons for the next week. Reluctantly, she inched her toes out of bed and onto the cool linoleum. Just as her toes touched the floor, she became aware of the sound of water running outside. She went into the bathroom and turned on the tap. Nothing.

Moving to the kitchen, she tried those taps with the same results. Damn, something was wrong. The toilet flushed but did not refill.

After hastily throwing on jeans and a sweater, Ann went outside. She circled the trailer looking for running water but could find nothing until she came to the rear of the old trailer. A huge puddle was forming under her bedroom window. Checking under the skirting boards, she located the source of the flow. It seemed as though something had come loose from the pipeline that came from the well.

She had no tools and even less of an idea as to how to fix the problem, so she dialled the store and asked Herb if he knew someone who could make the repairs that day.

"Sure, Ed's a good plumber and he knows about pumps. Is it the actual pipe or did your pump burst a valve?"

"I have no idea. Water's just gushing out and spreading all over the ground. It is coming from under the trailer, though," Ann replied.

Two hours later, Ed, a rough-hewn cowboy, showed up looking apologetic.

"Sorry, having trouble with one of my best bulls. Coughing and hacking like you wouldn't believe. That guy's worth over a thousand. Had to wait for the animal vet to come from the other side of Belmont," he said as he shook her hand politely.

"No worries. I'm just glad you could come. I know nothing about plumbing, pipes, or wells. I grew up a city girl," Ann stated anxiously.

Ed pulled off more skirting board and shimmied under the trailer. He appeared a short time later with a puzzled frown creasing his forehead.

"Found your problem all right. The intake pipe's been severed. Cut clean through. It couldn't have happened accidentally. Is someone fooling around?"

Ann gasped and then wearily shook her head. "I've been having some trouble. Figured it was young kids trying to play tricks on me," she told Ed as he ran his hands through his greying hair, getting rid of leaves and bits of debris.

"No kid around here would do that. First, they'd have to have the right cutter, and second, it'd be way too much trouble. We got good kids round here." Shrugging his shoulders, he turned and went back to his truck. He came back with a new length of pipe and some heavy industrial glue, and then set about repairing the break.

A short time later, his work was done. "That should do it. You never heard anyone under your trailer?"

"No, but I wasn't home until late last night. Then I watched TV. You don't hear much over the TV," Ann stated flatly. She was annoyed at herself for starting to let her guard down. If someone was trying to frighten her, they were doing a good job. She felt vulnerable. Her space, her private sanctuary was being invaded.

"Thanks. How much do I owe you?" she asked.

"Make it an even fifty. It'll cover the material, and the job didn't take long."

Ann waved as Ed drove away. The phone was ringing insistently. She ran inside and lifted the receiver.

"Water, water everywhere. I have a message from Sean ... he says to stay away from Bates if you know what's good for you," a sinister whisper echoed through the earpiece.

"Who is this?" Ann furiously demanded. "Who in hell are you?"

A dial tone reverberated in her ear. She froze. Whoever was tormenting her knew about Sean.

She pulled herself together. She hadn't come all the way to Wolfsburg to be frightened away from her new life.

***

After spending the rest of her day working in her classroom, Ann drove home to get ready for her date with Patrick. Choosing a long wraparound skirt, she added a simple boat-necked blouse and a small pendant that her sister, Evett, had given her for Christmas.

One look in the mirror assured her that she would please her companion. She found Patrick very attractive and looked forward to the evening. Perhaps they would come back to her place after dinner in town.

With that in mind, she quickly tidied up and spruced up the bathroom, finishing just as she heard Patrick drive into the yard.

"Hey, there," he greeted her and then gave her a lingering kiss. "You had company?" he asked as he pointed to the tire marks from Ed's truck.

"Oh, yes. A pipe burst under the trailer, and Herb got Ed to come and fix it." She studiously avoided mentioning the phone call or telling him that the pipe had been cut. Unless she felt in immediate danger, she wasn't going to involve Patrick in her problems anymore. She'd have to put on her big-girl panties and deal with it.

They had a lovely dinner and ended up seeing a show at the theater. It was an entertaining but very amateur production of the *Lion King*.

After drinks in a local lounge, Patrick suggested they stay in town rather than drive all the way back to Wolfsburg in the dark.

Ann readily accepted the invitation. She wasn't anxious to return to her trailer, and it was always a strain to drive the dirt roads after nightfall, constantly on the lookout for moose and deer that might dart into the vehicle's path.

"I don't have a toothbrush or anything to sleep in," Ann said as she got into Patrick's SUV. Then she laughed as Patrick reached into his coat pocket and extracted two toothbrushes still in their packages. "You'd make a good Boy Scout," she teased.

"One problem solved," whispered Patrick. "And I think the dress code will be clothing optional."

***

The following morning, Patrick drove Ann home. "Out you go," ordered Patrick with a grin. "I'd better at least pretend to do some work. The community is getting pretty fed up with the lack of progress on the murder case. Think I'll go over to Shane Howsers's slough where we found Susan's car and look around some more. Have combed that area dozens of times, but you never know. See you later." With a wave, he reversed his truck and sped off down the road.

Ann scanned the yard. Everything seemed to be normal. There was no sign that anyone had been there while they were in town. Her car was fine, and the only tire marks on the drive were Ed's or Patrick's. She unlocked her front door and threw her keys on the kitchen counter.

***

Ann worked all day at the school. Some days it seemed as though she would never get caught up with the paperwork, marking, and now the report cards were looming on the horizon. She knew the first year in a new position was always the worst, but she hated this feeling of running like a hamster on the wheel, never getting anywhere, never feeling quite in control of the preparation. She shut her daybook, then stretched and gathered up her books. It was time to go home and get some supper. Night came quickly here in the north. It was not yet six o'clock, and the sun had already disappeared.

Slipping out of her sweatshirt and jeans, she drew a warm bath, adding sea salt and a bit of lavender oil to the steaming water. As a treat, she lit a lavender-scented candle and placed it on the edge of the tub.

She sank into the fragrant bath, closed her eyes, and let her thoughts drift back to the previous evening. Patrick sure knew how to treat a lady. He was kind and attentive, and he made her laugh. She reached over to the tap in order to add a touch more hot water to the bathtub.

Suddenly, the room was plunged into darkness. Her eyes gradually grew accustomed to the flickering light from the small candle on the side of the tub. The power had gone out.

Stepping quickly out of the tub, Ann reached for her towel, accidentally knocking the scented candle into the tub. It was really dark now. The faint glimmer of light that filtered through the small bathroom window barely showed the outline of the window.

She wrapped her towel tightly around her dripping body and then felt her way over to the door and down the hall to the kitchen. Her feet made wet fish noises as she moved cautiously, trying not to slip on the linoleum. Fumbling in the catch-all drawer beside the stove, she managed to find her supply of emergency candles and some matches.

Relief swept over her as she lit the first candle and placed it in a shot glass. Then she lit three more of the thin tapers, sticking them into melted pools of wax in larger water tumblers. Cheerful flames danced in the kitchen. Ann moved through the trailer placing the candles where they would be the most effective.

Already she could feel the poorly insulated trailer growing colder. She knew that she would have no water since the pump was driven by electricity. She couldn't even refill the toilet if she flushed it. *Darn*, she thought as she realized just how dependent she was on power. Even more annoying was the fact that one of her favourite shows was coming on in half an hour, and of course, the TV wouldn't work.

It was strange that the wind wasn't howling and no heavy rain was falling. She peered out into the yard and couldn't see any downed trees that may have taken out the wires. Assuming it was a general power outage in the area, Ann dressed quickly in her pyjamas and sat down to read by the light of the candle on the end table.

Half an hour later, she was rubbing her eyes. *How did the pioneers manage back in the old days?* She wondered. Reading and sewing by candles or kerosene lamps must have been very tiring. Of course, kerosene lamps would have been better than candles. She made a note to herself to buy one of those lamps for emergencies the next time she went to town.

It was getting uncomfortably cold. Ann changed into a set of heavy fleece lounging clothes and thick, gray woollen hiking socks. Glancing at her watch, she saw that the power had been out for well over an hour. She dug out her cell phone from her packsack and dialled Patrick.

"Hey, how are you doing? How long do you think the power will be out?" she asked when he answered.

"Hi, Ann. I've got power here at the store. There are lights on over at the school grounds too. Must be something wrong at your end."

Ann felt the remaining warmth leave her body as she realized there was a very good chance that someone had sabotaged her trailer again. Keeping her voice steady, she asked, "Do you think you could come over and check out my electric panel? I checked the fuses, but they were all fine. There's no power anywhere in the house."

"Yup, be right over," he said and hung up the phone.

Patrick jumped in his truck and started out on the now very familiar route to Ann's place. He could see evidence of lights in every house as he drove along the main road through Wolfsburg.

Switching on his flashlight, he mounted the stairs and rapped on the front door. Ann greeted him wearing her unfashionable fleece suit.

"Pardon the attire," she said ruefully. "It's bloody cold in here." She led him into the utility room where he examined the fuse panel.

"You're right, nothing wrong here. I'll take a look outside where the line comes in," Patrick said, moving towards the door.

A few minutes later, he was back inside looking concerned.

"The hydro meter has been yanked away from the trailer. There are some footprints where someone stood when they destroyed the connection. I don't like the feel of this at all. I think you should come back with me and spend the night at my place."

"I can hardly do that in this small community. Teachers are supposed to be above reproach," Ann said at this suggestion. "It simply wouldn't look right. No, I'll be okay until tomorrow when I can get the maintenance guys to fix the damage."

"I could stay over," offered Patrick.

"I have to get to bed soon. I have playground supervision duty in the morning. I'll just crawl into bed and keep warm that way. Can you escort me to my outhouse before you leave? That way I don't have to flush the toilet … there's no water here when you have no power. I'm on a well, and the pump, of course, is run by electricity."

Patrick helped Ann find her way to the outdoor loo and waited a discreet distance away while she used the long-abandoned facilities.

"You sure you're going to be all right?" questioned Patrick after ushering her back to the trailer. He was reluctant to leave her alone but could readily understand the implications if he were to stay, or she were to go to his room over at the store.

"You could bunk down in the medical room at school," he suggested.

"Yes. That's an idea. If I get too cold, I'll do that."

Patrick spent a few minutes collecting evidence. He dusted the meter for prints but found nothing. The perpetrator had been wearing gloves. He measured and photographed the footprints. Noting a significant amount of white sand in the tread marks, he scooped up a portion and placed it in a clear evidence bag. He was quite certain it was sand, but the lab would be able to provide more specific details. An old flathead screwdriver lay a short distance from the bedroom window. Patrick bagged this as well.

"Is this yours?" he asked, holding out the bag with the screwdriver in it.

Ann shook her head, "No, but there's all kinds of junk like that lying around this yard. It could have belonged to a previous tenant."

"I really don't like leaving you alone," he murmured as he gathered her into a quick embrace. "Those footprints belong to someone who's quite tall, and judging from the depth, quite heavy. Keep this flashlight handy and don't hesitate to use our signal, Ann."

"Don't worry, I'll be fine," Ann replied with more confidence than she actually felt.

"Lock this door behind me," he ordered as he left.

Ann drew the deadbolt and checked to make sure the curtains were pulled tightly across the windows. After compulsively rechecking the front and back doors, she blew out the candles and crawled into bed with all her clothes on. Patrick's flashlight and her cell phone were securely stashed under the edge of her pillow. She lay wide awake throughout a night filled with peculiar noises, waiting for the dawn.

The next morning, Ann sat in the staff room cuddling her coffee cup and looking like a wreck. Her makeup was almost non-existent, and her clothes looked as though they had been put on hastily. She glanced up as Colleen came through the door from the workroom.

"Oh hi, Ann. Didn't expect to see anyone here so early. Usually it's just Malcolm and me here first thing in the morning. He must be late today."

"Hi, Colleen," Ann mumbled. "Sorry, did I scare you? No power at my place, and I came in early to warm up. That old trailer gets freezing cold when the power goes out."

"My goodness. Why didn't you call me? You could have stayed at my place. It's only a one-bedroom, but there's always the couch."

"Didn't think of it. I'll get Robert to put a call into maintenance when he gets in. Hopefully, they can come out today," replied Ann wearily.

Both women looked towards the front door as they heard it swing open. Robert was stamping his feet and scrubbing his shoes on the entrance carpet. He hated having to change his shoes. Every morning, he carefully coordinated his outfit. He had more shoes than most of the women teachers on staff.

"Hi, Robert," Ann said. "Am I ever glad to see you. The meter to my trailer was damaged last night, and I have no power. Can you phone maintenance and get them to come out and fix it please?"

Robert stared at Ann with satisfaction. She looked as though she hadn't slept, and her usual careful appearance was decidedly messy.

"What happened? A tree come down?" he quizzed.

"No, some kids must have vandalized the meter out the back of the trailer. Maintenance will have to replace it and some of the wiring. It was so cold with no power. I hardly slept all night. I couldn't even make coffee this morning."

"You'd never last long in the bush. Poor little princess needed someone to keep her warm," he said.

Ann lost her temper. "For God's sake, just call maintenance. I don't need any of your smart remarks today. I'm tired and fed up."

Robert smirked as Ann stormed out of the staff room. Turning to Colleen, he smiled and said, "Can't take a joke, can she? Best she watches how she talks to me. I might not remember to call the repair guys."

At recess time, Colleen caught up with Ann as she left her classroom. "You better check to see if Robert phoned. I don't trust that slimy character. It'll take all day to fix the damage if the wires are destroyed."

As she came in from recess duty, Ann asked Robert if maintenance was coming out to fix her power. She was dismayed to learn that Robert had conveniently forgotten to call.

"I'll have to call at lunch time," he said as he hurried into his classroom.

As usual, Robert went over to his teacherage at lunch time, forgetting again to put in her request.

Ann watched him leave and turned to Malcolm. "Can I call maintenance myself or does Robert have to do it since he's head teacher?"

"The maintenance department is really fussy about requisitions. Why don't you call Carolyn and ask her to put in the order?" suggested Malcolm. He knew that Robert was probably pulling a power trip.

"Good idea, thanks," said Ann, heading out to Carolyn's office to place the call.

Carolyn answered on the second ring, and Ann explained the situation.

"Sure, no problem. I can put in a requisition right now. Only thing is they probably won't be able to get out there today. It's late," Carolyn said. "Why don't you move into the medical room for the night? Grab supper at the store and put in for reimbursement. I'm so sorry about this. Things like this have never happened before. Are you sure it was kids?"

"Pretty sure. I think I'll bunk down in the school tonight. Amy offered to put me up, but I would prefer to manage on my own," Ann said appreciatively. She knew she could count on Carolyn's support.

She had just ended her conversation with Carolyn when Robert walked into the office.

"What are you doing in here?" he asked.

"Oh, I called Carolyn about the power problem. You went home for lunch, and I figured there would be very little chance of getting anything done today if I didn't call. As it is, they won't come out now until tomorrow."

"You interfering little bitch," exploded Robert, shaking his fist. "You just want to make me look bad. Think that's going to get you further ahead in the head teacher thing, don't you? You've got a lot to learn, you stupid cow."

Appalled, Ann just stared at him open-mouthed as he stormed off down the hall towards his room.

Right after school, Ann drove over to her trailer. She needed to pick up her toiletries, clothes, and a couple of books while it was still light out. After pulling into the small yard, she quickly got out and headed towards the stairs.

Something didn't feel quite right, but she dismissed her concerns, blaming her feelings on being tired and the blow up with Robert. She opened the door and stepped inside. Her foot kicked a manila envelope that had been shoved under the door. Stooping down, she picked it up and with trembling hands tore it open. She pulled out the sheaf of paper that had been stapled in one corner and studied the forms in front of her. They appeared to be notes from a police report.

In the official-looking documents, details of the incident in Alton were displayed in stark black and white. Dates, times, and names were listed. It was noted that the accused had left town and that the whereabouts of Maria Santos were unknown. Other points listed included the fact that although the plaintiff had withdrawn his complaint, the police reserved the right to press charges if and when they saw fit. The damning papers concluded with the declaration the file was being left open pending further investigation. Ann sank to her knees.

She tore the documents into shreds, dropping the bits all over the floor. Moving as if she were in thick molasses, she drew a plastic bag out of a kitchen cupboard and began to gather up the scraps of paper. Her hands scrabbled over the floor seeking every last shred of the damaging text. Rising to her feet, she knotted the bag and found some matches.

Her automated movements took her behind the trailer where she held a match to the white plastic. Flames leapt and destroyed the evidence.

She found herself back inside her trailer sitting at the kitchen table. As dusk settled, the shock of discovering the police report began to wear off and she felt the cold interior grow even more frigid. Unable to deal with her problem, she tried to push it out of her mind. Time would help her figure out her next move. Obviously, someone had found out about her past. She might be able to persuade them to keep quiet once she knew who had discovered her secret.

She collected her clothes, sleeping bag, and a few necessities, and then left her icy home and climbed into her car. Five minutes later, she settled into a chair in the store's small café.

"Herb, I'll have whatever's on special and a big mug of coffee, please."

Just as her meal arrived, Patrick entered the store and saw her sitting by herself. He crossed over and spoke softly. "Don't feel like company tonight?"

Ann startled for the second time in as many days. "Hi, I didn't notice you come in," Ann said. "Come sit down. I'm having supper. No one could come out to fix my power until tomorrow. I'll be sleeping over at the school tonight. Too darn cold at my place."

"You okay?" he asked as he sank into the chair opposite her.

"Sure, I'm fine," Ann hastened to reassure him. They chatted quietly while she ate the house special, meatloaf.

A little while later, she excused herself and went to buy a couple of muffins for the morning and a sandwich for tomorrow's lunch. Then Ann made her way over to the school. She was so tired. Last night had been endless, and she was actually looking forward to the medical room's cot.

Sleep did not come easily in her unfamiliar surroundings. The noise from the school's furnace was surprisingly loud, and the empty halls amplified every sound. The lumpy mattress smelled faintly of vomit and sick children, and the cheap clock ticked relentlessly. Tossing and turning in the cramped room, she eventually gave up and dragged her sleeping bag to the staff room. After settling down on the couch, she finally fell asleep.

Very early the next morning, Robert entered the staff room quietly and stood beside the couch looking at the still-sleeping girl. She was lying on her side snoring softly. She was dead to the world, oblivious to her surroundings. It was apparent that she had finally gotten to sleep after a very restless night. He lifted his load of books high over his head and then let them drop to the floor.

Ann bolted upright and frantically looked around.

"Serves you right, you stupid cow," he rasped. His face materialized inches away from hers. "Last night won't be your last sleepless one if you keep on trying for the head teacher position. It's mine. Don't you forget it." He scooped up his books and left as quietly as he had come.

Ann struggled to slow her breathing. As she calmed down, she began to understand that Robert was certainly enjoying her discomfort. She wondered if he was responsible for the power outage. Was he the one that cut the water pipe? Then the dreadful thought that Robert might have been the one to slip the envelope under the trailer door crept into her mind.

She woke with a jolt as she realized the front door of the school was being opened. As Ann climbed out of her sleeping bag, Robert entered the staff room.

"Morning," he said as he stashed his recess snack in the refrigerator. "I see you abandoned the medical room in favour of our couch. Did you have a reasonable night?"

Ann shook her head in disbelief. *Had she imagined the whole incident?*

"Oh, good morning. I'll clear out of here. I didn't realize it was so late." Hastily jamming on her sneakers, she fled to the medical room to retrieve her school clothes.

Ten minutes later, she was blow drying her hair after having washed it in the sink. Colleen came in to the staff bathroom and stared at her in surprise.

"Sorry, didn't mean to interrupt. Have you been here all night?" Colleen asked.

"Yes, I slept on the couch."

"You should've come over to my place," said Colleen. "More privacy there."

"I wish I had taken you up on your offer—I just didn't want to impose. It was a miserable night."

"Hey, what are friends for. You know I consider us friends even though we haven't known each other very long, right?" Colleen said sympathetically. "Are you all right? You seem upset ..."

Ann nearly burst into tears at Colleen's concern. Fighting for composure, she nodded silently, and Colleen put a supportive arm around her.

"Rough times, eh? If you ever need to talk, you know where to find me." With an encouraging smile, Colleen left to start the coffee maker.

She was becoming increasingly worried by Ann's jumpy, tired, and forgetful behaviour.

***

Nathan, the maintenance man, brought the school district's electrician, John, with him. They were mirror images of each other. Both men were short and slight. With their black coveralls and work boots, they looked as though they belonged on a construction site rather than in a school. First they stopped by Ann's classroom to get her keys, and then they headed towards her isolated trailer.

John had been quite taken with the attractive teacher. He quizzed his companion. "She's new out here, isn't she? Know if she's single or what?"

"She's single all right, but I think Herb over at the store said he's seen her out with the cop ... Bates," replied Nathan. "Why? Want to try your chances?"

"Wouldn't mind. It's been a long time since Sophie and I broke up. A man needs company, if you know what I mean."

"Wouldn't know, got all the company I can handle. My gal is one hot mama," Nathan boasted. "Here we are."

The men pulled into Ann's driveway. Litter and garbage were strewn everywhere.

"Christ, what a mess. Looking at her you wouldn't think she'd live in such a pig pen."

"No, I've been here before. Last month I had to put some weather stripping around the back door and change the locks," said Nathan. "It wasn't like this."

The garbage can had been upended, and the slight wind was lifting the papers all over the yard. Crows had already gotten into the household trash. Heavy footprints led up to the porch where the garbage cans had been stored.

"Someone's had a great time," observed John, stepping over the trash on his way around the trailer. "Let's have a look at what's wrong with the wires."

It took them several hours to repair the extensive damage. Then they checked out the entire wiring system of the home to ensure that no further mischief had been done. Returning to the school just after the closing bell, Nathan and John found Ann shepherding her students out to the bus.

"You're all fixed up. We restarted the furnace, so the place should be nice and toasty by the time you get home," Nathan reported. "Your site's a mess. Garbage chucked everywhere. Think a bear or something did a number on your garbage cans. Sorry we didn't have time to clean it up. Gotta get back to town."

"Thanks, guys. I really appreciate you coming out all this way. No one out here does electrical like that—plumbing yes, electrical no."

"You had plumbing problems as well?" asked John.

"Yes, some kids cut a pipe under the trailer. Water got everywhere," Ann replied.

"Sounds like you need a man to help you out," joked John. "I'm available."

"Oh, I'll be okay," Ann said with a smile. "Think I'm going to get one of those 'fix-all' books. Better yet, I'll put the school board maintenance on speed dial. Thanks again." She made a mental note to bake some cookies. She could ask the high school bus driver to drop them off at the maintenance building for Nathan and John. Who knew when she might need them again? Besides, it never hurt to show appreciation.

After she got home, it took her the best part of an hour to clean the mess from around her yard. As she was finishing, Patrick drove up.

Putting on a brave front, she explained away the gloves and garbage bags by saying a bear must have been attracted to the fish she'd put in the can a few days ago. "Should've known better. Guess not all the bears are asleep yet."

Patrick scanned the area.

"Bears with the same footprints as the ones that tore apart the junction box I would say," he said with chilling certainty. "Sure don't like what's going on here."

Chapter Twenty-Four

Robert got up from the breakfast table. Ignoring Betsy as she scuttled out of his way, he strode into their bedroom. He hauled an expensive leather suitcase out of the closet and placed it on the neat bed that Betsy always made as soon as he got up.

He carefully folded a variety of clothing. Then he packed the silk shirts, pressed pants, and highly polished shoes into the sleek black suitcase. After adding a selection of socks and underwear, he threw in his toiletry bag and shaver.

Robert went to his sanctuary and withdrew a large amount of cash from the cashbox hidden in the bookcase. Five hundred should do it, he thought. He'd charge the room and most of his meals to his credit card. This money was for incidentals. Some of the "incidentals" had blonde hair, some were brunettes. He wasn't fussy. He returned to the bedroom to finish packing.

"Are you going somewhere?" Betsy asked tentatively, coming to stand by the open doorway. It was the weekend and they needed groceries. She had been hoping they would go to town as a family.

"None of your bloody business!" he yelled. "None of your damn business," he repeated, shoving her against the dresser and closing his suitcase with finality.

"Okay, okay," Betsy quietly said. "Can you bring back some milk and eggs if you go into town? We're all out, and you know how expensive the store is. Also, there's no money in the household jar. Can you get some out of the bank?"

"Shut your whining mouth, bitch. Here—take this and get the stuff at Herb's. I won't have time to go grocery shopping. Too much to do," he said as he snatched a couple of twenties out of his Italian leather wallet.

"When will you be back?" Betsy whispered, knowing full well that he hated being questioned.

Robert glared at her. "When I'm good and ready. Going to get me a little action," he said as he Michael Jacksoned his crotch.

***

Robert had overheard Ben, on Wednesday, telling Ann that he was going to Clearville for the weekend. Apparently Jake had arranged for them to go to the Gilbert concert. Ben had offered to get tickets for Ann and Patrick Bates, but she had declined. She and Patrick were heading to a play that night at Belmont Fine Arts Theatre.

Robert crossed the parking lot. He smiled when he noticed the duffel bag in Ben's car. Good, everything was going according to plan.

Shortly after three on Friday afternoon, both Ben and Robert left the school and drove to town. In Belmont, Ben stopped to get a snack at the service station, but Robert carried on. He tooted his horn cheerfully as he drove by.

***

Ben rapped on the door to number five. Glancing around the motel's parking lot, he was relieved to see that none of the vehicles were familiar. Jake answered quickly and ushered Ben into the suite.

"Not bad, eh?" Jake gestured with his arm. The room was tastefully decorated in hues of gold and deep red. A large flat-screen television occupied one wall with some comfortable-looking easy chairs conveniently arranged in front of it. A mini-bar stood at the ready, and Jake had already chilled the glasses.

"What do you feel like? Red or white?" he asked as Ben tossed the duffel onto the luggage rack.

"Red please," he said as he sank into one of the chairs. "That was a long drive."

They passed the time cheerfully chatting and catching up with each other's week. Soon it was time to leave. They had made reservations at the new steakhouse on 54th Street.

"I'm pumped to try a new place," declared Jake. "Roma's nice but a change will be great."

Dinner at the new steakhouse they tried was quite expensive and mediocre in quality. Ben's steak was overdone, and the vegetables were cold. Both of them were rather tired, so they returned to the motel and relaxed. They enjoyed a mystery movie on the big flat screen TV, while finishing the rest of the wine. They were looking forward to the concert the next evening.

A cold and windy morning put an end to their plans for an early jog around the lake. Instead they headed over to the indoor pool attached to the motel. They enjoyed being the only clients in the pool, tearing up the lengths with mock races and showing off their diving skills from the five-meter board. Finally exhausted, they made their way into the change room with their arms around each other. Soaping up in the shower led from one thing to another.

Ben caught some movement out of the corner of his eye. He turned his head fully and saw the back of someone hastily retreating with a camera dangling from his arm. Pushing Jake away from him, Ben grabbed a towel and started after the intruder. He was too late. The man quickly ran to the pool house entrance and disappeared.

"Let's get out of here," Ben said. "Bloody stupid of us anyway."

Jake shrugged his shoulders. "Chill out. We thought we were alone. He didn't see much anyway; I was only kissing you."

Ben stared at his partner. "How can you be so calm? My job could be on the line if anyone finds out about us. Come on; let's get out of here—*now!*"

They dressed and headed back to their suite. As they made their way through the parking lot, Ben noticed a truck similar to Robert's backing out of a stall. When the driver turned and waved, he was certain. Robert had a huge grin plastered across his face.

"Christ—that was Robert Doyle. You know, the nasty bastard that teaches at Riverside. It may have been him in the change room. He'll spread rumours all over the community."

Jake lost his temper. "You're such a weak knee! It's *way* past the time you should have come out. Man-up. What's the worst that could happen?" He shook his head. "I really hoped that I meant more to you than a job. Besides, you could always transfer into town if the religious nuts revolt."

"I know I could transfer, but I like teaching out there. I was going to put in for head teacher next year. Why can't you understand? I'm not like you. I don't want to advertise my sex life. I want to keep it private," Ben said. "Why can't you understand?"

Jake unlocked the door and stormed inside. After yanking open the drawers and the closet door, he pulled out his clothes and stuffed them into his suitcase, leaving Ben's stuff scattered all over the room.

"I'm out of here. Call me when you get some balls."

Ben watched as his lover drove out of the parking lot, disappearing from sight. He sank down on the bed and stared at his discarded clothes. Finally, he gathered everything up and left the room. He paid the bill and made his way back to his tiny house in Wolfsburg.

***

Monday morning in the staff room, Ann took one look at Ben's haggard, forlorn face and dishevelled appearance. She could tell that his weekend had not gone well.

"God, Ben, what's up with you? Someone die?" she asked as she sat down beside him.

"No, no one died. Just had a falling out with my brother, Jake," Ben answered softly.

"Your brother?" Ann said with a smile. "Come on, Ben, I'd like to think I mean a lot to you. Jake isn't your brother is he ... and he's more than a friend, isn't he?"

Ben scanned quickly around. Seeing that they were still the only two in the room, he said, "How did you know?"

"A girl knows. It doesn't matter to me. I only ever wanted for us to be friends. We are friends, aren't we?" she quizzed, squeezing his shoulder lightly. "Come on, tell me what happened."

"Not here. Let's go to my classroom. We can talk better there," replied Ben with another glimpse around the still-empty room.

They made their way to his classroom, and after telling Ann his woes, Ben felt better. The world didn't seem so empty, and his troubles didn't feel quite so insurmountable.

Ann persuaded Ben to call Jake; her logic made sense to him. She agreed that it was impossible for him to come out in this tight-knit community, but she was convinced that Jake *did* understand Ben's difficult situation. She reasoned that they had both been badly upset by the intrusion. Since both of them wanted the relationship to continue, it was just a matter of waiting for their tempers to cool and discussing the problem. Communication was the key.

The clock in his classroom read 8:10. If he hurried, he might be able to catch Jake at the high school where he taught. The high school sessions didn't begin until 9:00. With a long, heartfelt hug, he thanked Ann and fled to Carolyn's office. After shutting the door carefully behind him, he placed one of the most important phone calls of his life.

***

After school, Robert placed three boxes of books on the workroom table.

"Here are the freebies from the government," he said, referring to the annual shipment of new books the Ministry of Education sent to every school library. "We'll have to go through them carefully to make sure they meet with the guidelines of this community. We don't need any parents finding anything that even remotely represents gay lit." He shot Ben a meaningful glance.

"I don't want to censure the books," Malcolm said with authority. "Our union feels strongly about representing all minorities, sexual persuasions, and the like in school libraries." He was on the committee that represented social equality. "If the parents object to some of the books, they can remove them. I won't have any part in it."

Several others shared his views, and a lively discussion followed with most of the staff refusing to sort through the books.

Robert threw up his hands in frustration when it appeared that no one was willing to cull the books. "Listen, you lot. Carolyn said we should go through the books. Do you want me to tell her how uncooperative you are?" He stared at his colleagues. "For Christ sake, it'll take me forever to do this by myself."

"Tough. That's what you get paid the extra money for," Malcolm said. "If you want it done, you do it." The others nodded in agreement.

Robert quickly closed the gap between Malcolm and himself. Leaning over the table, he hissed in Malcolm's face, "Watch your step, you pompous ass. I'll make you regret the day you showed up in Wolfsburg. That reserve will seem like paradise compared to here." Jerking his middle finger in the air, Robert exited the room.

Malcolm went white. Pale and trembling, he looked around at the others. Shocked and puzzled teachers stared back at him. He rose to his feet, shook his head, and went to his classroom.

Chapter Twenty-Five

Later that afternoon, hoping to clear his head from the tension caused by the confrontation with Robert, Malcolm took Sassy for a long walk along the back road bordering his place. In spite of the decided chill to the air, they enjoyed their ramble through the countryside. Sassy nosed in the decaying leaves, occasionally stirring up a half-dormant shrew or field mouse. Excited little yips filled the air as she showed off her hunting skills.

"Way to go, girl," he laughed. "Quite the clever hunter when the critters are almost asleep."

They carried on down the road a bit farther, but it was getting late and they were losing the light. All too soon they had to return home. It had been a pleasant diversion.

Sassy's hackles rose as they mounted the steps. She whined anxiously and sniffed around under the porch. Finding nothing, she allowed herself to be enticed into the kitchen where Malcolm had dished out her supper.

"Here you go, girl. Stop being a little piggy. Take small bites." Malcolm chuckled as Sassy practically inhaled her food. He fixed himself a fried cheese sandwich and poured a glass of milk. For the first time in a while, he didn't feel the need for booze. He was pleased that he had taken Sassy for the walk instead of popping open a beer or slamming down a shot.

Halfway into the documentary on wolves, the phone rang. Although he didn't recognise the number on the call display, he answered it thinking it was a response to the fundraiser he was working on.

"Diamond Collection Agency," a voice identified itself. "May I please speak to a Mr. Malcolm McDermitt?"

Malcolm sighed. "Speaking." He knew it was useless to try to evade these calls. At least they were phoning his home and not the school.

Several minutes later, Malcolm hung up. He had promised a payment by the end of the month. It meant that he would have to go to one of those cash advance places and take out a loan. The cost of borrowing like that was exorbitant, but he had no choice. The agency was threatening to garnishee his wages.

Any residual pleasure from his afternoon walk evaporated as the tensions from the day gripped him. He lifted the bottle from behind the cereal boxes in the cupboard and then poured a full glass, not even bothering to add ice.

Settling morosely into the La-Z-Boy chair, he sipped the amber liquid. The howls of the wolves on the screen filled the room. At the harsh interruption of the advertisement for biodegradable dish liquid, he powered off the television and chose a disc to play on his stereo instead. Sweet, relaxing sounds of Enya failed to ease his mind. He saw that the newly opened bottle was now half gone.

"Come on, girl, out you go," he encouraged Sassy as he opened the door. "Hurry up. I've gotta get some sleep." He stood on the stoop impatiently waiting for Sassy to finish up her task. "Good girl. Now come to bed." Stumbling into his bedroom, he stretched out crosswise on the bed, still fully clothed.

"Maaalcolm ... Maaalcolm ... "

Raising his head, Malcolm listened carefully.

"Maaalcolm ... Maaalcolm ... " the sound came again and again.

Struggling to his feet, he searched the house thoroughly. Nothing seemed to be out of the ordinary. He watched Sassy as the sound repeated itself. Her ears twitched, but the soundly sleeping dog didn't wake up.

Then all was silent again. Realizing that he was still in his clothes, Malcolm changed into his sleep shorts and T-shirt and then clambered back into bed. Closing his eyes, Malcolm drifted off to sleep.

"Maaalcolm ... Maaalcolm ... " Once again, the sounds woke him up. He went into the kitchen, sat down at the table, and poured a glass of courage. After a while, he pulled on his coat and some rubber boots, went outside, and slowly circled the barn. Scrabbling noises came from under the porch. Malcolm suppressed a scream as a mangy, grey tomcat streaked out into the night.

Shaken, he went back inside and hung up his coat. Returning to his La-Z-Boy, he sipped the whiskey steadily until a warm oblivion sucked him into its depths.

Rousing from the heavy fog of booze, Malcolm sat holding his head in his hands. His temples throbbed, and he was desperately thirsty. *To hell with it all*, he thought as he sank back down into emptiness.

***

Ann looked at the clock. It was half past eight, and school started in less than half an hour. Malcolm had yet to show up for work. She looked at Ben seated on the sofa across from her in the staff room.

"Hey Ben, did Malcolm say he was taking today off?" she asked. "He's usually here way before now."

"No, he's coming in today. We're going to set up the reading buddy system for our classes—you know, that peer-tutoring recommended for the older grades."

"Think I should give him a call?" Ann asked.

"Better you than Robert," said Ben, referring to yesterday's altercation.

Ann took out her cell phone and dialled Malcolm's number. Just when she thought it was going to voicemail, he answered.

"Hey, Mal, you coming in today? ... What's wrong?" Ann said. "Food poisoning? Oh, how dreadful. Of course I'll call you a sub."

Ann shook her head. Something in his voice concerned her. His speech wasn't at all steady, and he seemed to be drifting off as he talked to her.

"Want to come with me after school, Ben? I think we should go check on Malcolm to see if he's okay. He said he has food poisoning, and that can be pretty brutal."

***

Malcolm was reluctant to let his visitors in, but he could see no way of putting them off without appearing rude and raising suspicion. He ushered them into the kitchen and put on the kettle.

"Thanks for coming by, you guys. You shouldn't have worried. I'm feeling good now. Must have had a stomach bug or something. Could be the age-old leftovers I ate last night. Could easily have been those."

"No worries, Malcolm," insisted Ben. "Ann and I were going for a drive out this way anyway."

When Ann's eyes fell on the bottle of whiskey sitting propped up beside the easy chair, she quickly realized the truth.

As they drove away after finishing their tea, she told Ben of her suspicions.

"Ben, he's hung over. He must have been self-medicating after the hassle with Robert yesterday."

"Poor guy. I had no idea he had a drinking problem. I knew he had migraines but that's all. Robert going after him must have pushed him over the edge."

"Robert's such a nasty piece of work," agreed Ann. She shivered, as if to shake thoughts of him off. "Oh well, let's carry on up past the turn-off and enjoy the last of this beautiful Indian summer day."

Ben swung onto the dirt road and rolled down the windows so that they could enjoy the warm breeze. Ann was such good company. It was a relief to find out she didn't care that he was gay. He was thankful that he had someone to talk to, someone who wouldn't judge.

***

Ben unlocked the school door and went straight to his classroom in the intermediate wing. He was so immersed in his preparation work, he scarcely noticed that Malcolm had entered the school and was striding down the hall. The loud crash as Malcolm dropped his books trying to open his classroom door made Ben jump.

"You drop your teeth?" called Ben from his desk.

"Oh, hi. You're in early," Malcolm commented as he poked his head around Ben's door. "Thought I was alone. Didn't see your vehicle parked outside."

"Walked this morning," replied Ben. Then he stared at Malcolm. The man was in total disarray. His shirt was buttoned incorrectly, and his hair looked as though a squirrel had spent a restless night. "You okay?"

Malcolm lost his balance slightly as he turned to try to unlock his door again. Ben got up quickly and crossed over to his friend, catching the strong odour of alcohol as he neared him.

"Malcolm," he said softly, "you're in no shape to teach. Here, let me drive you home before anyone else gets here."

"Oh, Ben, I don't know how it got this far. It's just not worth it anymore," Malcolm muttered, shrugging his shoulders and looking downwards. His whole being mirrored his defeated attitude.

Malcolm reluctantly agreed to let Ben drive him home. On their way out the door, they passed Robert.

"Malcolm's still not right from the food poisoning. I'm taking him back to his place. Can you get a sub for him?" Ben asked as they made a wide berth around Robert.

When they reached Malcolm's place, Ben steered him up the steps and into the kitchen. Sassy dashed outside before either man could prevent her exit.

"Oh, get her quick!" exclaimed Malcolm. "Something's taken up residence under the steps and is keeping us up all night. Can't get any sleep. That's why I'm like this. Had a couple of nips last night so that I could get to sleep."

"Christ, Malcolm, you shouldn't touch the stuff. My uncle was an alcoholic and kept going in and out of rehab."

"I know...I know better, but things are just getting so awful. Robert's always on my case, and I hate confrontation. It won't happen again. Please don't tell anyone ... *please*."

Ben nodded. Pity welled up in his chest as he reached out to his friend and drew him into a quick hug. He turned and ran down the steps to catch Sassy before she ran off down the dirt road.

"Here she is. None the worse for wear," he said gently as he placed the little dog in Malcolm's arms. "She sure loves you, doesn't she?" Sassy was licking Malcolm's face with her frantic tongue.

"Yes, she does. Listen, please don't tell anyone about my drinking. The school board would probably fire me and the community wouldn't tolerate it," Malcolm begged, his voice thick with emotion.

"Ann figured it out the other day, but she won't let on. What are you going to do now? Can you stop drinking? We're your friends. Let us help you if we can."

"Thanks, Ben, but I've been here before—lots. I'm grateful for your support, Ann's too, but there's only one person who can help me, and that's me," said Malcolm, shaking his head miserably. "Grab that bottle over there and find the other one behind the cereal boxes. Get rid of the stuff. Just get rid of it," he pleaded. "I'll phone my sponsors and head in to the AA meeting as soon as I'm sober. Just don't tell anyone."

Ben stood up and shook Malcolm's hand. He could see the steely determination in his eyes.

"It's okay, man. You're secret's safe with us. I have to get back—school's in session in a few minutes, but here, I'll make you some coffee before I go. Why don't you go take a shower?" Ben started the coffee maker and waved good-bye to the broken man.

A morose Malcolm stuck to his words. Over the next two weeks, he desperately clung to sobriety, despite Robert's bullying and numerous phone calls from the collection agencies. Although Ben could see him struggling, he could do little to prevent his friend from spiralling deeper into depression. It was a miracle that Malcolm remained sober. He never smiled, never slept, and hardly ate—but he did not take a drink.

Chapter Twenty-Six

Bates downloaded the forensic report from the lab in Jackson. The three-page document stated that the soil sample collected near the destroyed hydro meter contained sand with traces of organic materials similar to those found near sources of freshwater, such as lakes, rivers, streams, dugouts, sloughs, and creeks. The footprint was that of a man's medium-width, size eleven boot. One side of the footprint showed more wear than the other side.

Other than that, there was no more viable evidence. No fingerprints were found on the handle of the old screwdriver. It had either been out in the elements too long, or as Bates suspected, the intruder had worn gloves.

Anxious to share the lab results, Patrick phoned Ann.

"Hey there, feel like grabbing a bite at the store tonight?" he asked.

"Oh, hi, Patrick," she said, smiling as she heard his voice. "Sure, I'm always looking for an excuse not to cook. Shall I meet you around six?" It had been a long day, and she could do with a break.

At dinner that evening, Patrick went over the results sent from the Jackson lab. Ann was disappointed but secretly pleased as well. Little evidence meant that there was less chance anything could be tied to the manila envelope she had found under her door. She hadn't told Patrick about it and still had no intention of doing so. Her past was her business and had nothing to do with him. With luck, it would stay that way.

Sitting in her trailer later that evening, Ann heard the wind howl and whip through the grove of spruce trees behind her trailer. Occasionally, the lights flickered, but fortunately they didn't go out. This part of the country was known for wild autumn winds that funnelled across the wide river valley. The leaves had long since dropped, leaving the aspen and poplar trees standing starkly against the evening sky.

Pulling on her oversized grey sweater, Ann settled into her grandmother's rocker with her latest book. There was nothing good on television, and besides, the satellite reception was dismal lately.

The evening ticked away peacefully. When she got up to put the kettle on, she noticed that the wind had ceased and the stars were speckling the night sky. Standing at the open front door, she breathed in the fresh air that had followed the windstorm. While she gazed at the pinpoints of light, she saw that the door to the outhouse had blown open. Drawing her sweater closer around her shoulders, she crossed the small yard. She closed the outhouse door with a bang and then pulled on it to make sure it was latched with its wooden peg. *It must have been quite a strong wind to blow the heavy wooden door open,* she thought. Branches and leaves littered the ground confirming the wind's earlier strength. Thankfully, the night was clear and calm now.

The insistent screech of the whistling kettle drew her back to the porch and inside. She put a tea bag in her cup and poured the steaming water over it. Reaching into the fridge for the milk, she froze in horror. There on the center of the top shelf was a squirrel carcass. Blood was dripping everywhere, and its entrails tumbled out of its body cavity. Her stomach roiled as the stench of still warm blood rose from the remains.

Gasping with shock, she frantically looked around. She could see no sign of anyone, but the back door was wide open. Instinctively, she slammed it shut, scrabbling frantically to turn the lock.

She turned back to the horrible sight in the fridge. Thrusting her hands inside a plastic grocery bag, she scooped the sopping mess into the bag and inverted it. Then she tied the ends tightly and threw the revolting mess into the kitchen trash container. It took a good ten minutes to rid the fridge of the spilled blood. With trembling hands, she scattered baking soda over the shelves hoping it would absorb the cloying odour.

Still shaking, she rushed around inside the trailer ensuring the doors and windows were secure. If this was a prank, it was not funny. This was downright terrifying. Hesitantly, she called Patrick.

"Hey, pretty girl, what's up?" Patrick Bates smiled as he realized who was calling. Ann had been a bit distant lately, but he had put it down to report card time and a heavy workload. His tone changed abruptly as he listened to her frantic story. Within five minutes, he was pounding on her door.

"Ann, Ann. It's me, Patrick. Open up ... open the damn door."

Ann opened the door and fell into Patrick's comforting arms. A search of her property and the trailer itself yielded nothing of value.

A small half-tread of a boot was left in the bloody trail from the back door to the fridge. Some bloody smears had been left on the side of the fridge door, but these had been obviously been made by a gloved hand.

Examining the squirrel remains in the plastic bag, Patrick concluded that it had been caught in a trap and had been eviscerated while it was still alive. Its heart had been pumping hard, spraying blood everywhere. Whoever did this was some sick bastard in more ways than one.

"I don't care what you say. I'm staying over tonight," Patrick declared. "You're way too shook up to be on your own."

Ann didn't need much convincing. She kept seeing the dreadful sight over and over in her head. "Okay, thanks. But just for tonight. You'll have to leave as soon as it gets light, before the farmers get up to milk."

In the cold light of early morning, everything seemed much better. Ann had convinced herself that this had been the work of kids. She would just have to be more careful with locking her doors in future. Patrick wasn't so sure, but he didn't want to alarm Ann unnecessarily. He left quickly, taking the back road home.

Ten minutes after Patrick entered his room behind the store, Ann got the first phone call.

"Hello," she said as she picked up the phone. A dial tone hummed in her ear.

Five minutes later, another call came. This one was longer. Music played eerily in the background as a voice said, "Best you look after yourself, bitch. Leave Patrick outta this if you know what's good for you. It'll only get worse if you don't. There are more copies of that police report, and one could find its way into your lover's hands, as quick as quick."

"Who is this? What do you want?" Ann shouted. A dial tone replaced the strange, rough voice.

When the third call came, Ann picked up the phone and just listened. She could hear nothing but breathing.

"Leave me alone, you sick bastard!" she yelled as she slammed down the receiver. Her trembling hands made it nearly impossible to fasten her blouse as she dressed for school.

***

Robert observed his fellow teachers with a great deal of satisfaction.

Ben was jumpy and high strung. Ever since his weekend in Clearville, he appeared to be on edge.

Ann looked as though she hadn't slept in a week. Large circles marred her pretty eyes, and she had lost at least ten pounds. Those bouncing tits didn't jiggle quite so much.

As for Malcolm, it was obvious he was hanging on by a thread. His hands shook when he reached for his coffee cup, and he positively leapt out of his skin every time the phone rang. A mere mention of collection agencies was enough to give him one of his infamous migraines.

They were all falling apart. Even Carolyn had noticed how tired and distracted they were. She had summoned them all to a staff meeting this afternoon.

***

Standing at the head of the staff room table, Carolyn tapped lightly on her glass, calling the meeting to order. She began putting her plan in motion. She was determined to find out what was wrong with the staff—in particular, with Malcolm, Ben, and Ann. She also had some news to share from the school board.

"I know you're all busy and are probably wondering why we're having an extra staff meeting this month. There are two things to bring to your attention.

"First, I pride myself in providing a happy work atmosphere, but I've noticed that there's been considerable strain amongst the staff lately. I'll be holding confidential talks with each one of you over the next week. This will be an opportunity for you to address any concerns or problems you may be having with your workload, a member of staff, the parents, the students, or any other matter. If you'd like, you can bring your union representative with you, but rest assured I view this talk as private and confidential."

She paused and then continued.

"Secondly, the school board has requested that we move up the deadline for head teacher applications. There have been some concerns brought to the school board by some of the parents in this community. While the board has utmost confidence in our school, they feel that changes might be in order. Robert has been head teacher for well over two years. They're looking for a qualified individual to spearhead a review of the discipline policies and goals of Riverside Elementary. The new deadline for applications will be the second week in December, with the head teacher position becoming effective at the beginning of the January term."

Robert flushed with anger. *How dare they try to replace him… and so soon!* His shoulders stiffened and he sat ramrod straight in his chair.

"What kind of complaints?" asked Malcolm.

"Right now, the complaints are quite general in nature, and the board has asked me not to go into detail," answered Carolyn. "If the complaints are concerning an individual teacher, I'll address this in my confidential conference with that teacher."

Much to Robert's pleasure, he saw Ben, Ann, and Malcolm go pale. His plan was working well. Still he wondered what complaints had reached the board. He hadn't told anyone any of the information he had gleaned about the threesome.

Still, he was worried. Maybe the parents were objecting to *his* discipline. This new bunch of students certainly seemed to be weaker and more likely to wimp to their parents. Doug, in fact, had broken down in tears the other day. That kid was such a loser. No worries, nothing could be proven. It was Doug's word against his, and Robert felt invincible.

However, there was the matter of the head teacher position. That job belonged to him. He was by far the best qualified, the most experienced, and he knew Riverside better than anyone else on staff.

Knowing the timeline was now shortened, Robert began plans to make sure Ben, Ann, and Malcolm wouldn't be tempted to apply for the posting. It was time to up his game.

Glancing out the window, his gaze fell on Sgt. Bates hurrying up the steps of the teacherage. As he watched, Robert saw Betsy peek through the living room curtains. Sgt. Bates raised his fist and insistently rapped on the front door again. Several moments later, Betsy, in her housecoat and slippers, opened the door. Robert saw Bates wave a piece of paper, and Betsy reluctantly let him inside.

Tapping his fingers impatiently on the cool surface of the staff room table, Robert sighed loudly. "Can we get going here? It's past four, and I for one would like to get home. I'm here first thing every morning, and it's been a long day."

Carolyn frowned. Deliberately she leaned forward into Robert's space, and sensed him back up just a bit.

"Sorry to keep you, Robert. You can go if you like, but I'm going to discuss the new requirements of the job posting. You don't have to stay if you're not going to bid," she said sarcastically.

Bates hadn't come out of the teacherage, but Robert knew he couldn't leave now. It was gnawing away at his insides. What did Bates want? Damn, what were the new requirements for head teacher?

"Damn right I'm putting my hat in the ring. No one's better suited that I am. I've got the experience, knowhow, and the parent support.

I've got the chairman of the board on my side, as well. He and I go way back."

Carolyn looked at the teachers with compassion. Knowing how hard they worked, she sympathized with their tiredness. Everyone wanted to go home.

"I'll make this as quick as possible for those who want to stay. Time is of the essence because the deadline for applications is coming up quickly. If you want me to supervise some of your lessons, you should speak to me soon. Christmas concert practice has a way of using up lesson time." She waited while several teachers, including Colleen and Barb, stood up and quietly left the staff room. Only Robert, Ben, Malcolm, and Ann remained seated, waiting to hear what she had to say.

Robert ground his teeth in frustration. Bates *still* had not left his place, and these jokers were still trying to steal his job. Fuck them, life was about to get a lot tougher around here.

***

"What did Sgt. Bates want?" he asked as soon as he got in the door. "He was here long enough."

Betsy stole a quick look at her husband's face as he shucked off his boots and hung up his coat on the padded hanger reserved especially for him. He seemed okay.

"Nothing much. Said he needed to see your boots. Something about checking all the men's boots in Wolfsburg."

"You didn't show him any of my boots did you?'

"Just your outside work boots. You wore your favourites to school today. The others are in your room. You know I can't get in there."

"What was he checking out boots for? Did he say why?"

"No, just said something about eliminating suspects. I guess they must've found some footprints or something. I gave him coffee. It seemed rude not to offer him anything."

Taking care to appear disinterested, Robert went over to the stove and lifted the saucepan's lid. Steam rose, tickling his nostrils.

"See you made chowder. Did you follow my mum's recipe or did you wing it like usual?"

"No, I used her notes. I know how you liked your mum's cooking," Betsy whispered. She seldom talked about his mother unless he had already mentioned her.

"Have it on the table in five. I'm taking a shower. It's been a long day."

Robert felt the hot water cascade over his shoulders. Watching the suds pool in the cubicle, he remembered that he hadn't been wearing his favourite boots when he killed Susan. He was pretty sure he hadn't worn them at Ann's trailer either. Those were his good boots. They fit him like a glove and were the best if his foot gave him trouble. His second-best pair also had the support he needed. He often wore them if it was raining or muddy out. Those boots stood in the corner of his sanctuary out of sight from prying eyes.

Timmy quietly watched his parents. He ate the chowder slowly, blowing each hot spoonful cautiously.

Robert casually questioned Betsy at supper. Plying her with an extra glass of wine, he listened carefully as she related her interesting visit with Sgt. Bates.

"Had a pleasant chat did you? I saw you answer the door in your housecoat. Little late for not being dressed, wasn't it?"

Sensing a trap, Betsy stammered, "I had just got out of the shower. He waited in the living room while I changed into something decent."

She quickly pushed her chair back, stood up, and moved towards the kitchen.

"You want coffee now or later?" she asked.

"Later," growled Robert as his fist caught her on the side of the head.

Timmy sprang between them, trying to protect his mother. His soft body absorbed the next blow. With a muffled grunt, the child crumpled to the floor. Small whimpers escaped from his lips, and Betsy's stomach lurched as she bent over her son. Tears rivered down her reddened cheeks, and her breath came in harsh, ragged gasps.

Furiously, she whirled around, punching and scratching at Robert.

"You bastard! You bastard! That's our son! You hit our son!"

Robert deflected her blows and reached out for her. His hands circled her throat as he dragged her towards the bedroom. He slammed the door and began to teach her a lesson.

Ten minutes later, emerging from their bedroom, Robert shook his head to clear it from the overwhelming fog. He was surprised to see Timmy lying curled in a fetal position on the floor beside the kitchen counter.

"What's wrong?" he asked as he bent over the prone child. "Why are you lying there like that? Come on, get up. Mum's got a headache, so she's gone to bed. Let's see if there are any cartoons on TV."

He vaguely remembered hitting Betsy. Timmy must have gotten in the way. God help him if he was starting to take after his old man. Vivid scenes of childhood beatings filled his mind as he bent his head in shame. He held his son close.

Chapter Twenty-Seven

The next morning, dressed in jeans and a sweatshirt, Robert rushed into the staff room ten minutes before the bell. He dragged Timmy along by the hand.

"Amy, who's that women that looks after kids after school? You know... the one that lives over by the crossroads?"

Amy's head shot up. Peering at Robert over her reading glasses, she inhaled sharply. Robert looked like he'd slept in his clothes, and Timmy was still in his pyjamas.

"It's Mrs. Shamous. What's up? You look like you never even went to bed last night."

"Betsy slipped in the shower stall, and we've spent all night at the hospital in town. She fractured her arm, and they sent her to Clearville to the specialist. Something about a spiral fracture. Now what's that damn woman's phone number?" he demanded.

"Oh my, God, Robert, that's terrible. Why aren't you with Betsy?" questioned Amy.

"She can look after herself," Robert said. "Give me that woman's phone number. School starts in a few minutes. Timmy has to go somewhere. He can't stay with me."

Amy wrote down the phone number, handed it to him, and said, "Tim can hang out with my class for a few minutes. You call Mrs. Shamous and get her to come pick him up here at the school."

She draped a protective arm around the little boy. "Want to come see what we do in grade one?" she asked him. "So, Mommy got hurt in the shower. Don't worry; the doctors will take good care of her." Timmy burst into tears.

Terrified of discovery, Robert knelt down in front of Timmy and gathered him into his arms.

"If you want Mommy to be okay, you will keep your mouth shut," he whispered into the small ear.

"I'll make that phone call," he said as he gave Timmy a slight push and left him with Amy.

Amy held Timmy until the sobs lessened.

"Come on, little man. Let's go see if we can find some kids to play with until Mrs. Shamous gets here."

At recess, Robert called for a substitute teacher. They were releasing Betsy, and he had to go to Clearville to pick her up.

***

Pushing his foot on the accelerator, he set the radar detector and began the long drive to Clearville. It was frustrating to have to do the boring drive twice in as many days. Dr. Smith had called to say they were releasing Betsy this afternoon. Her arm had been set; there was no need for her to remain at the hospital. The longer she remained away from him, the more chance there was of her slipping up on the story they had patched together. He had told her to keep mum about the beating. If anyone asked about her arm, she was to say she fell in the shower. He was counting on her bruises not really showing until tonight at the earliest. By then he'd have her safe at home where she belonged.

Seeing that the nurse on duty had her head bent over paperwork, he slunk by the desk and down the hall to room 112. Darn, he noticed that three of the four beds in the semi-private room were occupied. He drew the curtains closed around Betsy's bed and sidled up beside her. Reaching out gently, he wrapped his arms around his wife. "Hi there, girl. How's my pumpkin feeling?"

Betsy tried to shrink back, but his arms held firm.

"Hi there, yourself," she murmured. "They said I could go home. It's a bad break, but the doctor in Belmont can check on it. They sent the X-rays." Trembling, she buried her head into his shoulder and willed herself to relax. They had been through this before. Nothing ever changed.

"Christ, Betsy, I'm so sorry. I never meant to hurt you. You just made me so mad. Why did you have to invite the son of a bitch in? You could have just talked to him on the step. Why'd you try to make me jealous?" He relaxed his arms slightly and stared into her eyes. "You didn't say anything, did you? You know your life would be worth zilch if you did. You'd never see Timmy again."

"No, no I didn't say anything. Just that I slipped in the shower like you said," Betsy whispered, scared that they could be overheard.

Sharp-heeled shoes echoed down the hall. Dr. Joanne Smith entered the room. As she drew back the curtain, her practised eye quickly assessed the situation. Knowing full well that she had no real proof of abuse, just her suspicions, she smiled and approached the bed.

"Well, Betsy, I see that your husband is here to take you home." She nodded to Robert.

"If you'd just wait outside in the waiting room, I'll do a last check-up on your wife, and then you two can go on your way."

Robert shot a pointed look at Betsy.

"Sure, okay. I'll go get us some coffees for the trip home. I won't be long," he said, bending over the bed and kissing his wife gently on her forehead.

Dr. Smith carefully examined Betsy. Feeling the patient stiffen as she gently probed her neck, she asked, "Is that tender? Is there something you need to tell me?"

"No, I'm fine. I slept awkwardly last night and I have a stiff neck. I'm fine," Betsy replied in a firm voice. Terrified of the consequences, she was determined to put on the best act of her life. Timmy was everything to her. Without her precious boy, her life would be meaningless. She had to keep him safe. She had to find a way to get them both out of danger.

***

Robert ran up the steps to the Shamous's house and pounded on the door. Mrs. Shamous quickly opened the door. Timmy stood behind her with his coat and boots already on. It was obvious that he had been waiting for them to return.

"Hi, we're back. Is Timmy ready to go? How much do I owe you?"

Timmy took a step backwards away from his father, his pale eyes wary.

"He's been pretty upset all day. Insisted on putting his boots on an hour ago. Misses his mom, I suppose," chattered the woman nervously. She was not very comfortable around most outsiders. Still, it was the proper thing to do, and she had been happy to assist someone in need.

"Oh, that's fine, don't worry about any money. It was an emergency. I was happy to help," the woman insisted. "Happy to help."

Holding out his hand to his son, Robert smiled his thanks and then led Timmy to the car.

When they arrived at the teacherage, with his arm around Betsy, Robert shepherded her up the stairs, and Timmy trailed behind. Once inside, Robert made her comfortable on the couch and set about making some supper.

"Is mac and cheese all right?" he asked as he noisily dug in the pot drawer for a large enough saucepan. "I know it's Tim's favourite, but is it okay for you?

Betsy nodded her head cautiously. Her neck was very painful. She dreaded looking in the mirror.

Ten minutes later, he set three steaming bowls of the orange-coloured noodles in front of each place at the kitchen table and slammed the ketchup down in the center.

"Come and get it before it turns to mush," he demanded. Betsy rose slowly, held out her hand to Timmy, and joined her husband.

"Mmm, smells great. I didn't realize how hungry I was." Smiling gratefully, she squirted some ketchup onto Timmy's portion, and they began to eat. Robert ate quickly, avoiding their wounded eyes.

After dinner, as he pulled on his boots, he called to Betsy. "I've got to go prep and see what kind of a mess the sub left for me. You guys head off to bed. It's been a long day. Don't wait up for me."

Once outside, he turned the key in the lock. Then he rounded the corner of the teacherage and ran his hand along the wall until he felt the telephone wires. With a quick yank, he stripped the wires from the connection box. Betsy was too vulnerable right now. He couldn't risk anyone seeing her or phoning her and asking questions. It was better she stayed put, as well. Let things blow over. Let things get back to normal.

The unwelcome memory of his father locking them in that northern Ontario cabin came flooding into his mind. He could smell the smoke from the wood stove and see the frost clinging to the small windows. He could feel his mother's hands on him as she forced him to scrub the kitchen and the old washstand beside the back door. Unconsciously, he shrank from her cruel grip as she sought to exert the only power she had left. Betsy might be a miserable lay, but she would never harm their son.

Robert saw that the substitute teacher had had a rough day. The masses of scribbled notes that littered his usually pristine daybook, the barely legible notes decorating the essays, and the complete disarray of his papers were all indicative of an inexperienced teacher at the end of her tether. He didn't recognize the woman's signature at the end of her very detailed summary. There had not been much choice for the substitute teacher, as most had already been deployed by the time he was able to call for one. Mary Banister must be either really inexperienced or uncertified.

Grabbing the essays, he sat down to re-mark them. His students had put in the least amount of effort. Angrily, he circled mistakes and added caustic comments. The imbeciles would have to do the assignment again tomorrow, along with their regular work.

It was well past ten when he passed by the office. Knowing that today had been one of Carolyn's days in the school, he wondered if there was anything new. Scanning the desk, he saw a series of memos neatly piled in Carolyn's inbox. He lifted them out carefully and then read each one. His name appeared several times. It seemed that Doug's mother had called wanting to see Carolyn. The meeting had been set up for tomorrow at three o'clock.

After replacing the notes just as he had found them, Robert turned towards the door. Beside the telephone, he noticed a glossy pamphlet from the University of North Rochester. It extolled the virtues of the university, in particular, its master's program. *Why would Carolyn be reading a booklet on a master's program?* Intrigued, he fired up the computer and entered the school district's site.

He scrupulously read Carolyn's profile as it came up on the screen. It reflected a well-educated teacher who earned an undergraduate degree from the University of Manitoba and a master's degree from Gonzaga in the States. Her experience was listed according to years, but curiously, her education was not.

He pulled up the website for Gonzaga and scrolled through the lists of graduating students for the ten years since Carolyn had graduated high school. There was no record of her master's degree. He searched further but could find no trace of Carolyn Myers. Unless she had changed her name, she had not been to Gonzaga.

Checking her school board profile again, he discovered that Carolyn had not changed her name when she married three years ago. *The bitch must have falsified her credentials.* He felt the corners of his mouth form a huge grin as he understood the value of this information.

***

Late the next night, Robert sat in his room nursing his scotch. He brooded over his situation. Betsy didn't turn him on. She hadn't for years. If it weren't for Timmy, he'd have been shot of her long ago. His wig certainly came in handy when he trolled for girls in Belmont's red-light district. It would never do for a teacher of his standing to be recognized. Now with Betsy's broken arm, he wouldn't even be able to get some at home. He thought of her pathetic eyes that seemed to follow his every move.

Then there was Timmy. He had really screwed up this time. A wave of remorse flooded his gut as he remembered Timmy lying on the kitchen floor. He thought about how both Betsy and Timmy now shrank from his touch. It would take a lot more than making macaroni and cheese to regain the child's trust.

Swinging around in his chair, he saw the lights on the school grounds shut off for the night. It was getting late. However, Robert knew that sleep would be elusive tonight.

The head teacher position seemed tenuous indeed. Even though Ann, Ben, and Malcolm were constantly on edge, suffering from sleep deprivation and appearing overwhelmed, they didn't seem dissuaded from applying for his job. In fact, they had remained long past the usual end for the staff meeting just to hear the details of the listing. Now the memos on Carolyn's desk pointed to the parents kicking up again. He wracked his brain to figure out what had gone wrong this time. Doug was a little wimp. The kid couldn't take anything. Perhaps he'd been on the kid's case a bit much lately, but he deserved it. He was such easy pickings. You don't get anywhere these days being a sissy boy and a pain in the ass.

The parent complaints were coming at the wrong time. Given enough time, he could ride it out and wait for things to die down, but the job deadline was fast approaching. He wouldn't win many points with the board if the parents were upset, and Carolyn couldn't be depended on for a reference.

He thought back to the work that the students had passed in while he was away. None of it was up to standard. Tomorrow they would regret their stupid behaviour.

With a sigh, he realized that the situation looked more and more depressing. He knew he had to do something soon. He had to make his competitors back off. Slamming his hand down on the desk's wooden surface, he muttered, "When the going gets tough, the tough get going." It was a good motto. Malcolm, Ann, and Ben had no idea just how tough things were going to get.

He reached over and switched on his computer. Pressing the favourite tab, he quickly navigated into his preferred porn site.

***

"Sit up straight, you morons. You'll regret what you did yesterday for sure. How you could imagine getting away with such crap is beyond me. Mrs. Banister may not be the sharpest tack in the box, but you guys are even dumber to think you'd get past me," he berated the students as he flung their tests at them. The children had to duck to avoid being struck by the flying missiles.

As they struggled to redo yesterday's assignment, Robert enjoyed their silent efforts. Gathering up the first papers, he quickly slapped more work on their desks.

"May I go to the washroom, Mr. Doyle?" asked Doug as Robert gave him his second task.

"Like hell you can. Get on with your work."

A few minutes later, Doug asked again. "May I please go to the washroom?"

Robert smirked, "Are you deaf, boy? I said no, and I haven't changed my mind."

"Please ... I really have to go," begged Doug, his face red from embarrassment.

"No."

Scraping back his chair, Doug rose and shot out of the classroom.

Robert slammed down his textbook and followed Doug into the boy's bathroom. Waiting quietly beside the sink, he watched as Doug emerged from a stall. In a second, he was over to the frightened boy twisting his arm behind his back.

"I said no, you asshole. I said *no*," he whispered with his hot breath bouncing off Doug's face. He shoved the student towards the sink. Thrusting his knee behind Doug's knees, he forced Doug's face into the bowl. With his free hand, he turned the water on full force, soaking the student. Doug sputtered and coughed as he struggled to free himself from Robert's grip and the icy torrent that threatened to drown him.

"There's more of this learning in store for you if you dare say a word. While you're at it, call off your parents. I don't need any more trouble from them. Have your mother cancel her appointment with Ms. Myers." Robert released his hold on Doug, turned, and left the bathroom.

***

Five minutes later, Doug returned to the classroom with his head down, never glancing at his friends. Water was still trickling from his hair down into his collar. He had made a quick call to his mother begging her not to talk to Ms. Myers. He sat down quickly and got down to work.

As concerned whispers started up, Robert raised his voice. "Get to work if you know what's good for you. There's no recess break today for you morons. Anyone not finished by noon will be joining me and Master Doug here after school."

It was past five o'clock when Robert finally allowed Doug to go home. Escorting the sullen boy out the front door, he locked the school behind them.

"No blabbing to Mommy now, kid. Man-up and behave yourself. Anymore disrespect from you and you'll wish you'd never been born."

***

Doug scuttled away in the direction of the store. Robert watched him go, then crossed over to his teacherage and unlocked the door. Betsy's accusing eyes met his as he sat down in his chair.

"What's wrong with you, bitch?"

Barely audible, she asked, "Why did you cut the phone and lock the door? What if Timmy had gotten hurt or sick? You may not give a damn about me, but you can't put your son in danger like that."

Robert paused and then sank his face into his upturned hands.

"You're right. But I can't have you blabbing our business to anyone. What goes on here is our business, no one else's."

"I won't say anything. I never have in all these years. I never have."

"Damn straight, woman. If you do, you'll never see Timmy again. I can promise you that. Now where's supper?"

Timmy got quietly up from the sofa and began gathering the knives and forks. He started to set the table for supper. If he was a good boy, maybe they wouldn't fight.

***

Patrick watched from his usual table, as Doug entered the store and went over to the payphone.

"Yah, Mom," he heard Doug say, "I had to stay in after school to make up some work … Yah, I can wait for a little while … Okay, see you then." Doug went to stand over by the door.

"Hey, kid. Feel like a soda while you wait?" Patrick asked.

"Oh, hi, Sgt. Bates. Sure that'd be real nice after the day I've had. My teacher was on my case and kept me in after school," he said with a grimace.

"It sure can suck sometimes. What'd you do?"

Doug glanced around fearfully and then just shrugged his shoulders.

"Nothing much, just missed some assignments." He was unsure as to how much he could tell this man. Cops were from the outside world, and most outsiders could not be fully trusted. They were often judgmental as to the ways of his faith.

Patrick suspected there was more to the story than Doug was letting on, but unless the boy felt comfortable, there was no use in pressing for details.

"Never mind then. I guess you're all caught up now. What will you have? Pepsi or something else?"

Patrick waited until the boy was halfway through his drink, and then he casually said, "You guys have a counsellor at your school? Or is there someone you could talk to? I usually feel better after I've run my problems by someone I trust. I sure like Mr. McDermitt and that guy who teaches grade seven ... Ben ..."

"Mr. Smith. Yah, he's a nice guy, but Mr. McDermitt is good to talk things over with. He's my homeroom teacher this year." With a slurp, Doug concentrated on his drink, raising his head as he saw his mum's van pull into the parking lot.

"There's my ride." Doug extended his hand to Sgt. Bates. "Thanks for the soda and the advice."

"My pleasure, kid. See you around," Patrick said as he shook the proffered hand. He felt a twinge of concern for the boy as Doug went out the door. Teenage years were difficult enough. Having problems getting along at school made it doubly hard. He reached for his cell and called Malcolm.

"Hey, Malcolm, Patrick Bates here. How's it going? Listen I have a concern with Doug Weibe ... No, he's not in trouble with me. No, he's had some kind of trouble with his teacher, and I was wondering if you'd chat with the boy."

Patrick waited and listened as Malcolm responded.

"No, don't make it too obvious. Doug doesn't know I'm calling you. I think he's afraid ... Okay, thanks." With a satisfied sigh, Patrick signed off and went to pay for his supper.

***

Doug begged his mom to drive him to school early the next morning. After their long conversation last night, she was more than willing to help her son. Doug was terrified that Mr. Doyle would somehow make things worse if his mother kept her appointment with Ms. Myers. He had persuaded her to let him see if Mr. McDermitt could straighten things out.

With a wave of thanks to his mum, Doug ran up the steps and tried the front door. Locked. He sat down on the steps to wait for the first teacher to arrive. After only a few minutes, he slowly got to his feet as Mr. McDermitt rounded the corner and parked in front of the school.

Wasting no time, Doug called out to Malcolm. "Hi, Mr. McDermitt. Can I speak with you for a few minutes?"

Malcolm looked up surprised. He seldom met anyone this early in the morning. Doug must have purposely come to school early and had been waiting for him. One glance at the student and he could see misery cloaking his shoulders.

"Sure, Doug, what's wrong?" Malcolm quickly closed the gap between them and put his arm around the boy.

"Nothing, everything," stammered Doug as the last of his reserve broke down under the kindness shown by his favourite teacher.

Malcolm unlocked the school, and they went to his classroom. Malcolm pulled a chair next to his desk, then sat down in his own chair and motioned for Doug to have a seat. Anger and frustration flooded Malcolm's brain as he listened to Doug sobbing and quietly telling him about Robert's abuse. Standing up suddenly, Malcolm began pacing. Doug sat morosely beside Malcolm's desk, studying his hands.

"That son of a bitch. He's what gives teachers a bad name. Sorry, Doug, I know I shouldn't swear, but this makes my blood boil."

He crossed back over to Doug and placed his hands on the boy's shoulders. Looking deeply into his eyes, he said, "Leave it up to me, Doug. I'll sort this out."

***

Carolyn Myers began her meetings with the Riverside staff that afternoon. Malcolm was one of the first to be interviewed. She was extremely worried about this pleasant man who had been through so much since the beginning of the school term. It must have been dreadful to find Susan bludgeoned like that.

Malcolm rapped on the door to Carolyn's office and waited to be welcomed. He had been anticipating this meeting, and his jaw tightened compulsively. He knew that Ann and Ben would never have divulged anything about him showing up at work under the influence, but he couldn't help worry that she might know about the creditors phoning him. God knows what Robert would have said, but thankfully his appointment was after Malcolm's.

"Come on in," called Carolyn. "Please shut the door so we can have some privacy."

Malcolm sat in the proffered chair and shifted uncomfortably. He glanced around the sparsely furnished office. Carolyn had made an effort to make the office warm and friendly. Pictures of her husband, herself and their three German Shepherd dogs casually faced the visitor's chair. A small vase of dried flowers and an ornate wooden pencil holder were placed beside the computer. As some pastoral pictures scrolled over the computer's monitor, he felt himself let his guard down a little.

"Relax, Malcolm. I'm really pleased with your work here at Riverside. Today I want to talk about the atmosphere among the staff members. I've noticed strain, and you for one seem to be under a lot of pressure. Is it Susan's murder that's bothering you?"

"No, it's not Susan's murder; Patrick Bates is doing what he can to get to the bottom of it. Something will break soon. He's a good man, and he's working hard." Malcolm sighed deeply.

"So then what is it? Remember, everything here is confidential between us. If I can help in any way," Carolyn gestured with open palms.

"Some of it's personal," stammered Malcolm. "Some debts from last year have followed me to Wolfsburg, but I'm working on a repayment plan … No, that's not the main thing. It's Robert. The man is impossible to work with. Not only does he bully the staff, but he also victimizes the children. As adults, we can stand up to him, but kids like Doug don't stand a chance."

Carolyn sat up stiffly. Robert's name was coming up more and more frequently.

"Tell me what's going on. What happened to Doug?"

After Malcolm left, Carolyn sat staring out the window. The sky had already darkened, and it was getting late. Reaching over to the intercom, she punched in Robert's classroom and spoke firmly. "Mr. Doyle, are you still here?"

Robert slammed the last of his papers into his briefcase. He was tired and fed up with waiting for Carolyn to call him in.

"Yes, of course I'm still here. I've been waiting for over half an hour for our meeting."

"Good. Give me five minutes and then come to my office. We'll get this over with today." Flicking off the switch, she sat down again and called her husband.

"Hi. I'm going to be late. I have some unpleasant business to do … No, I'll tell you later. I can guarantee that I won't feel like cooking, so do you want to meet me at the Grill? … Okay, see you at seven."

Robert strode into the office and sat opposite his principal. Everything irritated him about this office, from her fancy box and her happy family pictures to the insipid wilderness scenes dripping over the computer screen. Crossing his arms angrily, he said, "You've kept me waiting long enough. Let's get on with it."

"Do you want to get Colleen back over to the school as a union representative?" Carolyn asked quietly. "I think you might need someone."

"Hell no. What would I need the union for?"

"There have been several complaints from the parents that you bully the students. Several staff members have also made allegations that you abuse your power. I'm here to tell you that you're on notice. Any further complaints will lead to an investigation and possible dismissal. Also, you can forget any ideas of keeping the head teacher position after the Christmas break. If I can replace you, I will. There are several promising candidates."

"What kind of complaints?" Robert demanded to know. "Who's been making these so-called allegations?"

Carolyn, reading from her notes, slowly went over each and every complaint that had been filed over the last term. The complaints were anonymous, but Robert knew they could easily be verified. He felt his face redden and his breathing become laboured. His career seemed to be slipping away, and he couldn't afford to lose this job. Each job change had been more and more difficult to cover up. Now that the Susan thing seemed to be blowing over, if he could just deflect these criticisms away from himself and towards his rivals, everything might work out.

He took a deep breath and stared at Ms. Myers.

"Have you heard of professional autonomy? How I deal with my students is up to me. So long as I deliver the mandated curriculum, evaluate the students, and show up to work on time, you have nothing to say."

"That's where you're wrong, Robert. How you treat the students is entirely my jurisdiction. Legally, I must protect each and every student in this building. By law, teachers must report even suspected child abuse to the appropriate official. That's called professional ethics," countered Carolyn, her eyes never leaving his.

Robert opened his mouth and then closed it. She was right, but could she prove it? Suspecting that someone must have ratted him out, he said, "Who's been telling lies about me? Who's been trying to damage my reputation? Malcolm? Ben? No, I bet it was Ann. Those guys just want my head teacher job, that's all."

Carolyn simply sat there watching Robert self-destruct. She had no intention of falling into the trap of divulging her sources.

"Bloody hell," Robert swore. "I'll find out who's been spreading the lies. Just you wait."

"Like I said, Robert. You're on notice. If we speak about this again, it will be to set up a disciplinary hearing."

"Don't you worry. There's nothing to these lies and innuendoes. My record is exemplary, and you can't prove otherwise. Now if you'll excuse me, I'm done. I'm heading home for supper. Goodnight."

He got up from his chair and stalked out of the room. Pausing only to drag on his coat and boots, he made his way out into the now-dark schoolyard.

Carolyn watched him go, knowing that this was not the end to the problems. Glancing at her watch, she noticed that it was already quarter to seven. It took at least an hour to get to town and then another fifteen minutes to get to the Grill on the other side of town.

"Hey, Don. I can't get there until closer to eight. Want to wait on supper or do you want to grab something on your own? ... Okay, see you there. Love you." She smiled. Don was her rock and could always be depended on for solid advice and comfort.

***

Out in the parking lot, Robert circled Carolyn's car. Reaching down, he stabbed at the front tire with his open pocket knife. It glanced off and clattered to the dirt. Retrieving it, he punched harder this time and successfully stabbed it through the rubber wall. He pulled the knife out, and grinning with satisfaction, he swiftly walked over to his steps, cuffing the dog as it rose to meet him.

***

"Hey, Don. I've got a flat. Can you come and help me fix it? The lug nuts are on too tight and I can't budge them ... Okay. I'm just past the substation this side of town."

Chapter Twenty-Eight

Towards ten o'clock that night, Robert stuffed the black wig and his olive skin-coloured makeup into a plastic bag, and left his home quietly. Both Betsy and Timmy had fallen asleep on the couch.

Betsy opened her eyes as she heard the door snub. Breathing a sigh of relief, she was thankful he didn't lock them in. If ever there were a fire or if Timmy hurt himself, they would have trouble getting help. She looked around at the tiny home, seeing very few possibilities for escape. She supposed she could break a window or take the door off its hinges, but both of those solutions would take some time to do.

"Come on, little man, let's get you to bed," she whispered as she gathered her son into her arms. His small arms circled her neck as she carried him into his bedroom.

"Night, night," she cooed. His innocent child smell caressed her nose as she bent to kiss him.

"Night, Mom."

***

Standing shivering in the cool night air, Robert flipped open his cell phone and dialled Malcolm's home phone.

"Hello, Mr. McDermitt," a small, threadlike voice whispered into the phone. "It's Doug. Can you meet me at the school?" He quickly snapped the phone's lid shut, got back in his truck, and drove the short distance to Malcolm's barn conversion. After parking several yards past the building and in the shadow of the church building, Robert pulled out his supplies and began to apply his disguise. When he was done, a quick check in the back mirror assured him that no one would recognize him except Malcolm—and he would think Robert was the man from in the casino.

His feet crunching on the frosted gravel echoed loudly in the still night. As he approached the barn, Robert made an effort to quieten his footsteps. Relieved when he saw that Malcolm's truck was gone, he bounded up the steps, thrust a screwdriver in the lock, and popped the catch.

Over at the school, Malcolm waited for over half an hour. He grew anxious when Doug didn't show but reasoned that Doug had been unable to get away. Concerned, he turned back towards his home.

The door was slightly ajar. He couldn't remember leaving it like this, but he was in such a hurry. *Bloody careless of me*, he thought. *Sassy could have easily escaped. Where is she anyway?*

Robert perched silently on the chair, one hand holding onto Sassy's collar. As she heard her master enter, Sassy began to bark and whine to be let down.

Malcolm's eyes shot to his visitor. With a start, he saw that it was his gambling buddy from the casino.

"Hey, what are you doing in my place? Let my dog go!"

"Nice to see you too. You haven't been at the casino for a while, and I was wondering where you got to." Robert let the little dog go, and she bounded into Malcolm's outstretched arms.

"Gonna offer your guest a drink?" the stranger asked.

"Don't have any booze. I'm on the wagon. What are you doing here? How'd you know where I live? What do you want from me?"

"Plenty," Robert said. Lifting his hand to his forehead, he began to remove the black wig. Malcolm stared in horror as he started to recognize who sat in his kitchen chair.

"What the hell?" Malcolm gasped.

"Yes, it's me. And hell is where you'll wish you were."

Robert stood up quickly and grabbed Malcolm by the jacket sleeve. Sassy dropped to the floor. "Come and sit. This is gonna take a while," he said as he thrust him into the wooden kitchen chair.

With one hand gripping Malcolm's shirt in a vise-like grip, Robert began systematically slapping him with his open hand. Malcolm reeled from the blows. As his cheeks reddened, he began to plead. "Stop, please stop," he begged. "What do you want?"

"What do I want? *What do I want?*" He shifted his weight slightly so that his blows reined downwards, causing even more pain.

"Please, tell me what you want," Malcolm cried. "Please stop hitting me."

"Listen, you boozer. I know about your problem. You can't leave it alone, can you?" He shook his finger in Malcolm's face as he continued his tirade. "I've seen you going into the AA meetings. I know you showed up to school so drunk your pals had to cover for you." Moving still closer to Malcolm, he whispered, "I know the reason why you had to leave the Tine Reserve."

In a slow, menacing voice, Robert spelled out the hold he had over Malcolm.

"Yes, I know. I know about the gambling debts too. Those collection agents can be very informative. What is it—$45,000 now? How much did you skip out on at the reserve? Not that it matters to me, but you can rest assured the school board would take a dim view of it."

Malcolm looked like he was about to pass out cold.

"Best you do as I say," Robert threatened him.

"What do you want?" repeated Malcolm.

"Don't put in for the head teacher position. You know that job is mine. If you even fill out the application, I'll make sure the board, the teachers, and the entire community know what a boozer and gambler you are. I'll tell everyone about Tine Reserve, about you coming to school plastered, and about your gambling debts. Mark my words, they'll run you outta Dodge faster than you can roll the dice."

He backed away from Malcolm and scooped up Sassy.

"Put her down, put her down," begged Malcolm as he saw Robert's hands reach around the dog's throat. "I'll do whatever you want. Just don't hurt her."

Robert flung Sassy against the wall and once again reached for Malcolm. His fist caught the side of his victim's head, driving it backwards.

"Your headache pills are on the counter—or would you prefer a mickey of rye?" Robert taunted as he made his way past the table.

Sassy whined and struggled to her feet. As Robert left through the front door, Malcolm picked up his trembling dog and held her tightly. She squirmed to get free, but he held her firmly.

Once he was certain that Robert had left, he felt Sassy all over, beginning with her back and working his way towards her paws. Thankful that she had no injuries, he finally let her down on the floor. She headed straight for the front door, barking furiously.

As he washed the blood from his nose, Malcolm could see the bruises starting to form and welts appearing below his eyes. He reached for the phone and ordered a sub for the morning. Then he reached behind the cereal box to find his bottle of rye. Cursing, he remembered Ben and Ann had stripped his home of every last ounce of booze.

***

Tuesday night when Malcolm was driving home after a trip to the dentist in town, lights appeared in his rear view mirror. Harsh blue and red flashes pierced the darkness.

"Pull over, pull over," commanded a voice over the megaphone. Malcolm steered towards the side of the road and shut off the engine.

The uniformed police officer got out of his cruiser and quickly closed the gap between his vehicle and Malcolm's car.

"We've had a report of erratic driving. What have you had to drink tonight?"

"Nothing, nothing at all," stammered Malcolm. They were right in front of the school. The monthly parent and teacher meeting had just ended and he could see the teachers and parents staring in fascination as they got in their cars.

"Please get out of the car, sir. Blow into this breathalyser. If you haven't been drinking like you say, you have nothing to worry about."

Malcolm stood submissively, quietly blowing into the hand-held machine while what seemed like the entire community filed past in their vehicles.

***

As he sat at the staff room table, Malcolm hung his head in embarrassment. His colleagues had all seen the incident last night and deserved an explanation. He had none to give them.

"I'm hugely embarrassed. They must have been looking for someone else," was all he could think of saying.

"Of course," echoed Ann and Ben.

"Don't worry about it. We'll make sure the community knows it was a mistake. We'll get the word out," Ben said confidently.

"Sure, don't worry yourself about it," Robert said. "It's not like anyone thinks you have a problem. You made someone mad lately? I wonder who tipped off the police." He reached over and squeezed Malcolm's shoulder. "Don't worry about a thing. Just keep your nose clean, and maybe it'll all blow over."

Malcolm shrank back from Robert's touch. He could still remember the pain these hands had inflicted. He had taken four days off work, not wanting to show his battered face at school. Struggling to put on a brave front, he smiled at the rest of the teachers.

"Thanks, you guys. I certainly appreciate your concern. Thanks again." Malcolm shrugged his shoulders helplessly and left.

The teachers could hear him making his way down the hall and then heard his classroom door close. What they didn't see was Malcolm sitting at his desk with his head buried in his hands. Muffled moans mingled with the tears that leaked between his fingers.

Chapter Twenty-Nine

Robert washed his hands thoroughly with the harsh, pink liquid soap that the economical school district supplied. It was a wonder his hands didn't fall off using the foul stuff. More than once, he had considered bringing over his own soap but was reluctant to do that because someone else might use it. He abhorred other people's germs on his personal things.

Ben came out of the stall and went over to the sink to wash his hands.

"Hey, Ben." Robert gestured to Ben's crotch. "Been putting it where the sun doesn't shine?"

Ben stared incredulously at the ignorant man. "What the hell are you on about?"

"Hiding the wiener, stoking the fire, poking the pig. You know what I mean," said Robert, leering and enjoying the younger man's discomfort. "Or are those not the terms you fellas use nowadays."

Ben turned off the tap and dried his hands on the paper towel. Ignoring Robert, he threw the waste paper into the garbage can and left in a hurry.

Robert smiled as he followed Ben out the door.

***

Hurrying to put the finishing touches on his project, Robert copied the last of the pictures into his home computer. He had spent the last hour sifting through the images stored on his camera's memory card. Using his tiny digital with its powerful zoom, he had over the last few months recorded quite a few incriminating pictures of Ben and Jake engaging in decidedly unbrotherly behaviour.

Loading his printer with good quality photo paper, he started to print the damaging images one by one. As the prints emerged from the machine, he smiled. These were his winning lottery tickets.

Robert carefully stowed the prints in his briefcase and switched off the light. It was time for bed. He was sure Betsy would be asleep already. Lately, he had been avoiding any physical interaction with her. She no longer turned him on with her flabby arms, pooch belly, and accusing eyes.

The image of his mother, in her cotton housedress, bending over the stove with her white arms jiggling as she stirred, came flooding into his memory. Often as not, those arms would wield the spoon and connect with his buttocks as she lashed out in anger. He had learned to avoid her as well.

***

Trying to finish his lesson preparations for the next week, Ben worked late on Thursday afternoon. It was well past five when Ben startled and looked up as Robert came barging into his classroom. He watched as Robert closed the door with a decided thump.

After checking through the classroom window to see if anyone was on the playground, Robert strode swiftly over to Ben's desk.

"Time you and I had a little chat," he said as he bent across the space between them.

Ben moved his chair back slightly trying to get to his feet. Robert reached over and grabbed Ben's shirt near the collar. "Whoa. Where are you off to? Set yourself back down. I said it was time for a chat."

"Some other time, Robert. I've got to get going. I'm meeting Ann in town for dinner."

"Oh, so that's why you're in your fancy duds," commented Robert, taking in Ben's crisply pressed burgundy shirt and grey flannel pants. "Well this shouldn't take long."

He reached into his briefcase, extracted a file folder, and dropped it onto the desk. Then he took the pictures and laid them in a row facing Ben. "Let's see what little gay boy's been up to, shall we?"

Ben gazed in fear as each picture came into focus. They showed Jake and him coming out of a motel room, the two of them running in the park, and them sitting cosily at dinner at Roma.

"These are pictures of my brother Jake and me in Clearville," bluffed Ben.

"They get better," hissed Robert as he placed the last two damning photos on top of the others.

Shocked, Ben saw one was a picture of him kissing Jake at Robin Lake, while the other showed Jake fondling him in the change room at the hotel pool. His head swirled as he realized he was holding his breath. Weakly, he slouched in his chair. Desperate thoughts whirled through his mind. There was no escaping from the evidence before him.

"What do you want?" he whispered.

Robert permitted himself a short laugh and then leaned forward into Ben's personal space.

"How would this community react to a homo teaching their kids? A homo hanging around their boys after school, supposedly running a basketball club. To their minds, the equation is simple: homo equals pedophile, pedophile equals homo."

"Okay! Okay, I get it. What do you want, Robert?" Ben asked desperately. "I need this job. I'll give you what you want … money … just tell me."

"I want what's rightfully mine. I want to keep the head teacher job. If you apply for it, that bitch Carolyn will give it to you in a heartbeat. Don't throw your name in the hat. Don't apply for the job if you know what's good for you," Robert shouted.

By this time, Ben was sobbing, and tears were streaming down his face, pooling in his neatly trimmed beard. It was no longer the handsome face of a blond Adonis.

Robert pressed home his point once more.

"Can you imagine," he said, waving his arms at the pictures displayed on the desk. "Can you imagine them falling into the right hands? One pinned up on the store bulletin board or perhaps a copy left in a church pew?"

Ben raised his face towards Robert.

"Please," he begged. "Don't show anyone, don't tell, please. I won't go for the job. It's yours, all yours. I need this job, please, please don't say anything."

"Keep your word, gay boy. Keep your word." Robert left, striding out of the room, relishing his newly found confidence.

Chapter Thirty

Ann knew without a doubt that she would have to distance herself from Patrick. The danger of his knowing about her past was too great. The threatening phone calls were unnerving. It was clear that someone was trying and succeeding in scaring her. Now, she was certain, this person had access to her trailer. Lying awake at night was taking its toll on her. Since sleep was so elusive, she was forgetting things.

"Hey, girl, did you stay up all night watching movies?" Colleen had commented, noting the dark circles under her eyes. Just yesterday, Carolyn had called wondering why her data for the math survey was late.

Ann sighed as she turned into her small yard. It was frightening to know someone had a key to her place and that person had discovered her secret. She had to do some immediate damage control, starting with Patrick.

As soon as she got into the trailer, she called him and told him she needed to cancel their dinner date on Friday. When Patrick asked if everything was okay, she insisted that nothing was wrong, she just needed to work on report cards and catch up on things.

"You can't work all weekend. Listen I'll bring some pizza back from town and we can cosy up at your place," he suggested, hearing the regret in her voice. When they did get together, they got along well, but lately Ann had been coming up with excuses not to see him.

"No, sorry I can't. Talk to you soon." Ann hung up quickly, afraid that she might change her mind. As much as she liked Patrick, she had to cool the relationship. Shivering, she recalled the sinister voice on the phone telling her to stay away from Bates. There was something familiar about the cadence of the voice, but her tormentor's identity escaped her.

The next morning, she shoved her feet into her new fleece-lined boots, yanked open the trailer door, and quickly got into her car. The harsh, accusing grating of the starter reminded her that she should have plugged her car in.

"Come on, come on," she encouraged the cold vehicle. Late already, she didn't have time to walk to school. After several tries, she finally started the engine and drove the still-cold car to school. Arriving in a panic, she saw that it was already time to ring the bell to bring the students in for classes.

"Hi, Ann. Don't worry I covered for you," Ben said as he hung up his jacket.

With a start, Ann realized that she had forgotten that she had morning supervision.

"Sorry, Ben. Thanks. My car was hard to start. Took several goes and I was beginning to worry about running down the battery."

"Didn't you plug in? No offence, but older cars like yours need to be plugged in overnight. The temperature dipped quite low last night."

"Yes, I forgot. Too much on my mind these days, I guess."

She saw Robert watching the entire interaction with a slight smirk on his face.

"Poor little princess. Not prepared for a winter in the frozen north? It might be the least of your worries."

"What? What did you say?" Ann asked Robert, having caught only half of what he uttered.

"Nothing. Best you remember to keep plugged in here and at home once the temp goes down to minus 10. We wouldn't want you to be stuck without a car."

***

The quiet hiss of the open intercom roused Ann. She had fallen asleep in the classroom's overheated warmth. In the several moments it took her to orient herself, she became aware of the slight crackles and sounds coming from the speaker in the ceiling. Someone had left the intercom system on or was listening in on her classroom. Since it was way past six o'clock, she knew it couldn't be students. The staff and the janitor had probably left an hour ago.

Getting up slowly, she moved to the door and peered out into the darkened hall. She could see no movement at all. As she turned back towards her desk, the intercom fell silent.

Well, it was time to get going. She gathered up the few remaining journals that she had to grade and went down the hallway and entered the dark workroom. There was just one more worksheet to run off and she'd be ready for the next day.

Guided by the light from under the lid of the photocopier, she lifted the cover and started to place her master copy on the glass. As usual, someone had forgotten to remove their master, so she picked it up off the glass. Turning over the paper, she gasped in surprise. It was a picture of Sean, and scrawled underneath the image were the words *Maria Santos charged with molestation.*

Suddenly she became acutely aware that she wasn't alone. In the still-darkened workroom, she turned to the doorway. Robert lounged against the door jam, his body silhouetted by the exit light.

A small involuntary cry of fear escaped her lips as she saw he was blocking the only exit from the tiny workspace. Struggling to maintain her composure, Ann managed to slide the incriminating picture into her pile of papers.

"Oh, Robert, you gave me a fright!" she exclaimed. "I didn't know anyone was still in the building."

"I was waiting for you, princess," he said quietly as he moved closer.

"Oh, you needed me for something?"

As he closed the gap between them, she tried to flatten herself against the photocopy machine. Panic filled her as she felt his body crushing hers and his hands groping at her breasts.

"Leave me alone! Stop!"

"Why should I? You're mine. I know your secret."

Desperately pushing away, Ann turned and ran. Robert caught up with her as she reached the entrance doors. She could feel the cold glass and the rigid steel panic bar in her back as he slammed her against the outside doors.

With his hot ragged breath pulsating inches from her face, she heard him dictate his demands.

"Don't apply for the head teacher job. It's mine. No one wants an upstart like you in that position anyway. I won't work with a woman. Women are only good for one thing. He pushed harder. The panic bar bit into her shoulder blades. If you know what's good for you, you'll start looking for a job elsewhere. How do you think the board, your friends, and the parents around here would react to a child molester in their midst?"

Ann, suddenly losing all will to fight, slumped in defeat.

"I didn't do anything. Sean made it all up."

"Who's going to believe that after I spread the word?" Robert whispered. "Where there's smoke there's fire. Isn't that how the saying goes?

Step outta line, princess, and everyone around here will find out what you did."

Ann tried unsuccessfully to stifle her sobs. The smell of his after-shave threatened to overwhelm her as she slid further towards the floor. She felt him grab her shirt and fumble with the buttons.

"Let's see what you got for Robert."

Ann brought the edge of her hand up and into Robert's nose. With an angry cry, he let go of her shirt, clamping his hand tightly over his spurting nose. Blood poured everywhere as he staggered towards the washroom.

Leaving her coat and boots behind, she snatched her purse from the staff room table and dashed out into the cold night. Her hands trembled violently as she yanked the cord from her outdoor electrical socket, and then struggled to unlock her car. She cranked the starter and roared off along the road to her trailer. By the time she threw the deadbolt, her whole body was shaking from the cold. Cradling the phone in her hands, she fought against calling Patrick.

Chapter Thirty-One

Robert nudged Betsy awake.

"Get up and make breakfast," he demanded as she raised her head off the pillow. Her dirty blonde hair was sticking out in all directions.

"Take a brush to that hair before we head off to church," he said as he caught sight of her appearance.

"If you want me to go to church, I'll have to wear a scarf over my hair," she explained. "It's too dirty to comb out. I can't wash it with my arm in a cast."

Robert thought of his mother and how she had dressed so carefully to attend services each Sunday. It didn't matter what had gone on all week; she made sure she was presentable for church. He wished Betsy had the same pride.

***

Patrick surveyed the congregation. Each Sunday, he had made it his habit to attend one of the churches in the community. Not that he was a religious man, but it sure helped get people on his side, and he could also observe the interactions between his neighbours.

Today as he looked around, he saw Doug and his family take their places in the Weibe pew. Robert, Betsy, and Timmy came in shortly after them. As Betsy reached awkwardly with her left hand for the hymn book, he could see her right arm was encased in plaster. Her hair was covered with a headscarf, and she was keeping her head down. He couldn't tell if she had any other visible injures. Ann had said Robert told them Betsy had fallen down the steps to their house. His gut twisted as he reflected on the miserable life that woman must have. Still, no one could help her until she laid charges or actually asked for assistance. He made a mental note to go and visit her again soon.

***

Monday morning, Robert stared at his class. An atmosphere of dis-respect and bravado permeated the classroom. Several students were carrying on a conversation as he waited for them to settle down.

"Hurry up and get ready. Any more chitchat and you'll forfeit gym period," he threatened, knowing they were anticipating playing basket-ball against Malcolm's class.

Suddenly the door opened and Doug entered with his head averted from his friends' sympathetic looks. He had not spoken to anyone except his best friend, Frederick, and then had sworn him to secrecy. The word had spread that Robert had done something to Doug, but details were few.

"Nice of you to join us, Mr. Weibe," Robert said sarcastically. "You can spend recess with me since you're ten minutes late."

Doug's head jerked up and he stared at his tormentor. Then just as quickly, he dropped his challenging stance and slunk into his seat. Dragging out his spelling text, he waited for Robert to assign their practice pages.

"That's right, Mr. Weibe, I'm the boss. Your attitude has just lost you lunch period, as well."

Mutterings of "no fair," "leave him alone" and "what'd he do?" reached Robert's ears.

"Anyone want to keep Mr. Weibe company?" threatened Robert in a steely, low voice. "I'll be happy to accommodate them."

The students settled into their math work with resignation. Mr. Doyle could and would make your life miserable.

Throughout the very long day, Robert kept picking on Doug. When Doug involuntarily let a small sigh escape his lips, Robert pounced.

"Enough of the attitude Mr. Weibe," declared Robert. "That just earned you an after-school session."

***

"It's past six o'clock. You can head home now," Robert said, finally letting Doug go home for the day. "Keep your trap shut or there'll be more days like today."

Doug sullenly gathered up his things and shuffled off down the hall. He could feel Mr. Doyle watching him, so there was no opportunity to talk to his mentor. He passed Malcolm's door quickly and made his way over to the store to call his mother.

Doug chose to wait for his mum just inside the store entrance. Since he had no money for a drink or anything, he didn't feel right lingering in the eating area. Herb noticed this was the second night lately that Doug had missed the school bus.

"Hey, Patrick," Herb commented when he saw the detective walk in for his supper. "Doug missed the bus again. It's strange for that kid to do that. He's always on time because he's got chores to do before supper. It's a big spread they got to look after. Well over three hundred head on their home pasture alone."

"Yah, he was some upset the other night. Said something about his teacher keeping him in."

"His teacher is Mr. Doyle. Doyle can be mean. He runs a real tight ship. Has several of the parents complaining every year. Guess this year's no different," Herb said as he wiped off the counter.

"Can't be tougher than my old geography teacher in high school," Bates said as he launched into a tale from his own childhood. Soon both men were laughing and trying to outdo each other with stories of back in the old days.

Chapter Thirty-Two

Ann returned from her grocery trip to town and was greeted by the smell of smoke drifting on the wind. As she looked around her yard, she could see footprints leading towards the outhouse behind the trailer. Curious, she followed the tracks around the trailer. She had not been in the backyard since the snow fell on Tuesday.

She watched in terror as voracious flames erupted into the crisp night, consuming the decaying structure. Intense heat drove her back towards her trailer. Afraid it would catch fire as well; Ann scrabbled in her purse for her cell phone. After punching Patrick's number on the speed dial, she waited impatiently for his response.

"There's a fire. My outhouse is on fire. What do I do? Who do I call out here?" she quickly asked as soon as she heard his voice on the other end.

"Whoa...Calm down. Take a breath," he said. There was no point in panicking.

"It'll probably be okay. The outhouse is quite a distance from your trailer, isn't it?" he asked.

"Yes, but I'm not sure it's far enough away. The fire is really intense. Flames have to be at least ten feet. They're shooting out all over the place. Who do I call?"

"No point in calling into town. It would take them too long to get here, even if they would come from town. There's no fire protection out here. I'll get Herb and we'll figure it out."

Ten minutes later, three trucks loaded with several men came screeching around the corner and into her yard. Within minutes, the night was filled with clanging shovels and grunting men as they showered the now-consumed biffie with snow.

"Oh my God, Patrick. What would have happened if it had been my trailer on fire?" she asked as they surveyed the charred remains.

Patrick put his arm around her as he replied, "Nothing would be left. Just like this. That's the danger of living in a community with no fire station. They have a first aid base and some trained personnel, but no fire trucks."

Ann shuddered, thinking of the possibilities. Gathering her wits about her, she turned to thank her helpers.

"Thank you so much for coming so quickly. I'm sorry if I panicked, but the flames were so fierce," she said and then collapsed against Patrick as tears coursed down her cheeks.

"No worries, Ann. No worries," comforted one of her neighbours. "Country folk help one another. You're one of us now. No worries." With a wave of his hand, he climbed into the cab of his truck and the other men followed suit.

Ann drew a shaky breath as she pulled away from Patrick's comforting arms.

"Did you hear what he said? I'm one of them. It's so nice to feel that I belong somewhere at last."

As she spoke the words, she knew that she wouldn't do anything to jeopardise the welcome she felt in Wolfsburg. They definitely wouldn't feel the same way about an alleged child molester. She was darn sure Robert would tell them what he knew—and what he didn't know, he was quite capable of making up.

Patrick accepted her offer of coffee but left shortly after finishing it. He had to complete his monthly reports and could tell she was exhausted from all of the shock and excitement.

***

Ann sat in the easy chair sipping a brandy. Somehow she didn't think tea would do the trick. As the liquor pooled in her veins, she began to doze. Her head dropped towards the soft blanket that she had wrapped herself in.

Gradually, she became aware of a cold draft under her feet and the smell of wet charred wood. Shucking off her toasty blanket, she rose and looked around. Ann's body stiffened when she saw that the back door was wide open.

"Quite an exciting evening, wasn't it?"

Ann stifled a scream as she spun around to see Robert seated at her kitchen table.

"Get out! Get out!" she demanded as she reached for her phone.

Robert got to his feet and stood within inches away from her.

"Enjoy the rest of your evening," he smirked. "Remember what I told you. I know everything, and if you're not careful, so will Bates and all of Wolfsburg." He grabbed her chin with his gloved hand, bringing her face close to his. Crushing his mouth on hers, he held her fast as she struggled to breathe.

"Next time, I'll want more."

As he went out the back door, she slammed it behind him and dragged the washing machine over in front of it. She checked the deadbolt on the front door three times before she sank to the floor. Overwhelmed, her shoulders shook with ragged sobs as she realized the hopelessness of her situation. He had a key, he knew where she was most of the time, and he knew her secret.

Vowing to be more careful, she decided to never be alone at school again. She would call the school maintenance department in the morning and arrange for them to change the locks to her trailer. However, there was nothing she could do about his discovering her past, nothing at all.

***

Pretending to be interested as the whole staff buzzed on about Ann's fire, Robert made a joke. "Some hot seat you might have had, princess."

Ann looked at him in amazement. It was incredulous that the man could appear to be so innocent. She had no choice but to laugh at his poor attempt of humour.

***

As evening came, she got ready to go home. Luckily, she had already seen Robert going towards his teacherage. She and Malcolm were the only ones in the school, and when she saw him in the boot room, she stopped to chat.

"You're late tonight. Feel like grabbing a bite at the store?"

"Sure, I'm beat. Sassy will be okay for a little while longer," Malcolm replied, grateful for the possibility of company. The evenings stretched out long and dismal these days.

When they got to the store, they joined Patrick at his table. The time passed cheerfully as they all began reminiscing about their childhoods. Both Malcolm and Ann were very careful not to give away any specific information. All too soon, it was time for Herb to close the store, so they bid one another goodnight.

Ann climbed into the cold car and turned on the heat as soon as the engine gauge registered any sign of warmth. Up here in the northern part of the province, it was getting colder quickly. Already there had been a skiff of snow, and the forecast for next week promised at least 10 cm more.

She slowed down to take the corner onto her road. Her eyes shut as suddenly the interior of the car filled with blinding light. The shuddering, grating noise of the brakes shot through the floorboards as she jammed her foot on the brake, managing to come to a stop.

As her eyes adjusted to the glare, she saw a truck opposite her close off its lights. It backed off and started forward again. Once again the lights came on. The glare filling her car forcing her to look away. With its horn blaring, the truck swerved at the last minute, avoiding crashing into her.

Gradually relaxing her white knuckled grip on the steering wheel, Ann sat immobilized with fear. Robert drove a truck.

Chapter Thirty-Three

Since Betsy was still in no shape to be seen in public, Robert left for town as soon as school had finished on Thursday afternoon. She had given him a list of groceries and other items they needed. He was also planning on visiting his favourite corner to see if his girl Sadie was available for a quickie. Betsy had whimpered and whined when he tried to have sex last night. She was a complete turn-off.

Ann caught some motion out of the corner of her eye. Knowing that Robert had left for town and that the other teachers had also called it a day, she put down the dry erase pen and stepped quickly over to the doorway. She could see Doug poking his head out of Malcolm's classroom.

As she watched, Doug left the room and ran quickly towards the exit.

"Hey, Doug, can I help you with something?" she called at his retreating figure.

"Oh hi, Ms. Santos. No, I was just looking for Mr. McDermitt. I guess he's gone for the day."

"Yes, he left already. Want me to tell him something for you?"

Doug looked down at his feet and silently shook his head. He approached her slowly, and then whispered, "Just give him this note in the morning, please."

Ann was concerned as she took in his pale face and saw his hands tremble.

"Can I do anything for you, Doug? You seem very upset."

"No, Mr. McDermitt knows what's going on. I'll see you later." With that he turned and left through the entrance doors. Snow was just starting to fall. The predictions of freezing temperatures and a snowfall of several inches appeared to be correct.

***

The next morning just after recess, Ann caught up with Malcolm as he walked down the hall to his room.

"Hey, Malcolm, Doug was looking for you after school yesterday. He gave me this note to give to you."

Malcolm's face paled as he read the hastily written note.

"Oh my God, Ann. Doug didn't show up for school this morning and this doesn't look good," he said as he handed her the scrap of paper.

"Let's not panic yet," Ann said after reading the note. "We should call his parents. He's probably home with the flu, or maybe they needed him to help with the livestock. There was a lot of snow last night, so he was most likely needed at home."

After a call to Doug's parents, who had been out looking for him all night, and a call to Carolyn, Malcolm and Ann summoned Patrick Bates. The detective arrived several minutes later and took charge of the situation. He called all the teachers into the staff room.

"What does this mean, 'I can't take it any more'?" he asked Malcolm as he read Doug's message.

Malcolm filled Patrick in on Doug's latest problems with Robert. However, he was careful not to paint too bad a picture of the insensitive bully.

Turning to Ann, Malcolm said, "What do you think he meant by 'I've got to get away. Don't look for me, I'll be okay. Maybe someday I'll be back and we can fish in the lake.'?"

Convinced that Doug had gone to the lake, Ann offered to drive out and see if he had made it that far yet. It was a long way on foot, but Doug had had a huge start on them if he left after school yesterday. She shuddered, thinking of the boy out in the snow overnight in these temperatures.

"There isn't much chance of him going out there. He's got no wheels," suggested Patrick. "But go ahead and check while I call in some of the men from the community. Drive slowly and check the roadway and ditches as you go."

Malcolm and Ben took off towards town, while the rest of the staff thoroughly checked the school and surrounding buildings.

Waiting until Patrick was busy on the phone to Herb, arranging for a search party, Robert declared to the other teachers, "I'm heading out to the lake, as well. No telling what problems princess could get into. She's not used to these road conditions." He headed out to his truck without waiting for the detective's approval.

After asking Colleen and Barb to gather all the students into the gym, Sgt. Bates addressed the children.

"I'd like to talk to his closest friends, but if any of the rest of you have an idea where Doug may have gone please let us know. I don't want to worry you but it is really cold out there. The sooner we find him the better. These teachers will be supervising you while the rest of us begin the search," he said indicating Barb and Colleen who were standing beside him. "I know I can count on your best behaviour in this crisis."

***

Driving slowly, Robert made his way along the snow-covered road following Ann's tracks. As her vehicle came into view, he eased back. He watched as Ann made the right-hand turn into the small car park at the boat launch.

Ann got out of her car and stared hard at the ground, trying to see any evidence of footprints in the deep snow. Other than some narrow deer tracks leading to the water's edge and away again, the snow seemed undisturbed.

She called Doug's name several times, but only an echo from the opposite cliff face replied. Reaching into her pocket, she withdrew her cell phone.

"I guess you were right, Patrick," Ann said. "There's no sign that anyone's been here. I've called his name several times, but there's only me and the snow ... Yes, I'll head back."

The scrunch of the snow was the first sign that she was not alone.

"Doug?"

***

Patrick had just hung up from Ann's call when Malcolm reached him.

"We've got him. He's safe. Some trucker picked him up hitching on the way to town. Dropped him off at the garage this side of town. He spent the night at the owner's house. They were just about to phone the cops when we stopped for gas. He wouldn't give his name, but they were glad we were looking for him."

Relaying the happy news to Doug's parents and the search teams, Patrick called off the search. He was glad that it had been Malcolm and Ben who had found the boy. No telling what would have happened if Robert had reached him first. Doug would have probably run again.

Uneasiness crept over him like a chill. Colleen had said that Robert had gone looking for Ann at the lake. Patrick's gut instinct was telling him she was in danger. Throwing on his parka and boots, he raced out to his vehicle.

Fifteen minutes later he approached Robin Lake. The sight of two figures in the distance, struggling in the snow, triggered his foot to press harder on the accelerator. The heavy SUV skidded as he turned towards the lake.

"What the hell are you doing?" he hollered as he raced across the snow. "Let her go!"

"It's all right. I'm just trying to stop her from dashing off alone into the bush," gasped Robert, staring deeply into Ann's eyes. "The silly cow thinks she heard someone reply to her hollering. I was trying to make her wait for the search party instead of going off half-cocked and getting herself lost."

"It's okay, Ann," Patrick said. "We've found him. He's safe." He grabbed her from Robert's grasp.

"Stupid cow," Robert repeated, striding towards his truck. Swinging into the cab, he turned and waved to Patrick and Ann as they stood in the snow.

"You okay, Ann? What's going on?"

"I'm fine. It's like he said. I wanted to go look for Doug. I thought I heard something over the other side of the lake." She fought hard to keep herself from breaking down.

"I'm going home. This cold is getting to me and I need a warm bath," Ann said, getting into her car. The look in Robert's eyes had been bone chilling. She was deathly afraid of what he was capable of doing.

As Patrick stood in the cold, watching her blue car disappear from sight, he looked down. His eyes were drawn to the uneven footprint left by Robert's boot.

Chapter Thirty-Four

Robert felt his face flush and could taste the bitterness of stomach acid making its way into his throat. Without bothering to knock, he thrust open Carolyn's office door. Storming over to the chair opposite hers, he sat down and glared at his adversary.

"I'm here. What did you want me for?"

"I've spent all weekend thinking about this situation," Carolyn replied. "I can't imagine the anguish Doug's parents have gone through. Doug could have easily frozen on his way to town."

"It serves him right. That kid has no brains to take off at minus 20 degrees. Instead of playing on the basketball team, he should join a drama club."

Carolyn stiffened at Robert's insensitivity.

"The child is crying for help, and that's the best you can come up with? For all I know, it was your bullying ways that caused this crisis. I'm putting you on notice. There's going to be a full investigation into this incident. I've had too many complaints and now this mess. I'll get to the bottom of this, Robert."

Blind rage flooded his gut. He stood up, shaking his fist in her face.

"Investigate all you want. None of your little pets will say anything. They're all too weak. Besides I know stuff about you as well."

As Robert slammed his way out of the office, Carolyn looked on in amazement. The man was impossible. She knew there was a lot more to Doug's situation than she had uncovered. The quicker she got to the bottom of this, the better. Reaching for the phone, she called the superintendent of schools. The board needed to know that she was placing Robert on notice.

***

Betsy's head jerked up as she heard Robert slam his briefcase down and begin to kick off his boots. Timmy dropped the crayon he'd been using and watched it roll under the couch.

"Get my supper on the table," snarled Robert, gesturing with his arm wildly. He turned and went into the bathroom to shower. The full force of the scalding water cascading over his stiff shoulders did nothing to relieve his tension. After briskly drying himself with his plush towel, he dressed in his grey pants and favourite at-home sweater.

Any semblance of calm evaporated as he sat at the table contemplating his supper, congealing on his plate. His appetite had vanished as bile once more filled his throat.

"You aren't hungry?" Betsy asked quietly. "Is there something wrong with the meatloaf? Timmy liked it."

"Well then, Timmy can eat mine!" Robert shouted as he threw the plate full of food towards Timmy.

Betsy managed to gasp, "Timmy, go! Go now!" Robert loomed towards her.

Timmy cast a fear-filled look at his father and then dashed into the bathroom, locking the door behind him.

Robert brought his fist up, sharply catching Betsy in the diaphragm and knocking the wind out of her. Relishing in the sound of his fists pummelling her flesh, he methodically beat her.

Memories of his father laying a beating on his mother invaded his rage-fuelled haze. His anger sharpened as he transferred his frustrations onto Betsy. It was her fault he was like this. If she behaved better, these things wouldn't happen.

He watched as his boots connected with her hips. He laughed at the sight of her casted right arm hanging loosely at her side while she tried to protect her face with her left. Finally, as his leather-encased foot delivered a hard blow to the side of her head, he saw the light leave her eyes as she lapsed into unconsciousness.

Dragging her inert body into their room, he threw her onto the bed and went in search of Timmy.

"Open the damn door, Timmy! Open the damn door!"

Silence filled the small house.

Robert scrabbled through the junk drawer coming up with a finishing nail. He slowly approached the locked door and then inserted the nail into the safety hole. One click and the door flew open. Timmy scuttled backwards like a crab. Snuffling like a piglet, he tried to squeeze into the space between the toilet and the wall.

Robert easily reached his son and pulled him into his arms.

"Relax, kid. Daddy's not going to hurt you. I won't hit you. You'll learn that's what women are for."

Timmy peed himself.

"For God's sakes, Tim, stop being such a whimp." Robert said as his flat hand smacked Timmy. Once again, Robert saw the look of abject terror cross his son's face. He had struck his son—again.

After changing Timmy into dry clothes, he fed him his favourite snack, a grilled cheese sandwich. He plied him with hot chocolate. Marshmallows floated on the milky liquid.

Holding his son on his lap, he read story after story until the little boy's eyes closed with fatigue. As he stared at the sleeping boy, he felt desperately sorry. Things were getting out of control. Lifting his child carefully, he carried him into his tiny bedroom and laid him on his bed. He smelled a mixture of hot chocolate, marshmallows, and tears as he kissed his son's forehead.

"Night, little guy. Daddy's so sorry."

After checking on Betsy, Robert disappeared into his study. He was gone by the time Timmy woke the next morning.

***

Timmy crept to his bedroom door and listened carefully. Hearing nothing, he opened the door quietly and dragged his blanket into his mother's room.

Betsy tried to sit up only to sink weakly down into the bedding, the stale metallic smell of dried blood filling her nostrils. Frantically, she struggled to sit up again.

"Timmy, Timmy where are you?"

"Mommy, are you hurt bad?"

She felt his little hands patting her face.

"Mommy, there's a lot of blood."

She drifted back into oblivion, coming to once again as she became aware of his feeble attempts to mop the dried blood from her forehead.

Forcing herself to shake off the protection of the comforting fog that threatened to overtake her, she slowly got out of bed. Her hands clutched at her swollen stomach. Her body trembled with pain as she made her way into the bathroom. There in privacy, she stripped and examined her battered body. Purple bruises were beginning to surface. Welts and cuts were everywhere. She realized that he hadn't bothered to be careful to hit her where it wouldn't show. Robert had really lost control this time.

"Mommy, Mommy," Timmy's concerned calls came from behind the door.

With shaking hands, she dressed and opened the door. To her horror, Betsy saw a large red welt on Timmy's pale face. Robert had struck their child again.

***

She was surprised to find Robert's private sanctuary, his study, unlocked. Turning the handle, Betsy let herself in. He must have been in a hurry this morning to have forgotten to lock his room.

One flick of the computer mouse and the screen leapt to life. The garish colours of a porn site filled the screen.

She checked the history, finding more pornography and all the sites Robert had checked as he researched the other teachers. She saw that her friend Ann had been accused of touching a child. She read through the evidence on Malcolm and Ben.

Her eyes found Robert's favourite boots slung in the corner. Remembering Sgt. Bates's last visit, she instinctively knew that these were the boots he had been looking for.

As she sat in the old chair, rocking her son in her arms, all the damning evidence that she found in the study, coupled with what he had done to their son, piled up. Betsy knew what she had to do.

"Listen, Timmy, I need you to do something for me. I'm going to fix things. I'm going to make it safe for us."

As Timmy stared wide-eyed at her, she told him she would lock him in his room and he wasn't to call out or say anything until she came and let him out.

"It might be a very long time, but you have to be a good boy and do as Mommy says."

After shutting Timmy in his room, Betsy re-entered Robert's sanctuary. She searched the closet until she located Robert's shotgun that he used for grouse hunting, and then she found the shells.

With her stomach churning and head pounding, she dragged a kitchen chair over in front of the front door. The loaded gun was across her knees.

***

Patrick Bates hummed to himself as he drove back to Wolfsburg. The judge had been very accommodating and had issued the search warrant without many questions. Now, it was just a matter of searching Robert's

Audio Listing

Session 1:   Introduction and Romans 1:1 - 1:7

Introduction. Salutation. Attributes of the Trinity.

Session 2:   Romans 1:8 - 1:32

The Pagan Predicament. The Need for the Gospel. God's Righteousness Revealed Against Pagan Humanity.

Session 3:   Romans 2

The Righteousness of God Revealed. Condemnation of Moral Man.

Session 4:   Romans 3

Advantages of Being a Jew? Case Against the Entire Human Race. Why Does God Save Anyone?

Session 5:   Romans 4

God's Greatest Gift. Faith of Abraham and David. Salvation by Faith, not Works. The Resurrection.

Session 6:   Romans 5

Peace With God. The Sequence to Maturity. The Logic of His Love. Two Heads: Adam and Christ.

Session 7:   Romans 6

Two Masters: Sin Personified, and God as Revealed in Jesus. The Death of Defeat. Baptism. Sanctification.

Session 8:   Romans 7

Law School: The Law and Christ Risen. Dead to the Law. Spirit Is Willing, the Flesh Is Weak.

Audio Listing

Session 9: Romans 8:1 - 17

Deliverance from the Flesh by the Power of the Holy Spirit. The Holy Spirit's Inner Witness.

Session 10: Romans 8:18 - 27

The New Creation. Preservation in Suffering by the Power of the Holy Spirit.

Session 11: Romans 8:28 - 39

Our Eternal Security. Hymn of Praise for Victory. Certainty of Sanctification.

Session 12: Romans 9:1 - 5

Advantages of Being a Jew? Discussion of the Covenants. The Sceptre of Judah. Eschatological Heresies.

Session 13: Romans 9:6 - 13

Has the Word of God Failed? Doctrine of Election.

Session 14: Romans 9:14 - 33

God's Sovereignty. Moses and Pharaoh. Gentiles Called. Stumbling Stone.

Session 15: Romans 10:1 - 15

Rabbinical Expectations. Salvation by Faith Taught by Moses. "Whosoever..." Israel Present.

Session 16: Romans 10:16 - 21

Review of Post-Biblical History of Israel up to Modern Day.

home for the boots and his truck for evidence that could tie him to Susan Lloyd's murder. Everything was falling nicely into place.

Chapter Thirty-Five

"You've got no right to treat us this way!" yelled Fredrick, Doug's good friend.

Emboldened by Fredrick's bravery, several other students rose from their seats and began chanting, "No right, no right."

Doug's friend then walked up to Robert and said with a calm quiet voice, "He's our mate and we look after our own. My parents are going to report you to the school board."

Robert went white with anger.

"Sit your asses down and get to work," he demanded coldly.

The recess bell echoed in the hall. Robert watched as the class as a unit got up and left the room, heading down towards the gym. Several students saluted as they left.

When he reached the staff room, he was greeted by the sight of Carolyn, Ben, Malcolm, and Ann. Their heads were turned towards one another in serious conversation. They looked up and stopped talking as he entered the room. Paranoid and still shaken by his class's rebellion, Robert's gaze bounced off of each person in the room.

Slamming his fist down on the table, he glared at Carolyn and shouted, "You and your little lap dogs are talking about me, aren't you?" His voice rose to a fever pitch. "Think that you can steal my job, do you? Remember I'm the only good candidate. All you suckers have histories. Right, gay boy? Right, you alcoholic gambler? And you, princess? You like little boys so much that you can't keep your hands to yourself, can you?" he screamed as he stared from one to the other.

Carolyn stated flatly, "Keep quiet, Robert. We've had enough of you."

Robert shook with rage.

"Who are you to judge me? You don't even have your master's! You faked your credentials to get your job. The board will be happy to know about that."

Robert exploded out of the room. The other teachers looked around speechless, slowly coming to the realization that each of them had been Robert's victim.

As Sgt. Bates pulled his SUV into the school yard, he saw Robert charge up the steps to his home and turn the key in the lock.

A shotgun blast reverberated in the gathering dusk. Robert drew his last breath.